A Sampling of Praise for Brenda Novak

"What a wonderful love story....
An emotional, romantic journey you'll not want to miss!"
—*Rendezvous* on *Expectations*

Brenda Novak's "books are must-reads for those
hopeless romantics among us."
—Bestselling author Merline Lovelace

"In her first Superromance, Ms. Novak has given us a
wonderfully warm story. This is a definite keeper!"
—AOL Writers' Club Romance Group on *Expectations*

"...three-dimensional, very real characters
with realistic problems. These characters touched my
heart and had me reaching for the tissues."
—*Scribes World Reviews* on *Snow Baby*

Brenda Novak's "powerful storytelling voice
sweeps the reader through a stormy past
and a painful present, providing the novel with depth
seldom matched in this genre.... I very highly
recommend that you read *Snow Baby*."
—Cindy Penn, *WordWeaving*

"*Baby Business* is a heart-wrencher with a
knock-your-socks-off ending!...
One thing is for sure: I know I never, ever
want to miss a book by Brenda Novak."
—Suzanne Coleman, *The Belles and Beaux of Romance*

"This one kept me turning the pages. A tautly written
suspense plot, an interesting setting, well-drawn
characters and an enjoyable romance."
—Jean Mason, *The Romance Reader* on *Dear Maggie*

Dear Reader,

Sometimes we come to a point in life when we have to look honestly at our situation—and the decisions that have brought us to where we are—and face the fact that it isn't where we want to be. Maybe we took a wrong turn somewhere. Maybe someone else took the turn that threw us offtrack. Either way, changing requires a great deal of strength and determination. In *We Saw Mommy Kissing Santa Claus*, Jaclyn Wentworth is a woman who won't settle. She digs deep inside herself for the courage to do what must be done, and as she grows in wisdom and confidence, she eventually finds what we all want most— love and happiness. I hope you enjoy her journey.

I'd love to hear from you. You can contact me at P.O. Box 3781, Citrus Heights, CA 95611. Or simply log on to my Web site at www.brendanovak.com to leave me an e-mail, check out my book signings or learn about upcoming releases.

May we, like Jaclyn, find the courage to make the changes that are best for us!

Brenda Novak

P.S. Merry Christmas!

Books by Brenda Novak

HARLEQUIN SUPERROMANCE
899—EXPECTATIONS
939—SNOW BABY
955—BABY BUSINESS
987—DEAR MAGGIE

Don't miss any of our special offers. Write to us at the following address for information on our newest releases.

Harlequin Reader Service
U.S.: 3010 Walden Ave., P.O. Box 1325, Buffalo, NY 14269
Canadian: P.O. Box 609, Fort Erie, Ont. L2A 5X3

We Saw Mommy Kissing Santa Claus

Brenda Novak

HARLEQUIN®

TORONTO • NEW YORK • LONDON
AMSTERDAM • PARIS • SYDNEY • HAMBURG
STOCKHOLM • ATHENS • TOKYO • MILAN • MADRID
PRAGUE • WARSAW • BUDAPEST • AUCKLAND

ISBN 0-373-71021-6

WE SAW MOMMY KISSING SANTA CLAUS

Copyright © 2001 by Brenda Novak.

All rights reserved. Except for use in any review, the reproduction or
utilization of this work in whole or in part in any form by any electronic,
mechanical or other means, now known or hereafter invented, including
xerography, photocopying and recording, or in any information storage
or retrieval system, is forbidden without the written permission of the
publisher, Harlequin Enterprises Limited, 225 Duncan Mill Road,
Don Mills, Ontario, Canada M3B 3K9.

All characters in this book have no existence outside the imagination of
the author and have no relation whatsoever to anyone bearing the same
name or names. They are not even distantly inspired by any individual
known or unknown to the author, and all incidents are pure invention.

This edition published by arrangement with Harlequin Books S.A.

® and TM are trademarks of the publisher. Trademarks indicated with
® are registered in the United States Patent and Trademark Office, the
Canadian Trade Marks Office and in other countries.

Visit us at www.eHarlequin.com

Printed in U.S.A.

To my mother, LaVar Moffitt,
the inspiration for Jaclyn's strength and spirit.
And to Ted Novak, my own self-made man.
Cole has nothing on him.

PROLOGUE

THIS WAS IT, the absolute last straw. Jackie Wentworth couldn't take any more.

Numb, she sat in her new Suburban, the engine idling, as she stared in sickened wonder at her husband's 1997 Dodge Ram with its identifying Rodeo bumper stickers. She'd spent hours looking for him, worried when she'd returned home from her friend's place in Utah a day early to find their bed, their entire section of his parents' home, empty. Even though it was the middle of the night, she'd driven past his friends' houses, his two sisters' houses, and gone all the way out to Sand Mountain, his favorite weekend haunt.

But she'd been fooling herself, of course. His dune buggy, or "sand rail," as they were now called, was still in the garage. She just couldn't bring herself to believe the worst, at least not at first, not after all the counseling sessions and promises and hard-won confessions they'd been through—and finally, *finally* the forgiveness she'd managed to wring from her own heart.

What a waste. Jackie closed her eyes, hoping she'd see something different when she opened them again. But the scene was just the same. Her husband's truck sat in the dimly lit parking lot of Maxine's, one of the legalized houses of prostitution that stood neighborless in the barren desert just outside Feld, Nevada.

Behind her, Mackenzie and Alex were wearing their pajamas and fighting over the pretzels Jackie had bought to keep them occupied. Alyssa, the baby of the family at two years old, wailed miserably in her car seat. It was nearly three in the morning. Jackie couldn't blame them for feeling put out. But she heard the noise they made as though it came from somewhere far away. Her ears were ringing too loudly, her heart thumping too hard, to hear anything clearly.

Opening her door, just in case she was going to be sick, Jackie put her head between her legs and took long, deep breaths. *It's okay. You're okay,* she told herself.

But she wasn't okay. She didn't know if she'd ever be okay again. She only knew she'd leave Terry. She'd take the children with her if she had to crawl on her hands and knees and carry the three of them on her back. And this time she wouldn't let anything undermine her determination.

"Mommy? What's wrong with you? You look like you're gonna throw up."

"Mom, Alex is touching me."

"Shut up. You're such a pain."

"You shut up. You're the one who started it."

Jackie couldn't answer. She straightened, thinking of the movie classic *Gone with the Wind.* She pictured Scarlett O'Hara crying and angry and shaking her fist at the sky, swearing she'd never go hungry again, and finally understood the depth of that kind of resolve. Because she felt the same way.

"As God is my witness, I will never let myself become so dependent on another human being again," she muttered.

"Mommy? Why are you talking to yourself? What's wrong with you?"

"Just leave her alone. Can't you see she's sick?"

Alyssa cried louder. "Out, out, out!" she chanted.

"Yes, sweetheart," Jackie said, turning, dry-eyed, to

face the three of them. "We're getting out. Soon." *Out of Feld. Out of Nevada. Out of her loveless marriage.*

Her words did nothing to placate the baby. Alyssa had no concept of *soon,* except that it wasn't *now,* but Jackie felt infinitely better. Terry thought he had her where he wanted her. Since the car accident that had killed her parents six years earlier, she had no family to speak of. She'd spent what money she'd inherited attempting to leave him once before. And she'd married him right out of high school, so she had no college education, no marketable job skills—and three young children to care for.

What would she ever do without him? How would she make it? They lived with his parents on his father's ranch. Terry knew he'd inherit the whole operation someday, but they had no real money, not of their own. Her husband hung out with the same guys he'd known in high school, partied nearly as hard and cheated on his wife. And every time he got himself into a scrape, he ran to Daddy.

Her life had turned out so differently from what she'd planned. She'd married Terry Wentworth because she believed in his potential, the sweetness in him. She'd wanted to see him rise to that potential. But at eighteen she probably wasn't the best judge of character. Since then, she'd realized he was too lazy and too weak to fight the influence of having everything handed to him on a silver platter. He had no determination, no ambition, because no problem was too big for Daddy to solve.

Except this one, Jackie promised. Burt Wentworth was a formidable foe, but if he gave her trouble over the divorce—and she knew he would—she'd fight him.

She thought of marching into Maxine's to tell Terry so, then decided against it. Why embarrass him? Let him have his fun. Reality would intrude soon enough. But she couldn't leave without letting him know she'd caught him red-handed. Otherwise he'd claim she'd seen someone else's truck in the dark. He'd lie and cry and play the martyr. And she was done with all that.

Backing the Suburban out of the lot and parking it where the children could no longer see Terry's truck, she retrieved the large hunting knife they kept in the glove box, got out and methodically slashed all four of Terry's tires. The wheezing sound of escaping air followed her back to the Suburban. By now the baby was quiet, and her older children had stopped fighting, too busy turning in their seats, trying to see where she'd gone.

"What did you do?" Alex asked, as she climbed back in.

Jackie put the knife away and started the car again. "I just left Daddy a message," she said.

CHAPTER ONE

One year later...

JACLYN'S DIVORCE was final today, but she didn't feel much like celebrating. Her father-in-law and ex-husband had made her life hell with all their legal motions and expensive lawyers. She'd spent almost everything she'd earned waitressing on her own pathetic attorney—had run up a sizable bill, besides—and still she'd gotten no spousal maintenance, a mere pittance for child support and no more custody rights than Terry.

But she *had* escaped. Finally. She'd won in that regard and in one other: the court had given her permission to leave Feld, as long as she didn't go farther than a two-hour drive. Now she lived in Reno, Nevada, a mini-Las Vegas, self-dubbed the "biggest little city in the world." With a small strip of casinos, a constant influx of truckers, and slot machines in every gas station and convenience store, it wasn't exactly what she'd had in mind when she left the Wentworth ranch, but it was better than Feld. At least she was free to build a life for herself that didn't include Terry's family and their influence, or the sickening knowledge that her husband was warming someone else's bed. No more nights spent searching for him, wondering where or when he might turn up. No more heated arguments and denials.

And no more financial security. For better or for worse, Jaclyn was on her own. And being on her own could be downright lonely, she realized, rinsing off the knife she needed to slice pie for table number five. It was summer so the kids were out of school. Terry had come from Feld to pick them up, and now she was looking at three full days without them. She had to work tonight and tomorrow, but she was off, for a change, on Wednesday. What would she do with herself?

Maybe she should offer to take a shift for one of the other waitresses. She was already scheduled for forty hours this week, but heaven knows she needed the money.

"I just seated another table at your station," the hostess informed her. "Can you handle it? Or should I have Nicole punch in?"

It was late afternoon, before the dinner crush. Jaclyn was the only waitress on the floor and had three tables going already, but she could manage another. On a busy night at Joanna's, the manager assigned five tables to each server. Sometimes, when they were slammed, Jaclyn took six. "No problem. I've got it."

"Two men," the hostess responded. "And one looks good enough to eat."

Jaclyn didn't care if they were handsome. She felt no desire for another relationship, at least not yet. That they were male was significant, though. In her experience, men usually tipped better than women or families or seniors.

She delivered dessert to the four older women dining together at table five and approached the newcomers to find them both perusing the menu.

"Can I get you something to drink?" she asked.

"I'll have a cola," the man on her right replied. Heavy-set and about forty years old, he was resisting the loss of his hair by combing the few remaining strands over the dome of his head. *He* certainly didn't look good enough to eat. Which meant…

The man on her left lowered his menu. He had warm brown eyes, black hair and a ruggedly attractive face with a slightly cleft chin. His dark tan gave the impression that he worked outdoors, despite the business suit that fit his athletic body to perfection.

"Hey, don't I know you from somewhere?" he asked.

Jaclyn shook her head. Working in a café-style restaurant open twenty-four hours a day, she heard that line a lot. Only, it was usually after dark, not at four o'clock in the afternoon. Still, she had to admit it sounded better coming from a man who looked as if he could be plastered on a billboard advertising men's briefs.

"I doubt it. I'm new to Reno."

He frowned. "I never forget a face. Where did you live before?"

"A little town off the loneliest road in America."

"Highway 50. You're from Feld," he said. "You were Terry's girl."

Jaclyn blinked in surprise. "Yeah. How did you know?"

"I lived there for a while."

Even here she couldn't completely escape Feld or Terry. Jaclyn racked her brain, trying to remember who this man was. He looked about her age. If he'd lived in Feld long, she'd certainly know him.

And then it dawned on her. This was Cole Perrini, the boy who'd moved in right before their senior year. The wiry, rangy youth was gone. He seemed at least two inches taller and nearly fifty pounds of pure muscle heavier. But it was definitely Cole. The eyes and that cocky grin gave him away, along with a certain hard-bitten edge that seemed to warn everyone to keep their distance or take their chances.

"Oh, you're Cole," she said, remembering far more than just his name. The oldest son of a poor mining family, he'd lived in a cheap trailer just outside town and driven a beat-up old truck. Terry had been voted most likely to succeed that year. Had there been a category for it, Cole Perrini would have been nominated most likely to get someone pregnant. Which was exactly what he'd gone on to do. The girls loved him because he was handsome and dangerous and, from what Jaclyn had heard, good with his hands. Terry's crowd hated him—for the same reasons.

"You married Rochelle," she added.

He winced. "We're divorced."

"I know." The beginning of Cole and Rochelle's story was common knowledge, at least in Feld. Rochelle had loved Cole to distraction and chased him for more than a year. She'd gotten pregnant, and he'd married her. The rest Jaclyn had heard when she'd run into Rochelle years ago. Cole hadn't been faithful—which sounded all too familiar—and the marriage had ended in divorce just a few months after Rochelle miscarried.

"You still with Terry?" he asked.

"No." Didn't finding her here tell him that?

"I'm sorry."

"It's okay. My life's the way I want it," she insisted.

"Right. You were pregnant when I left Feld, weren't you?"

He remembered that? The last time Jaclyn had seen Cole Perrini was at the grocery store about ten years ago, a month before she'd given birth to Alex. Wearing an enigmatic smile, he'd shaken his head at her before strolling outside and driving away. And she hadn't seen him since. She'd wondered what he'd been thinking, and guessed he was letting her know how crazy he thought she was for marrying Terry. He'd actually told her once, back at a high-school football game, that she'd be a fool to do so. But she'd laughed and asked him who he thought would be better for her—him? He hadn't answered.

"I have three kids," she said. "Alex is almost eleven, Mackenzie is five and Alyssa is three."

"So the divorce is fairly recent."

"Very. It's final today."

He raised his brows and looked around the restaurant,

obviously taking in the fact that after twelve years and three kids, this was where Jaclyn Wentworth found herself.

Shame warmed Jaclyn's cheeks. Waiting tables wasn't exactly where she'd hoped to be at thirty-one. She'd wanted to be a wife and mother, to help Terry run the ranch, to grow old and gray with him. She'd never dreamed she'd need to be more than that. But life had a way of sending one scrambling for Plan B.

Not that her backup plan included waitressing forever. She was hoping to find something else once she got on her feet, someplace she could work during school hours, instead of nights and weekends. She just hadn't found anything yet that paid enough to support her little family.

She shot a look at Cole's friend, who was watching her curiously, before asking Cole, "You still driving semis?"

He chuckled. "No, I gave that up when I got divorced." As though her momentary distraction had reminded him that he hadn't introduced his companion, he said, "This is Larry Schneider with Reno Bank and Trust. Larry, this is an old friend of mine from high school, Jackie Rasmussen."

"Jaclyn Wentworth," she corrected, smiling a greeting at Larry. Everyone she knew in Feld called her Jackie, but she'd started using Jaclyn when she moved to Reno. She would have switched to her maiden name, too, but she didn't want her last name to be different from her children's.

"What are you doing now?" she asked Cole, even though part of her didn't want to know. He looked successful sitting there in his tailored suit. He'd escaped Feld and landed on his feet. For that she was envious. Especially because she'd just taken a flying leap and landed in the gutter.

"I build houses."

"You're a contractor?"

Larry gave a genial laugh. "Not quite. Cole takes a

pretty hands-on approach to his job, but he's not a contractor. He's a developer. And a damn good one. Haven't you ever heard of Perrini Homes?''

Jaclyn shook her head. "I've lived here less than a year."

"Well, he's got a subdivision near the golf course. Four- and five-bedroom homes. You should drive by and take a look if you're ever in the market."

Jaclyn doubted she'd be able to afford a home of that size in the next twenty years. She barely managed to pay the rent on the house they lived in now. It was only eight hundred square feet and older than the hills, but she'd rented it for the yard. Accustomed to wide-open spaces, she refused to raise her three children in an apartment.

"I'll do that," she said.

"I'd like to build a small development a few miles east of here," Cole said. "In Sparks. That's why I'm coming, hat in hand, to Larry, here."

Larry adjusted his silverware and smiled. "And I'll probably give you what you need. I've financed several of your projects already, haven't I?"

Working outdoors with his contractors explained the tan. A meeting with his banker explained the suit. "Sounds like things are going well for you," Jaclyn said.

Cole shrugged in a nonchalant manner. "Well enough, I guess."

The couple at one of her other tables kept swiveling their heads, looking for her and, no doubt, their check. And the food for table two was probably ready. She needed to get moving. "Would you like something to drink?" she asked Cole.

"I'll have an iced tea."

"It'll be just a minute."

Jaclyn left, feeling Cole's gaze trail after her. Who would've thought she'd run into him again? Especially here, now, when even pride was a luxury she couldn't afford.

She ducked into the kitchen and quickly tallied the tab for table three, but by the time she brought it out, the man was already standing.

"We've been waiting for ten minutes while you were busy flirting with that guy over there," he said loudly enough for half the restaurant to hear.

Aware of the attention he was drawing, Jaclyn flushed. "I'm sorry." She wanted to deny that she'd been flirting with anyone, but she handed him his bill and began to gather up the plates, instead. Sometimes it was smarter to simply apologize. She didn't want a scene, not with Cole Perrini less than ten feet away. And not while Rudy Morales, her manager, was on duty.

"I think we deserve a break here—for the wait," he persisted. "You've made us late for a movie."

Then, why didn't he pay his bill and hurry off?

The woman who'd eaten with him lowered her eyes, a sure sign that he was making a fuss over nothing.

"I couldn't have been longer than five minutes," Jaclyn said. "I just ran into an old friend, that's all."

"Well, maybe you should visit with your friends when you're on your break."

"I've apologized," she said. "If it'll make you feel better, skip the tip."

"I wasn't planning on leaving a tip."

Jaclyn felt anger course through her. This guy was an opportunist, and he was trying to take advantage of her. Her natural instincts prompted her to stand her ground. But the nagging worry of how she'd support her children if she lost her job kept her voice cool and polite. Rudy was already looking for any excuse to write her up.

"What if I send home a couple of pieces of pie with you? Will that help?" she asked.

"I don't want pie. I think you should comp our meals."

"For waiting five minutes?" Jaclyn asked. "You never even told me you were in a hurry."

"I don't have to give you my schedule when I sit down to eat. Now, are you going to work with me, here, or do I have to speak to your manager?"

A knot of unease lodged in Jaclyn's belly. When she'd first started working at Joanna's, Rudy had pursued her pretty aggressively. She'd gotten firm with her refusals, and he'd had it in for her ever since. "Fine. I'll take it out of my tips," she said. "Why don't you just go ahead and leave?"

"That's more like it," the man replied, slinging an arm around his companion and starting for the door. "Jeez, what kind of place are you running here, anyway?"

"It's a restaurant," a male voice replied. "In a restaurant, you order, you eat and you pay. Then you tip, generously."

Jaclyn looked up to see Cole Perrini towering over them all, and knew her day was about to go from bad to worse. Rudy would hear and... "This is my problem," she said quickly. "I'll handle it."

"Yeah, let her handle it," the guy said. "We were just on our way out."

Cole smiled and lifted his hands, but he blocked their path, and a certain hardness in his eyes belied his casual stance. "That's fine. You pay your bill before you go, and we won't have a problem, right?"

The man's face turned scarlet. He sputtered for a moment, looking as though he'd press the issue, but a glance at Cole's superior size and build seemed to convince him. Throwing a twenty on the table, he grabbed his companion by the arm and stalked out, pulling her along with him.

Before Jaclyn could say anything, Rudy appeared.

"What's goin' on here, Jaclyn?"

Jaclyn watched the door close behind the couple, then picked up the money and the bill. "Nothing, why?"

Rudy glanced doubtfully at Cole, who smiled and shrugged.

"That guy was an old friend of mine," he said, then made his way back to his seat.

WHAT WAS JACKIE RASMUSSEN—Jaclyn Wentworth—doing here, waiting tables?

Cole went through the motions of eating and tried to make a halfway-decent pitch for the funding to do the Sparks project, but he couldn't concentrate. Seeing Jaclyn brought back the most painful years of his life—memories that crept in between each sentence he spoke, wove through the whole conversation like an invisible thread. For the first time in eight years, he couldn't shut out Feld and the stifling, hot trailer he'd lived in there, the cloying smell of illness, his poor mother, pale and dwindling, his hungry brothers and absent father. And Rochelle. God, Rochelle. Just the thought of her made his throat feel as if it were closing up.

In a quick, desperate gesture, he loosened the knot of his tie and undid the top button of his shirt.

Larry glanced up at him in surprise. "Somethin' wrong, Cole?"

"No." Cole took a deep breath and a drink of water. He was free. Feld was history. Rochelle was on her own. His mother and father were gone...

"Would you like dessert?"

Jackie stood next to him, waiting with her pad. She'd left Feld, too, even though he never dreamed she would. He'd thought she would shackle herself to Terry and live under Burt Wentworth's thumb forever, or at least until she and Terry inherited his land and his money. All the girls in school had wanted Terry, and the family name and bank account that stood behind him. They'd wanted everything Jackie had just walked away from—for this. Who would have thought it?

"I'll just have a cup of coffee," Larry said.

"I'll have the same," Cole added, and Jackie soon returned with two steaming cups.

"Will there be anything else?"

Cole shook his head. He couldn't look at her anymore. When he saw her face, he saw Feld and the desert, and felt things he didn't want to feel.

"It was good to see you again, Cole," she said, slipping the check onto the table.

Cole wished he could say the same. "You look great, Jackie," he said, searching for some scrap of truth to offer.

She smiled, but it was only a ghost of the smile he remembered from high school. "Thanks," she said. "You always did have a way with the ladies."

Cole couldn't tell by the tone of her voice if she meant it as a compliment. But she walked away then, and he was free to pay his bill and go—and pretend he'd never seen her.

JACLYN WATCHED Cole leave and was glad to have him gone. She needed no reminders that her life had turned out far differently from everyone's expectations, including her own. She faced that fact every day when she put on her uniform, when she had to leave her children with Holly Smith, a young mother who lived down the street, when she wrote a check and knew it would barely clear her account.

Why did I have to run into him here? she asked herself, clearing off his table. Joanna's patrons paid at the cash register, but Jaclyn could see the edge of a crisp bill—her tip—stuck under Cole's plate. She slid the money out, expecting ten, maybe even twenty dollars, but found fifty, instead.

She stared at the 5-0 on the bill, amazed and sickened by what it meant. Fifty dollars was pure charity. Cole understood her situation—and he pitied her.

Damn. She was once the prom queen of Feld High. No one had doubted she'd marry Terry and live happily ever after. But she'd achieved no fairy-tale ending. She was divorced with three children and nearly penniless, her situation pathetic enough to make old friends feel obligated to give her money when they saw her.

Tears burned behind Jaclyn's eyes, and she began to wonder if she'd been crazy to try to escape Terry. She could have continued as his wife—but what kind of life would that have been? She had a right to fight for something better, didn't she? She longed to go back to school and become a nurse or a schoolteacher, *something* professional, to prove to herself and others that she could pull out of the tailspin of divorce and loss and regret.

If only she had the time and the money. She had four mouths to feed and bills that couldn't wait until she graduated from anything. Heck, she had bills that couldn't wait until payday.

Jaclyn shoved the money in her apron and finished stacking the dishes. Forget Cole, she told herself. He didn't matter. Nothing mattered except survival. So what if she felt as if the world were closing in on her and she was trying to run through quicksand to escape. She certainly wasn't the first woman to feel this way.

"Jaclyn?"

Turning at the sound of Rudy's voice, she found her manager standing at her elbow. At five feet five inches, he was just tall enough to look her straight in the eye.

"Yeah?"

He gave her an insincere smile, revealing eyeteeth that stuck out like fangs. It was her first indication of trouble. His words were the second. "I just had a gentleman call me. He claims a friend of yours threatened him with bodily harm when he was here just a few minutes ago. Can I see you in my office?"

The table next to them stopped eating to watch, but

Jaclyn ignored them. Too much fear prickled down her spine to worry about embarrassment now. "That's not true," she said.

Rudy nodded his greasy, dark head toward the kitchen. "In my office," he said, turning away.

And Jaclyn had no choice but to follow.

CHAPTER TWO

"I'M AFRAID I'm going to have to let you go."

Rudy sat behind his desk, gazing up at her with small eyes that were mere slits in his brown, fleshy face. His belly rested in his lap, and Jaclyn's personnel file was spread out in front of him.

Jaclyn stood near the open door, leaning against the wall for support, nearly leveled by shock, and horror, and myriad other emotions evoked by the injustice of his actions. "B-but you can't," she stammered.

He smiled, proving what Jaclyn had suspected all along. He was enjoying this. This was the moment he'd been waiting for ever since the last time she'd rebuffed him when he'd tried to talk her into coming over to his place after work.

"Actually, I can," he said, rocking back and steepling his fingers. "I'm the boss, in case you've forgotten. And the complaint I just received requires serious action."

"Serious action?" Jaclyn echoed weakly. "I've been a model employee ever since I started almost a year ago."

"A model employee doesn't threaten patrons."

"You know I didn't threaten anyone. And neither did—"

He held up a hand for her to stop. "A model employee shows up for all her shifts."

"I've never left you hanging—"

"It's all right here." He tapped her personnel file. "On August fourth, you didn't appear for work—"

"I had strep throat, and I called you—"

"You weren't here, that's what matters, and you received a written warning. On October tenth, you were late for work. A second written warning. On December ninth, your last and final no show—"

"And my third warning," Jaclyn finished. "But I couldn't come in that day. My baby was sick, and I couldn't get anyone to cover for me."

"Because you gave them no notice."

"The chicken pox gave me no notice! What did you expect me to do?"

"There's always some excuse," he said with a theatrical sigh. "But I have a restaurant to run here. I need waitresses who are dependable."

Jaclyn knew few waitresses were as dependable as she was. She'd missed a few days when Alyssa had the chicken pox, and she'd been late once when the bus had broken down and hadn't come to pick up Mackenzie and Alex for school. But she never called in sick unless it was a real emergency. She had a stack of customer commendations, and she was just about the only one who took the side work—filling salt and pepper shakers and ketchup bottles, scrubbing down tables and cleaning the kitchen—seriously.

Drawing an unsteady breath, she clung tenaciously to her temper. Even with Cole's fifty bucks, she needed the money she'd planned to make this week. She couldn't let Rudy, and his vindictiveness, cost her that.

"Come on, Rudy," she said. "That guy today was just trying to get a free dinner. I didn't keep him waiting more than five minutes."

"It was enough to make him and his wife miss their movie."

"So he says. Give me a break. It's only five-thirty now."

"He says he'll never eat here again!"

Jaclyn moved closer, but the smell of old sweat pressed her back. Rudy's office had no windows. It was more of a pantry, really. Small and close, with loaves of bread and other packaged items lining shelves that wouldn't allow the door to shut, it reeked of him. He was the kind of man with stains under the arms of every shirt.

"Then Joanna's is better off for it," she replied. "I wouldn't put it past that guy to plant a fly in his food."

"If he was so bad, why didn't you come get me?"

Because of this, Jaclyn wanted to say. *Because I need my job too badly to give you any reason to take it away from me.*

Aware of the cooks barking back and forth, the burgers sizzling on the grill, and the constant tramp of feet just outside, Jaclyn lowered her voice. "You've been out to punish me for a long time now, Rudy. This has nothing to do with the quality of my work, does it. What is it you're trying to prove?"

He laughed derisively. "That's pathetic, Jaclyn. I don't need your tight little ass running around this place. Now get your things and go."

For a moment, the kitchen clatter outside faded away, and Jaclyn heard only the beating of her heart. Its quiet tattoo seemed to echo the words: *Alex, Mackenzie, Alyssa.* As much as she hated to lower her pride any further, especially for a man like Rudy, she thought of all the things her children would need, and knew she had no choice.

"Please," she whispered. "You know I have kids who are depending on me. At least let me work out the week."

He snapped her file shut and hefted himself to his feet. "I'm afraid I can't do that," he said. "Now, if you'll go, I have to get back on the floor."

DAMN HIM, Jaclyn thought. She'd run into Cole Perrini for the first time in ten years, and he'd gotten her fired. Just like that.

Her eyes blurred as she scanned the want ads, and she paused briefly to wipe away two stubborn tears that rolled, one at a time, down her cheeks. As soon as she'd left Joanna's, she'd stopped by a convenience store to buy a newspaper. The checker had stared at her red, swollen eyes, causing her to chafe under the unwanted scrutiny, but it hadn't taken long to plunk down a buck seventy-five, grab a newspaper and a cola, and hurry away. Now she sat at her scarred wooden dining table, the sun fading to dusk outside, feeling the emptiness of her small house surrounding her like a shroud, and was both grateful for the privacy and terribly lonely.

Things'll get better, she told herself. *It's only been a year.* But it was hard to have much faith in finding a pot of gold at the end of this rainbow, when everything she saw in the paper either paid too little or asked too much. *Computer experience required. Medical experience required. Bachelor's degree required. Technical skills a plus...*

Her chair raked the linoleum as she rose to stare into the refrigerator. She hadn't eaten since breakfast, but with the children gone, there seemed little point in preparing a home-cooked meal. Retrieving a package of instant noodle soup from the cupboard, she set some water on the stove to boil, went to the bathroom to blow her nose, and returned to the kitchen table to resume her job search.

She'd never get ahead working as a waitress, she thought. She had to find something else, something with a future.

What about becoming a secretary? Though she was probably a little rusty, she'd taken typing in high school, and she still had some nice clothes left over from her married years. Office hours would be ideal, especially during the winter when the children were in school.

Problem was, most of the secretarial positions she saw required computer experience. She barely knew how to turn on a computer, let alone run Quickbooks or Excel or Microsoft Word or any of the other programs she saw listed so

frequently. Some companies demanded previous experience, as well, and she doubted having changed a million
dirty diapers would qualify her.

At last, Jaclyn saw an ad that made her pause:

Wanted: receptionist. Phones, light typing. $9/hr. No
benefits.

No benefits? Well, she didn't have benefits now.
Quickly, she did the math. If she worked forty hours per
week, she'd make $1,440 a month before taxes. Rent was
$850. Her car payment was $350. Car insurance, $100.
Health insurance, $340, utilities $180, and the list went on.
Even with Terry's $750 in child support, she'd be in the
red before she bought any gas or groceries or clothes for
the kids—she still had the credit-card bills she'd rung up
while they were married that the court had ordered her to
pay.

The pressure of tears began to build behind her eyes
again, causing a headache. Dammit! What now? She'd have
to go back to waiting tables. She had no choice. She could
have augmented what she made as a waitress giving piano
lessons, but she didn't have a piano. Terry had kept her
baby grand, along with almost everything else, when they
divorced.

The telephone rang, and Jaclyn looked at it with no intention of answering. But then she thought it might be the
kids, that they might need her, and picked up the receiver.

"Hello?"

"Jackie?"

Terry. Jaclyn's stomach tensed, the way it did whenever
she heard her ex-husband's voice. Their conversations were
never very pleasant.

"Is something wrong with the kids?" she asked.

"No. I thought you'd be at work. I was just going to
leave a message for you to call me."

"What for?"

"Alex says you returned the Nikes I bought him when he was here last and got him some cheaper shoes."

The accusation in Terry's voice was unmistakable. Jaclyn closed her eyes and shook her head. She wasn't in the mood to fight about the shoes. She'd just lost her job, and Terry's biggest concern was making sure Alex had brand-name sneakers.

"I did," she admitted.

"Why? You had no right to do that."

"I had every right, Terry. They were sixty dollars, enough to buy shoes for all three children, and you deducted it from my child support this month."

"That's what child support is for. To buy clothes and shoes and other things."

"But it's not up to you to decide how the money is spent. The kids are living with me most of the time, and we had other priorities."

"Like?"

Like food and electricity. But Jaclyn wasn't about to admit that things were quite that dire, even though she suspected Terry already knew. She figured the kids had to reveal in everyday conversation bits and pieces that gave her away, but Terry wasn't about to make life any easier on her. He wanted her as miserable as possible, and he didn't seem to care if his children suffered right along with her.

"It's none of your business how I spend the money," she said. "I don't have to account to you. Believe me, it takes every dime and then some to give the kids what they need. It's not like I'm spending the money on myself."

"But they don't have what they need. I don't want a kid of mine running around in ten-dollar tennis shoes!"

Jaclyn stifled a groan. "That's great, Terry," she said. "Then, I have a simple solution. Buy Alex the Nikes and don't charge me for them. You can buy him whatever you want. Buy him and the girls whole new wardrobes. I won't stop you, and I won't take anything back, as long as you don't deduct it from my child support.''

"You'd love that, wouldn't you? Then you might have the money to get a new dress and a manicure and go on the hunt for another man.''

"It's a tragedy that you won't be generous with your kids for fear I'll benefit in some way. It's the same thing with the piano issue. You won't let me have my piano even though, if I had it, I could teach the children to play.''

He chuckled bitterly. "I bought you that piano, and it cost me thousands. If you want it back, you know where to find it.''

"What's that supposed to mean?''

"If you don't like the way things are, you can always change them, Jackie.''

"By coming back?''

"That's all I've ever wanted.''

"You sure have a strange way of showing it.''

"Are you kidding? I've tried every way. I've begged, I've pleaded, I've promised—''

"And drank and philandered and lied…''

"I'm sorry about that, Jackie. How many times do I have to say it? I'm damn sorry. I wasn't thinking straight.''

"For twelve years? What's changed?''

"I've paid my price. You've taught me a lesson. That's what you wanted to do, isn't it? Now, come home. I want my kids back.''

That's what he thought the divorce was about? Revenge? Jaclyn could hardly believe it. What about the trust he'd destroyed, the faith, the love, the family ties? If he didn't understand by now what losing those things had cost them all, he never would.

"You get your kids whenever you want them," she said. "I've never tried to keep them from you.''

There was a long pause. "I want my wife back," he said softly. "I still love you, Jackie."

Jaclyn's stomach hurt so badly she thought she might throw up. "You and your high-priced lawyers have done everything possible to make my life miserable because you *love* me? That's not what I call love, Terry. Neither is how you treated me when we were married."

He cursed, growing angry again. "The lawyers were your idea, dammit. I'm not taking the blame for that. I never wanted the divorce in the first place."

Wordlessly, Jaclyn shook her head, feeling the dull throb escalate to a sharp, pounding pain. This conversation was certainly par for the day, but she and Terry had been down this road too many times. She thought about hanging up on him, but she had an issue she wanted to discuss, too, and now was as good a time as any.

"What about the decisions we made concerning the kids?" she asked.

"What decisions?"

"We agreed to make the divorce as easy on them as possible. We were going to speak kindly to and about each other. We weren't going to place blame. We weren't going to compete with each other for their affection. I've done my part, Terry."

"And you're saying I haven't done mine? What exactly are you accusing me of?"

He knew, but he was playing his favorite role—the innocent, persecuted martyr.

"Every time the kids come home, they seem angry with me, as though they blame me for something," she said.

"And you think it's my fault that they'd rather we were a family again?"

"Don't twist this. Alex told me what you've been saying about me."

Silence.

"How can you tell them the divorce was all my fault?" she asked.

"Who should they blame, Jackie? I had nothing to do with it. I can't believe you want me to be the bad guy."

"I don't think either one of us should have to be the bad guy. That's the whole idea. We're supposed to support each other, for their sakes. Don't you understand, Terry? You're not doing it for me. When you say bad things about me to them, you make them choose between us. That's hard on a child. And it's terribly selfish."

"Well, you should know about that. You've ruined all our lives with this divorce. How selfish is that?"

"What?" Jaclyn's blood pressure nearly went through the roof. "You're acting as though I was the one who was unfaithful to you!"

"I was never unfaithful to you, Jackie. Not really. I didn't care about those other women."

"And that makes it okay to sleep with them?" she asked, but she didn't wait for his answer. It wouldn't make sense to her. It never did. And no amount of arguing would change his mind. He wasn't going to take any responsibility for the divorce. He'd never had to take responsibility for anything in his life. Why start now?

She hung up and stared at the phone, breathing hard, letting the impotency of her anger drive away her earlier tears.

Come hell or high water, she would not let Terry starve her out. She would find a job, and she would make a success out of her life if it killed her.

Flipping off the stove, she ignored the water that had nearly boiled away to nothing and went back to the paper. She'd check each ad, no matter the column, and she'd apply for everything, whether she was qualified or not. Something had to go her way eventually, didn't it?

And that was when she saw it—an ad under Real Estate Sales.

Wanted: agent to work out of model homes near
Washoe County Golf Course. Must have R.E. license
and at least three years' sales experience. $36,000/year
plus commission, full benefits. Call 555-4108.

Thirty-six thousand dollars a year sounded like a fortune
to Jaclyn, but the salary wasn't what caught her interest.
Below the ad, in big, fancy script, was the logo of the
company that had placed it: Perrini Homes.

THE NEXT DAY, Jaclyn wiped her sweaty palms on a tissue,
straightened her linen dress, checked her lipstick in the
rearview mirror and climbed out of her Mercury Sable,
hoping she looked professional, capable, poised. It was
early yet, not quite eight o'clock, but finding Cole Perrini's
development had been easier than she'd thought. Blue-and-
white flags heralded the entrance, along with a huge sign
that announced five new model homes open to public view-
ing. The golf course was less than a quarter of a mile away.

Wow, she thought, squinting against the rising sun to
better see Cole's houses. They were big and made mostly
of brick. Steeply gabled roofs, dormers with black shutters
and lots of white-paned windows gave the development a
Georgian grace that was definitely unusual for Nevada, but
classy. Very classy.

"You're certainly not sparing any expense, Cole," she
murmured to herself, noting the expansive yards, recently
groomed to perfection with brand-new landscaping and
white, split-rail fences. She'd driven around the neighborhood when she'd first entered the development, and knew
there were at least fifty homes in varying stages of construction on a maze of streets and cul-de-sacs. She suddenly
felt foolish for having asked Cole if he was still driving
semis. Evidently he'd come a long way since then.

Her heels clicked on the aggregate walkway that led up
to the first home, set apart from the row of models by a

fancy stone fence with Oak Ranch Estates by Perrini Homes carved into it. A sign on the house labeled it as the office. Another sign in the window said Closed.

Jaclyn stood on the front stoop, wishing she could turn around and go home. But she wasn't about to lose her nerve now. Someone would be coming shortly. If Cole could afford to hire a real-estate agent for thirty-six thousand dollars a year, maybe he could afford a secretary to run errands and type and file for far less than that. Then she could learn the business, get a start and she hoped, become a real-estate agent someday. Showing homes was something she thought she might be good at. At least it was a job with a future.

A light glowed inside the house, but for all Jaclyn knew it had been on all night. She tucked a strand of fallen hair into the knot at the back of her head, fidgeted with her purse and watched the street for an approaching car. Then she glanced at her watch. Seven-fifty. Ten minutes more and surely someone would—

The door swung open behind her and a tall, long-legged man in jeans and a clean T-shirt nearly bowled her over on his way out.

"Whoa! Sorry about that!" he said, catching her before she landed in the flower bed. "I wasn't expecting anyone so early. You okay?"

"I'm fine. Didn't mean to surprise you." She gave a shaky laugh. "I'm looking for Cole Perrini. Could you tell me where I might find him?"

He rubbed his brow and frowned. "I think he might have forgotten you. He didn't mention having an appointment this morning."

"We don't have an appointment."

The newspaper sticking out of the side pocket of her purse caught his attention. "Are you here about the sales position?"

She nodded.

"Well, you're free to wait inside, if you want. Cole lives

here. Kinda convenient, since he works all the time, you know? But the phone rang just as I was leaving, and once Cole gets on a call, he can stay on it for hours. You might want to try the number in the ad and set an appointment. I think Rick's doing the interviewing.''

''Thanks, but I'm sort of an old friend of Cole's. I was hoping I could talk to him.''

Mild surprise lit his features. ''Oh, yeah? I'm Cole's brother, Chad.'' He stuck out a big hand, one with plenty of calluses and scars, and Jaclyn took it, feeling heartened by his friendly welcome.

''I'm Jaclyn.'' She didn't offer a surname, and he didn't ask for one.

''It's nice to meet you.''

''You sure look like your brother,'' she said, noting his wide shoulders, muscular arms and narrow hips. Chad didn't have a cleft in his chin, but he had the same raw masculinity as Cole, plus a couple of dimples that made him appear more fun-loving, if not more reckless.

''He's only half as good-lookin' as me,'' he teased, holding the door open for her. ''Go on in and make yourself comfortable. Rick'll be here shortly, so even if you don't see Cole right away, you'll get to talk to someone soon.''

He dipped his head in final greeting and strode off, leaving Jaclyn to search her brain for some kind of memory of him as the door banged shut. Cole had lots of brothers, she wasn't sure how many—four? five?—but they were all younger, and a high school girl didn't take particular notice of grade-school-aged boys. She couldn't place Chad and doubted she'd recognize any of the others, either.

Slipping into one of two modern chairs facing an expensive-looking desk, Jaclyn felt her tension start to mount again in the silence and willed herself to relax.

No sooner had she taken a deep breath than Cole came rushing down the hall from the back, holding what looked like a set of plans and wearing nothing but a towel around his hips.

"Chad! Wait!" he hollered. His hair was wet, like the rest of him, and dripping on the carpet, but he seemed to care only about catching his brother. Flinging the door open wide, he called after Chad again, but Jaclyn knew he'd missed his intended target when he cursed and pulled it shut again.

Then he saw her.

"Jackie?" His voice revealed his surprise.

Jaclyn jumped hastily to her feet, bumping her knee on the corner of the desk in the process but purposely swallowing the accompanying grunt of pain. "Hi, Cole," she managed to say, staring at all six feet two inches of nearly naked male. "I'm sorry. I didn't mean to catch you in the shower."

She tried to keep her eyes on his face, but it was impossible to avoid noting the lean, muscular build that started with bare feet and long legs and ended with an expansive chest sparingly covered in dark swirls of hair and a set of impressive shoulders. It was the thought, however, of what was hidden by the towel that rattled her the most. She hadn't seen a man this close to naked in over a year— and a year suddenly seemed like a very long time.

He looked down as though only now realizing that he wasn't fully clothed. But he must have considered himself modest enough, because he certainly didn't run for cover. "What are you doing here?" he asked, instead.

Jaclyn forced herself to stand tall and brave a smile. She didn't want him to know how difficult this was for her, how badly coming to him hurt her pride. "I just thought...well..." She indicated the paper she'd brought. "I saw your ad and thought I'd come over and..."

"Apply?" He frowned, his gaze traveling over her blue linen sheath dress and conservative shoes—an expensive outfit she'd bought while she was still married—before returning to her face. "You're a real-estate agent?"

Jaclyn swallowed hard, using every ounce of determination she possessed to keep her smile firmly in place. "Not exactly. I don't have my license…yet. I just thought maybe you could use a good secretary or something. You know, someone to run errands for you, do some typing—" her voice started to fade away, and she cleared her throat so she could finish strong "—answer phones, anything like that. I'm a hard worker and a fast learner," she added quickly.

"I'm sure you are, but…" He let his breath go in a soft hiss and ran a hand through his wet hair, shoving it back off his forehead. "What about your other job, at Joanna's?"

The story of her firing, and his part in it, hovered on the tip of Jaclyn's tongue. But the memory of his fifty-dollar tip stopped her from telling it. If Cole had pitied her yesterday, what would he feel today, when he found out she'd lost even that sorry job?

"Well, Joanna's is just a stop-gap, really," she heard herself saying. "A way to bring in some extra money and get out of the house." She laughed, praying he'd buy into her little charade, because she couldn't face the knowing in his eyes if he didn't.

"I may keep it, for weekends," she went on, "but I need something more…challenging. There're lots of interesting jobs in the paper, though." She patted it as if to convince him. "So if you don't have anything, it's no problem, really. I just thought I'd ask."

"I'd love to hire you, Jackie," he said, "but I'm not sure what I'd have you do. Except for a sales agent, I'm pretty well staffed here."

"Oh." She nodded. "Of course you are." Disappointment slashed through Jaclyn so strongly that it was a physical pain in her chest. Once the idea of becoming a real-estate agent had taken root inside her, it had bloomed quickly, seeming like the perfect answer to all her problems and raising her hopes higher than she had a right to let them go.

She should have known better. She'd been a fool to come.

"You're looking for someone with a license," she said, keeping the expression on her face as calm and pleasant as she could. But her smile was starting to wobble. She had to get away, fast. "I understand that. I just thought it wouldn't hurt to check. Anyway, I'll go so you can dress. I didn't mean to hold you up."

She grabbed her purse like a lifeline and started for the door, but he stood partially in her path and caught her by the arm as she passed.

"What is it, Jackie?" he asked. "What's going on?"

She could barely answer. Her throat constricted and her eyes—damn them!—were already filling with tears. "Nothing, Cole. Everything's fine," she insisted, blinking furiously in a last-ditch effort to stop the inevitable. "C-congratulations on all your success. I'm so…happy for you."

Then she twisted away and hurried out of the house, her only thought to reach her car before the first sob hit.

CHAPTER THREE

"WHO WAS THAT?" Rick asked, maneuvering around Cole to fit through the open doorway of the office.

Cole didn't answer. He was too surprised and confused by what had just happened. He'd run into Jaclyn Wentworth for the first time in ten years just yesterday, and this morning she appeared out of nowhere to ask him for a job. Stranger still, she'd nearly broken down in tears when he told her he didn't have anything.

What was going on? She couldn't need work *that* badly. The Wentworths were very wealthy. She had to have received a large settlement from the divorce, and there was always child support. She and Terry had three kids together.

Anyway, she certainly didn't look like she was hurting. That dress she'd been wearing was obviously expensive, and it fit her to perfection, hinting at feminine curves while revealing much of her long, long legs. Her thick russet hair was wound up into one of those sexy twists in back, and her light green eyes... God, those eyes. They were the prettiest he'd ever seen. He'd thought so in high school. He thought so now.

"Hello? Are you with me today, Cole?"

Jackie's car had disappeared around a corner, and Cole finally tore his attention away from the road. He closed the door. "I'm here."

"So what's up?" His brother indicated Cole's towel and grinned. "You have a guest last night? She must have been pretty good. You certainly stood in that doorway like a lovesick fool long enough. I guess that means things are really over between you and Laura, huh?"

Cole gave Rick a look designed to warn him away from the subject, but Rick only laughed.

"That evil-eye thing used to work when we were kids, but in case you've forgotten, I'm almost as big as you are now."

"Ha! That evil-eye thing never worked on *you*," Cole said. "You forced me to take you to the mat on everything. But you're twenty-eight now, and not likely to get much bigger. I've still got you beat by a couple of inches, so you'd better watch yourself or I'll whip your ass again."

Rick angled himself into a chair and propped his feet on the desk. "Like that time when I was fourteen and I wrecked Dad's truck?"

"I didn't whip you for wrecking it," Cole said. "I whipped you for stealing it."

Rick shook his head and put his feet down. "Creepers, Cole. How'd you keep us all in line? We were somethin', weren't we."

Cole laughed, because he could—now. The hard part was over. Despite his mother's illness, their poverty and his father's long hours in the mine, he'd kept his brothers safe. He'd seen to it that three out of the four of them—all except Rick—received a high-school diploma, that they learned the value of hard work, and that they stayed away from drugs and alcohol. As the oldest, he'd done his best by them, but he'd had to crack a few heads along the way, usually Rick's.

"It wasn't easy," he admitted, rubbing his neck. "And you were the worst of the bunch."

Rick started going through the papers on his desk; Cole took a moment to check the messages on the answering machine before heading back to dress for the day.

"Yeah, Andrew was the one you liked," Rick said. "He was always your favorite."

Cole shrugged. "He was the baby of the family and not likely to challenge me."

"And look at him now. He's going to college, just the way you told him to, right? Andrew's still a good little boy."

Cole noted the subtle change in Rick's voice, but wasn't exactly sure what to attribute it to. Was he jealous of Andrew's opportunity? Cole couldn't have afforded to put Rick through college seven years ago. He didn't have a high-school diploma, anyway. Chad had also missed out on any higher learning, but the younger Perrinis were now at the University of Nevada in Las Vaegs. "You could go back and finish high school, if you want," he said. "Then go on to college. Brian and Andrew would even let you room with them, if you hurry."

Rick didn't answer right away. He slammed one of the drawers in his desk and took a calculator out of another. "Maybe someday I'll overcome my wild past and do just that."

Cole grinned, pausing from his task of writing down the myriad messages he needed to return. "'Wild past' is right. Remember Mrs. Tiller? She invited us over for dinner, and you brought all those garter snakes in your pockets. I thought the poor woman was going to have a heart attack when one slithered past her plate."

Rick shook his head. "How could I forget? You gave me a whippin' the likes of which I'd never had before."

"Hers was about the only good home cookin' we ever got, besides what Granny Fanny gave us. And Mrs. Tiller never invited us back after that. I coulda killed you," Cole said, but he felt a prick of conscience all the same. Had he been too hard on Rick? Is that what stood between them? If so, it hardly seemed fair. Cole had been young and desperate to keep them all from winding up in separate foster homes. Maybe he'd forced Rick to knuckle under one too many times—but Rick had been so difficult. Riding him hard was the only way Cole could keep him in line. "I didn't pound on you because I liked it," he added, more gruffly than he'd intended.

Rick shrugged. "Hell, no. I deserved it."

For the first time in his life, Cole was tempted to share with him how heavy the load of raising his four brothers had been, how young and inexperienced he'd been at the time, how panicked. There were occasions he had gone without supper so his brothers could have more. Other days he took their turn sitting with Mom so they could get enough sleep to be ready for school. But Rick would never understand what life had been like for Cole. No one would ever understand. Which was why those years were better forgotten, along with Feld, the dusty little town where it had all happened.

"So, you gonna tell me about your lady friend?" Rick asked.

Cole ripped off the sheet of paper he'd been writing on and jammed the pen back into its holder. "She's just someone who's looking for a job."

"She got her real-estate license?"

"No."

"She a contractor, bricklayer, landscaper or roofer?"

"She look like a subcontractor to you?"

Rick chuckled. "Hardly." He punched a few buttons on his calculator and scribbled something down. "She was mighty fine, though. What *does* she do?"

"She married out of high school. She's recently divorced with three kids. I doubt she's worked many places."

"So did you give her the 'boy, did you screw up not getting a college education' speech?"

Cole chose to ignore Rick's needling. Whatever his brother held against him, he couldn't change the past. "I told her we don't have anything except the sales position right now."

"That's true."

Taking his messages with him, Cole headed down the hall. He needed to get dressed before anyone else arrived. "You think we could use some help here, around the office?" he asked, turning back.

Rick looked up. "Another salary wouldn't translate well on the projected profit and loss statement we need to provide the bank for that new loan."

"Yeah, you're right. Forget it."

Cole went to his room and dressed in a pair of jeans and a Perrini Homes T-shirt, then settled in his private office, where his primary tool was the telephone. Rick, with his natural talent for numbers, was the company controller and ran the front office, and Chad, as general contractor, handled most of the subs. But there were still a million details Cole felt more comfortable handling himself—like meeting with the county planners, coordinating inspections, dealing with the appraisers, signing the escrow papers when each house closed, approving new building plans and arranging financing for future projects. His days were long, but he loved his work. Nothing was more fulfilling than seeing a family pull into the driveway of a house he'd built, get out and water their flowers, or stand at the curb and talk to their neighbors.

But today Cole couldn't seem to settle into his usual routine. In his mind's eye, he kept seeing Jackie, the trembling of her lip, the proud tilt of her head, and knew he couldn't ignore whatever it was that was wrong.

Finally he picked up the phone and called information. They had no listing for Jaclyn Wentworth, but they had a J. Wentworth. He jotted down the number and dialed it. An answering machine picked up, and a child's voice told him to leave his name and number.

He hung up and grabbed his keys. It was time to return to Joanna's Restaurant.

COLE DOUBLE-CHECKED the address the waitress at Joanna's had given him, pulled to the side of the road and sat staring at Jaclyn's small house.

Damn. He'd had to go back to Joanna's, hadn't he. He just couldn't leave well enough alone. And now he knew Jaclyn had been fired and that she'd needed the job she'd asked him for, a whole lot more than she'd let on. Which left him with a decision. He could involve himself further and try to help her, or he could turn around and drive away.

His better judgment urged him to drive away. Jackie's problems weren't his problems. Lord knows, he'd had a hard enough time pulling himself and his brothers out of Feld, keeping food on the table, supporting his parents until they passed away and trying to build a new life and a business here in Reno. The last thing he needed was to take on more dead weight. It wasn't as if he had money running out of his ears. Perrini Homes was dangerously over-leveraged. If Oak Ranch didn't sell well, he could lose everything.

But Jaclyn's getting fired had come on the heels of his interference with that jerk who wouldn't pay his check yesterday, and he feared he might have cost her her job. Beyond that, he'd once been where she was right now—desperate, alone and new in town.

With a heavy sigh, Cole cut the engine and strode to the house. At his knock, the porch light came on. Jaclyn cracked open the door, then stepped back and swung it wide when she recognized him.

"Cole. How did you—"

"Hi," he said. "Looks like I've found the right place."

"How did you get my address?"

"Maddy at Joanna's gave it to me."

"You went back to Joanna's?"

"Yeah, I was looking for you."

"Oh."

"Can I come in?"

She hesitated, seeming embarrassed, but finally motioned him inside. "Of course. I was just doing some housecleaning. The kids are with Terry for a few days, so I thought I'd get some things done around here." She stripped off a pair of yellow rubber gloves. "Can I get you a drink?"

Her auburn hair was pulled back in a ponytail and she was wearing a simple tank top and denim shorts without shoes, but she looked even prettier than she had in her dress. Her firm, well-toned legs seemed to go on forever, and her skin, slightly damp with sweat, looked creamy and soft.

Cole tried not to notice that there was anything appealing about her. Jackie represented Feld and everything he'd escaped there.

"No thanks, I'm good," he said, moving past her.

The house was filled with old mismatched furniture, but it was clean. And it smelled like Jaclyn, a little earthy and definitely feminine, despite the hint of Lysol coming from the gloves she'd cast aside. Whether or not he wanted to admit it, Cole liked the smell. It reminded him of meadows and brooks and warm summer days. But from the looks of things, Jaclyn hadn't gotten a very big divorce settlement.

More bad news.

"You renting?" he asked.

She surprised him with a grin. "You think I'd buy this dump?"

"Beats a trailer." He smiled back, remembering, in spite of himself, the first time he'd ever seen her. She'd been sitting in his English class at the beginning of his senior year, and just the sight of her had thrown his boyish heart into overdrive. She had to be the only girl who'd ever made his palms sweat. Of course, that was before he knew she was a cheerleader, vice-president of the Honor Society, and captain of the debate team—exactly the type of girl who would never be interested in a tough, poor boy who missed as many days of school as he attended.

For a moment, the memories of Feld threatened to swallow him up again, but he focused on what Jaclyn was saying and pushed them aside.

"I wanted the kids to have somewhere to ride their bikes and set up a lemonade stand and run through the sprinklers," she said. "The neighborhood's not as bad as it looks, really. Mostly old folks on a pension." She sank into a seat across from him. "Of course, my three kids spice things up a bit."

"I bet." Cole noted that most of the pictures on the walls were crayon drawings, and wondered what Jaclyn's kids were like. After raising his brothers, he swore he'd never have any children of his own. He'd had enough of that kind of responsibility. But he'd bet Jaclyn's were cuter than most. Not that he wanted to meet them. He planned to offer Jaclyn the money she needed to get on her feet, and move on.

He cleared his throat. "I guess you know why I'm here."

She stared down at the threadbare carpet. "You found out I was fired yesterday."

"Yeah."

"Well, you didn't need to come."

She smiled, making another valiant effort to act as if she was fine, but Cole noticed how her hands fisted in her lap.

"Now that I'm on my own, I'd better get used to the ups and downs of it, don't you think?"

"How bad are things?" he asked, cutting to the chase.

Her eyes widened in surprise. "They're fine. I'm fine—"

"Jackie, I didn't come here for more of your stiff-upper-lip routine. I'm willing to help you, but I can't do that unless I know what you need."

"What I need?" She laughed, but there was no humor in it. "I need to go back twelve years, get a college education and not marry Terry. That's what I need." She paused. "You once warned me against doing exactly what I did. Do you remember?"

He remembered. He also remembered he'd warned her

against Terry because he wanted her himself. He'd had plenty of girls following him home from school and coming on to him at dances, and Rochelle calling him night and day, but Jaclyn was the one he'd dreamed about. "I was just a dumb kid. I don't know why I said what I did," he lied.

She folded her arms and leaned back. "Still, I wish I'd listened. Except, my children are great. I don't regret them."

The telephone rang, and she put up a hand to indicate she'd be right back. She carried the cordless phone into the kitchen to talk, but Cole could easily hear her, even though he stood and tried to amuse himself by figuring out what the pictures on her walls were supposed to be.

"What do you want now?... No, I didn't say that. I said she'd have to have her birthday party here... That place is too expensive, Terry, you know it is... Why do you always have to ruin everything for me?... Listen, I can't talk about this now because someone's here...Cole Perrini. You remember him, don't you? We went to school with him... What...?

She lowered her voice until Cole could barely hear her, but now that he'd heard his name, he strained to catch the rest.

"I can't believe you just said that. We're not doing anything. You have no right to even ask me that! Cole and I have never so much as kissed... Are the kids there? Did you just say that in front of Alex?... Forget it. I'm hanging up, Terry..."

Finally, in one frustrated-sounding burst, she said, "Well, he wouldn't have to be very good to be better than you." Then she hung up, leaving Cole wondering what he wouldn't have to be very good at. On the heels of her previous words, his imagination certainly presented some interesting possibilities. But they were possibilities he refused to entertain, because he knew that anything physical with Jackie would come at a price higher than he was willing to pay. He'd already raised all the kids he was going to raise. He wouldn't go through that hell again. And he'd already learned that marriage didn't suit him, either.

"Sorry about that," she said, returning.

"No problem. I've got to get going, anyway." He stood and opened his mouth to offer her the money he'd intended to give. He wanted to write her a check and be on his way. He didn't want to look back. But deep down he knew it couldn't be that easy. A woman with Jackie's pride wouldn't accept charity. So he did exactly what he'd promised himself he wouldn't do, and offered her the job she'd asked for, instead.

"I thought you didn't have anything," she said.

"Well, it won't be much to start with. You'll just have to fill in wherever we need you, and eventually we'll get you into the sales end of things. Once you get your license and some training, you can work anywhere."

Scowling, she said, "Cole, don't do this if—"

"Everyone needs a little help sooner or later, Jackie. When I came to Reno, there was a man who helped me get my start in real estate." His mentor. The one person who'd buoyed him up when he thought he'd drowned in responsibility. "I'm just passing on the favor. Besides, this isn't a handout. You'll work for your money. The position pays twenty-five hundred a month plus benefits. Can you get by on that?"

She nodded eagerly. "When do you want me to start?"

"Tomorrow, if you can."

A smile curved her lips. With hair falling from her ponytail in wispy strands, and hope and relief lighting her eyes, she looked incredibly attractive. She sure hadn't changed much since high school. Deep down Cole feared neither of them had changed enough. She no longer made his palms sweat, but she did strange things to his chest and caused a strong response in regions a little lower.

"I'll be there," she promised, then surprised him by standing on tiptoe to give him a quick hug. "Thanks, Cole. I'll do a good job for you," she murmured.

At least, that was what he thought she said. All he knew was that suddenly his nostrils were full of the scent of her, and his arms were full of the feel of her, and he could no longer regret hiring her.

He even thought about giving her a raise.

CHAPTER FOUR

THIS CAN'T BE HAPPENING, not on my first day! Jaclyn glanced at her watch, cringed when she saw she had only ten minutes until she was supposed to report at Perrini Homes, and frantically pumped the gas pedal of her Mercury Sable.

Come on, baby, start. Start!

The engine whined and chugged more slowly than before, then fell completely silent. Another turn of the ignition key caused nothing but a clicking sound. Her battery was dead. She'd have to go to the neighbor's and ask for a jump.

"Of all the blasted times," she muttered, getting out and trudging to Mr. Alder's next door. Careful to protect her best suit from the automatic sprinklers watering his lawn, she kept to the far side of the concrete walkway until she reached the porch, then gave his front door a hearty knock.

No one answered. She pounded two more times and had nearly given up in favor of Mrs. Lavender's across the street, when Mr. Alder finally opened up, wearing a tattered terry-cloth robe. He gazed at her in surprise, his white hair sticking up on all sides, the pattern of crumpled bedding imprinted on one whiskery cheek.

"Is it garbage day?" he asked.

Jaclyn cleared her throat, feeling a twinge of guilt for having dragged him from his bed to ask a favor. Retired for nearly eight years and a widower besides, he spent his time tinkering around his property. His days were probably long enough already. And it wasn't as though he particularly liked Jaclyn or her children. When they were home, Mackenzie, Alex and Alyssa disrupted the silence of the neighborhood, left their trikes and scooters in the road, sometimes picked his flowers as presents for her and generally pestered him at every opportunity. They considered any man over sixty a potential grandpa and were determined to win him over. But so far their efforts had done more to alienate than endear. Jaclyn had only chosen him as her savior today because she thought he'd be more mechanical than the little old lady across the street.

"I'm sorry to wake you," she said, "but I'm in a tight spot. I'm supposed to be at work in—" she checked her watch again and stifled a groan "—five minutes, and my car won't start. Is there any chance you could give me a jump?"

He angled his head to see her car sitting in her driveway with the hood up, and harrumphed. Then he muttered that he'd be right back and disappeared into the house. When he returned, he was dressed in his customary polyester slacks, short-sleeved, button-up shirt and wing-tipped shoes. A pair of jumper cables was clutched in one gnarled hand.

Jaclyn kept a vigilant but despairing eye on the time, while Mr. Alder moved his car alongside hers and hooked the jumper cables to both batteries. It was eight o'clock. She was late already. What was she going to tell Cole? Her tardiness might make him believe Joanna's was justified in firing her. She thought of going inside to call him, but didn't want to start her first day offering excuses. With Mr. Alder's help, she should be there soon.

Trying to keep calm, she climbed into her car, waited for Mr. Alder's signal and turned on the ignition. To her relief, the engine roared to life.

"Thanks," she called, as he removed the cables. "I'll bake you an apple pie this weekend, if you'd like one. Or maybe you'd prefer some strawberry jam. I make great strawberry jam.''

''Just tell your children to leave the rocks along the side of my yard alone,'' he said, his voice as gruff and cross as ever.

The rocks? What could her children possibly do to hurt some ugly old lava rocks? ''I'll tell them,'' Jaclyn said, sighing as she shifted into reverse and backed down the drive. Mr. Alder's patent disapproval was starting to get the best of her, but she'd have to deal with that later. She had more important things to worry about right now—like turning a seven- or eight-minute drive into no more than two or three.

Unfortunately, rush-hour traffic worked against her. By the time she arrived at Cole's office, it was nearly eight-twenty, and Cole wasn't anywhere to be seen. Neither was his brother, Chad. But the man she'd passed as she was leaving last time sat in the front office, talking on the phone. He lifted a finger to indicate he'd be with her in a minute, then bowed his head and jumped back into the conversation he'd been having when she entered.

''...I'm telling you we need those Sheetrockers there to-morrow. This house doesn't close by the fifteenth, it ain't gonna close, you know what I'm saying? Right, and in order to do that, we gotta get rid of these last few strag-glers... No, that's not good enough. The bank's watchin' us closely, wondering whether or not to plunk down an-other few mil. We need to convince them that their money's perfectly safe with us, and sales are the only way to do that. We have to close some escrows... That's right... Cole wanted it to happen yesterday...okay, see that it does...you got it...take it easy, man.''

He hung up and offered her a hesitant yet curious smile as he rose to his full height of nearly six feet and rounded the desk. ''You must be Jaclyn Wentworth,'' he said. ''Cole told me you'd be coming.''

He didn't add that Cole had said she'd arrive at eight, but Jaclyn feared he was thinking it. "Yes. I'm sorry I'm a little late. I'm normally very punctual, but my car battery was dead this morning and I had to get a jump."

Fleetingly Jaclyn realized she should have left her car running, given it time to recharge the battery. Instead, she'd pulled into the closest parking space, cut the engine and dashed for the office, which meant she'd probably need to get another jump come five o'clock. But there wasn't anything she could do about it now.

"I'm Rick, Cole's kid brother," the man said, offering to shake hands. "I'm the company controller, which in our case basically means I run the front office here, manage the cash flow and do the accounting."

"I think I remember seeing you a time or two in Feld." Jaclyn smiled as she accepted the big hand that momentarily engulfed hers. Unlike Chad, Rick wasn't the spitting image of Cole. He had the same lean, muscular build, the same angles to his face, but he had dark blond hair and blue eyes that held a certain wariness Cole had lost since high school. Jaclyn could sense other differences, as well, but couldn't yet place what they were.

"You probably did. I was a freshman when Cole was a senior. He said you were in his class."

"I was, but I certainly never expected to run into him again."

"It's a small world."

Folding his arms across his chest, he leaned one hip on his desk. "Um, just so I understand your capabilities, Ms. Wentworth, do you know how to use Windows?"

Jaclyn had seen that program mentioned a lot in the want ads. Everyone wanted a secretary who knew how to run Windows. "I'm afraid I don't. I haven't had much experience with a computer. But, please, call me Jaclyn."

"Jaclyn it is, then." He paused. "So you've never done any word processing?"

"No, but I can type. I—I took typing in high school."

"Okay. Do you have any accounting skills? Any book-keeping in your background?"

"Unfortunately not." Until she'd left Terry, Jaclyn hadn't even balanced her own checkbook. Terry's father had given them a monthly allowance, handled the credit-card statements and paid all the bills, but she wasn't about to volunteer that information. Rick's questions were already making her feel painfully inadequate.

"To tell you the truth, I've never worked in an office before," she admitted. "I think Cole hired me more on faith than anything else, because of the Feld connection. But I'm a quick learner and determined to be an asset here. I know it might be frustrating for you at first, but I hope you'll bear with me long enough to let me prove myself."

Jaclyn knew her sincerity had had an effect when Rick grinned and the hesitation in his manner eased. "I started with less. I think we can work with that."

"Great. Where do you want me to sit?"

He indicated a smaller mahogany desk next to a large map of the development. "That's your spot there, until we hire a real-estate agent and rearrange the place to accommodate three. For the time being, you can collect résumés for the position. Why don't you do the initial interview, too, then recommend the top three candidates to me? That would free some of my time so I can get caught up around here."

Jaclyn started to say that she didn't know what type of person they were looking for, but he raised a hand to let her know he anticipated such a response. "Cole told me you're not familiar with real-estate sales, but you can get some sort of feel for whether a person is reliable and well-motivated, and whether they seem experienced, right?"

She nodded.

"We'd prefer someone who's been in the business a few

years, but we'd stretch for a new licensee, if they're exceptionally sharp.''

"Okay.'' Jaclyn settled behind her new desk, which sat perpendicular to Rick's so that she saw him every time she looked up. An old-fashioned lamp, a black business phone, and a pad and penholder awaited her use on the polished surface; the drawers were empty, except for the recent addition of her purse and a Reno telephone book that looked as if it had been there since the beginning of time. "Will I be getting a computer?''

"I'll pick one up for you as soon as I can, but here's the bad news. There won't be anyone available to train you today until after lunch. I have to go to the county planning department and try to get the tree inspector to sign off on a couple of dying trees so we can have them removed and lay a foundation tomorrow. And Cole is out all day on appointments.'' He glanced helplessly around the office, and Jaclyn got the distinct impression that he didn't quite know what to do with her. "Any chance you could answer phones and do some filing until then?''

"Sure.'' Jaclyn gave him a reassuring smile that lasted until he headed out. But as soon as the door closed behind him, her confidence fizzled. She was sitting behind her new desk, wearing her best suit, gazing out at the perfectly manicured lawn and expansive Perrini Homes sign, feeling like a complete fraud. How much time would Cole—and Rick—give her to become comfortable with her position? Judging by the vast amount she needed to learn, she feared it would never be enough.

Dropping her head in her hands, Jaclyn massaged her temples to alleviate the headache that was already starting to pound there, then turned a doleful eye on the box Rick had set on the floor next to her before he left. It was overflowing with important-looking papers and business documents—profit and loss statements, escrow papers, house plans, bills, letters, litigation for God knows what, and receipts. Obviously, if Rick was the one in charge of the filing before she came, he was way behind.

Or he didn't know what to do with the stuff any more than she did. A daunting thought.

Jaclyn hauled the box into the next room and found a large photocopying machine and an entire bank of filing cabinets, just as Rick had promised. Hope momentarily raised its head as she gazed at the gleaming oak cabinets—they looked fairly innocuous—but then she opened the drawers. They were filled to bursting with hanging folders that weren't even in alphabetical order. And the papers inside them might as well have been written in Russian for all Jaclyn understood about what they were and why they belonged where they did.

What made her think she could do this job? she wondered, her insecurities returning full force. Rick had asked her to file, to *file,* for Pete's sake—which was supposed to be the easiest job in the world—and she couldn't even do that.

Feeling a little like the poor girl in "Rumpelstiltskin," who was locked in a chamber and expected to spin straw into gold, Jaclyn eyed the clock on the wall. She had three hours until Rick was expected back. She had to have something to show for them.

Tears of frustration brimmed as Jaclyn turned to the cabinet on her left and opened the top drawer, but she blinked them back. She'd wanted an opportunity, and Cole had given her one. She'd figure the filing system out somehow, even if it meant she had to read every piece of paper in the whole darn office.

IT WAS WELL AFTER SEVEN in the evening when Cole finally rolled into the driveway of Oak Ranch. He'd had a legitimately busy day meeting with engineers and architects and commercial real-estate agents, but he'd thrown himself even more wholeheartedly into his business than usual, hoping to forget that Jackie Wentworth started work today. After he'd left her place last night, he'd decided, for his own piece of mind, to ignore her as much as possible and let Rick deal with her. But it didn't look as though he was going to make it through the day without some sort of interaction. Her car was still in front of the office—and Rick's was gone.

What was she doing here so late?

Heaving a tired sigh, Cole toted his satchel-style brief-case and day-planner to the door and let himself in to find the desks empty, the place quiet. Where was Jackie? Had Rick taken her out to dinner or something?

It was certainly plausible. They were both single and attractive. But Rick and Jackie had nothing in common. And his kid brother was too young for her, anyway. There had to be—what?—three years between them?

Cole swallowed hard. Three years was nothing, certainly not the stretch it had been in high school.

Slinging his suit coat over the water cooler and loosening his tie, he sat behind his brother's desk, propped up his feet and dialed Rick's mobile. Cole hadn't checked in with the office today as he normally did, but Rick had given him an update on his voice-mail, so there hadn't been any real need to.

"'Lo," Rick answered.

"Hey, what's up?" Cole asked.

"Not a whole lot."

"Where you at?"

A pause. "Nowhere special, why?"

Cole could hear a dominant male voice and other conversation going on in the background. Was it a mall? More likely a restaurant. "You eating?"

"No."

"Jackie with you?"

"Who?"

"Jackie Ras—Wentworth, our new employee."

"You mean Jaclyn? Why would she be with me?"

"Because her car is here, but she's gone."

"Did you check the copier room?" Just as Rick spoke, someone near him said something about *Lady Chatterley's Lover*. At least, that was what Cole thought he heard. Where the heck *was* Rick?

"The what?"

"She was still in the copier room when I left," Rick shouted as the noise around him escalated. "I gotta go."

"Wait—" Cole said, but Rick had already hung up.

Puzzled, Cole stared at the phone. His brother used to stay at the office until ten or eleven almost every night. Lately he'd been coming in early but leaving promptly at five. He claimed he wasn't seeing anyone regularly but never mentioned how he spent his nights….

Something was up, Cole was certain. But what?

He shook his head. His brother was an adult now. Whatever it was, Rick could handle it—

"Who's here? Cole, is that you?" Jaclyn's voice resonated from somewhere down the hall, interrupting his thoughts.

"Yeah, it's me." Shoving to his feet, Cole went to see why his new employee was still at work. Didn't she understand that having a salary meant she wasn't being paid by the hour?

He found her in the copier room, just as Rick had suggested, sitting in the middle of a sea of file folders. Her shoes and jacket had been discarded by the door. Her hair was falling from a clip in back and, as he watched, she stretched her neck as though she had a kink in it. All in all, she looked like an overwrought librarian.

"What're you doing?" he asked, glancing nervously at the empty file drawer standing open above her head.

A proud smile curved her generous mouth. "I'm getting us organized."

Us? Cole felt his muscles tense. He'd never be able to

find anything again! What had Rick been thinking, turning her loose on the files on her first day? "Did Rick *tell* you to overhaul the whole filing system?" he asked, grappling for patience.

She indicated an empty cardboard box not far from her jacket and shoes. "No, he told me to file what was in that box until he had the time to train me. But when he *was* in the office, he was on the phone, so I kept myself busy in here. Once I got started, I realized this place needed some serious housecleaning."

Housecleaning? *Housecleaning?* This was his *business,* for God's sake, his sweat and hard work, and now… He gazed helplessly at the paper mess. "But you said you've never worked in an office before."

"I haven't." Her smile brightened even more. "It took me a long time to figure out how it should go, but once I started recognizing common elements, the sorting went much faster."

"I see." He hated the condescending tone that entered his voice, but he'd been up most of the night before, working on a proposal designed to interest private investors in his first out-of-town housing tract; he was too tired and irritable to deal with such an unexpected calamity. Obviously Jackie meant well and was trying hard to prove herself, but if she didn't go home soon, she'd learn just how unhappy he was with her little project.

He cleared his throat. "Do you know it's nearly eight o'clock?"

"Yeah. My kids are with Terry, so there's no real reason to go home. I'd like to finish here, as long as you don't mind."

He did mind. That was the problem. "But finishing could take all night, and then some," he said.

She followed his gaze over the cluttered room. "Actually, I'm almost done. I've already made the new file tabs, and everything is sorted into stacks, except this pile here—'' She indicated the papers closest to her, the ones she'd been poring over when he entered the room. "This is the stuff that doesn't seem to go with anything. Should I make a Miscellaneous file, or would you rather look through it and tell me where you want everything to go?''

He wanted everything to go back where it had been before the tornado that was Jackie Wentworth had hit his office, but he wasn't going to say so, not after seeing the pride she was taking in her work. Better to leave while he could still hold his tongue. "Actually, I haven't had any dinner. I think I'll go eat. Why don't you put them in a miscellaneous file for now, and Rick can have a look in the morning.'' *Right after he gets finished answering to me for letting you tear the place apart.*

"Okay. I'll finish up, then, and lock the office behind me when I go.''

Cole felt a muscle tic in his cheek with the effort it took him to smile. "That's fine. There's an extra set of keys in Rick's top drawer. You can keep them. Good night,'' he said, and left, cursing Rick for giving Jackie a free hand.

But deep down, he knew he couldn't blame Rick. Rick hadn't asked for Jackie's help; Rick hadn't wanted a secretary. Cole had hired her knowing she'd probably be more trouble than she was worth.

So he had no one to blame but himself.

FINISHING THE FILES took much longer than Jaclyn had expected. By the time she closed the last drawer, it was nearly midnight, but she felt a wonderful sense of accomplishment. She now knew more about Perrini Homes and how it was run than six months of training could have taught her. She'd read the closing papers on the first house Cole developed, the documents for his first loan and the appraisals of each project. She'd studied the maps of his developments, knew their location and size and sell-out information. Going through the files had shown her the history of Perrini Homes—and the past eight years of Cole's life.

Cole had to possess extraordinary business acumen to have built what he had out of nothing, Jaclyn thought, blowing a stray wisp of hair out of her face as she stood. According to Rochelle, he was a philanderer, like Terry, but at least he was a hard worker. At least he had dreams and knew how to make them come true.

She was going to make something of *her* life, too, Jaclyn decided, surveying the now tidy room. Taking Cole's entire filing system from chaos to order might have been a small step forward, but it made her more optimistic about her future. Heck, she already knew a lot more about real estate than she had fifteen hours ago.

''God, I feel great,'' she muttered happily, gathering her coat and shoes. She hadn't eaten since lunch, she was tired and her back ached from hunching over for so long, but the warm feeling she had inside made her smile. She wanted to traipse through the house and find Cole so she could show him what she'd done, but the house had been quiet for some time. Cole was probably asleep. She'd go home and celebrate her victory with a brownie from her own freezer—

Suddenly she had a terrible thought. What about her car? Would it start? She'd been so engrossed in her work that she'd completely forgotten about the depleted battery.

Fishing her keys out of her purse, she hurried outside and unlocked the driver's door. *Please start,* she prayed, slipping behind the wheel.

She pumped the gas pedal and turned the key, but nothing happened. The battery was dead, just as she'd feared. She was stranded at work on her first day, half starved and exhausted.

Imagining the sad picture she was going to make in the morning when Cole or Rick found her still at the office, wearing the same crumpled suit, she groaned. She had to get home. But how? It was too far to walk. She couldn't afford a taxi, not if she was going to have to buy a new car battery, too. And she didn't know how or where to catch a city bus. At this time of night, she wasn't sure she felt safe traveling on one, anyway. The places she'd lived had been too small for public transit. She'd never taken a city bus in her life.

Eyeing the back part of the office, the part that was Cole's living quarters, Jaclyn wondered if, by chance, he was still awake. His Lincoln Navigator was parked next to her car. If only she had his keys and a pair of jumper cables. She could be on her way in five minutes.

Can't hurt to check, she thought, getting out. She walked around to the back of the house, where she hoped to see a light or some indication that Cole might still be working, but everything was shuttered and dark.

Would he mind terribly if she woke him?

Motivated by hunger and an intense desire for her bed, she let herself into the office and tiptoed down the hall toward where Cole had gone. Outside a full moon hung bright and low, lighting those rooms that didn't have the blinds drawn. Jaclyn wandered through a state-of-the-art kitchen, complete with an island, a breakfast nook and white cabinetry, a formal dining room with hardwood floor and a den—judging by the expansive desk, leather furniture and fax machine—to confront a closed door that probably opened into Cole's bedroom.

Raising her fist, she took a deep breath…and knocked.

"Cole? Are you in there?"

No response. Maybe the door led to a pantry or laundry area, and not Cole's bedroom. She couldn't be sure.

"Cole?" she called again, rattling the knob. The door was unlocked, and she was halfway through it, thinking he must be somewhere else in the house, when she heard his sleep-filled voice from just a few feet away.

"It's okay, Laura. Come in. I'm glad you're here."

CHAPTER FIVE

COLE SMILED, content to remain half asleep as Laura slipped inside his room. He'd known she'd be back. She claimed she wanted nothing more to do with him, that she planned to marry and have a family with someone who was capable of making that kind of commitment. But she'd said similar things before. After a few weeks, she always called or came around, and they slipped into the same comfortable relationship they'd known for two years.

Tonight her timing was good. She'd been gone nearly a month, and he was missing the companionship and physical pleasure they shared. Not that he would have called her. It didn't feel right to press her if she wasn't happy with their relationship. But if she changed her mind on her own...well, that was a different story. He was perfectly willing to take up where they'd left off. For one thing, Laura understood and made allowances for his busy work schedule. For another, she'd been patient with him, considering. And he needed the distraction. He'd gone to sleep thinking about Jaclyn Wentworth and how angry he was at her for ruining his filing system. And how stupid he was for hiring her.

And how sexy she'd looked with her auburn hair falling down and that tired but happy smile on her face.

"Come here. Let me hold you," he said, reaching out to her.

"I'm sorry?"

Something was wrong with her voice. Angling his head

up, Cole squinted in an effort to see through the darkness, but he'd lowered his blinds before bed and couldn't make out anything beyond the basic shape of a woman. "Laura?"

"No, it's Jaclyn," the murky shape responded, hugging the wall as though he might gobble her up whole if she came any closer. "I'm sorry to bother you, but…um…my car needs a jump. I was hoping I could borrow your keys and some jumper cables."

"What?" In one swift motion, Cole snapped on the lamp, then groaned and shielded his eyes from the sudden burst of light. "Do you know what time it is?" he asked.

"It's after midnight. I…I just finished for the day and would be gone by now, but my car won't start."

Great. Not only had she decimated his file room, she'd stranded herself in the process. "Okay, give me a couple of minutes, and I'll be right with you."

"I can take care of it," she said quickly. "Just tell me where you keep your keys and where you might have a set of jumper cables."

Finally able to focus, he watched her gaze dip, which suddenly reminded him that he was wearing nothing but a pair of boxer-briefs under the sheet. During the summer, he rarely wore anything more to bed. It was too blasted hot.

Righting the bedding so he could cover himself properly, Cole sank back. He couldn't help her, regardless. He didn't have jumper cables. He didn't have anything like that. If he needed a jump, he called triple A. If he needed tools for anything else, he told Chad, and someone from the construction crew took care of it. Cole relocated too often to collect a lot of extra belongings. He packed light, and he wasn't particularly mechanical.

"I don't have cables," he said, looking for the easiest solution. "Just take my truck."

"Won't you need it in the morning?"

"I don't have any appointments first thing." *At least, not any I can remember right now.* "The keys are..." He racked his brain, trying to place them. "Actually, they could be anywhere. I'll have to find them for you."

She stepped out of the bedroom so he could get up, and he padded to the dresser where he'd emptied his pockets before going to bed. Credit-card receipts, small change, cash, some documents he'd meant to read before going to sleep, but no keys. Yanking on a pair of basketball shorts, he headed to the kitchen to check on top of the refrigerator.

Jackie was standing in the hall chewing her lip, when Cole passed. In the light spilling from his room, she looked tired and embarrassed but beautiful—always beautiful. He wanted to tell her to relax, that he didn't mind her waking him, but he hesitated to be too nice. He couldn't get involved with her, even as a friend. He was afraid it would evolve into something more. And he already knew that a confirmed bachelor wasn't what she needed.

"I really appreciate your help," she said, following him into the kitchen. "I'll get a new battery on my lunch hour tomorrow so this doesn't happen again."

"Are you sure you need a new battery? Maybe one of your kids left the overhead light on or something."

"I don't think so—they've been with Terry. And my car is pretty old. I don't know when the battery was last replaced."

"Have the clerk at the car-parts store check to see if it's still good, just in case," he told her, wondering why he felt the sudden urge to take over and handle the battery issue himself. It came from years of looking out for his brothers, he decided. But he wasn't about to extend that responsibility to anyone else, especially someone who might not understand it for what it was—a desire to help, nothing more. Jackie could certainly manage a new battery.

A loud growl came from the region of her stomach, and Cole glanced at her. "Haven't you eaten?" he asked.

She shrugged, turning red. "I was too engrossed in what I was doing to stop for dinner. Wait till you see the files," she added. "You're going to be so impressed. The documents in each one are organized by date, the oldest stuff at the bottom. The first cabinet houses all your closed and finished projects, in numerical order according to address. The next has your current stuff, organized the same way. The third has land packages and other information on properties you've looked into but haven't bought yet. The final cabinet contains employee records, receipts, bills, banking information and tax information. Each drawer is labeled, in case you forget. And tomorrow I'm going to do an index that will help you find any file you need in seconds."

An attack of conscience over his earlier reaction to her efforts on the files caused Cole to clear his throat and turn away. Discovering his keys on the counter, he dropped them into her palm and forced himself to thank her. "That was a lot of work. I appreciate that you went the extra mile," he said. "You know I don't expect you to stay past five o'clock, though, don't you?"

She smiled. "Oh, I know. I wanted to finish. And I'm glad I did. It really taught me a lot. I bet I know more about you now than most people."

When Cole met her eyes, he pictured Terry's arm slung casually around her shoulders, remembered seeing them dance at the senior prom as king and queen—right before he cut out of the dance for good. She didn't know anything about him. Not really. And if he could help it, she never would.

"I'd offer you something to eat," he said, "but I usually eat out so my cupboards are bare. I do have a microwave dinner, if you're interested."

"You eat microwave dinners?"

He used to cook every night, but only because he had to. When he was young, he had to feed his brothers. When he left Feld, he was still living on a shoestring and survived on macaroni and cheese and corn dogs—not that he called that cooking. Since then, things had changed considerably. "I don't have time for anything else."

"Who's Laura?" she asked. "Your girlfriend?"

"Just a friend."

"Doesn't she cook for you?"

"Occasionally," he said, because he didn't want to go into the fact that even if she had cooked for him at one time, she probably wouldn't be doing it anymore. He didn't like talking about Laura. She was a nice person who deserved a husband and children, if that was what she wanted. And he felt guilty for not giving her that. Sometimes he told himself it was pure selfishness that made him refuse her, but if he'd learned anything from Rochelle, it was that a sense of obligation wasn't a reliable basis for marriage. Bottom line, he wasn't walking down the aisle again for anyone. Marriage made him feel smothered, restricted, and only added to his burden of responsibility.

"Well, work comes early in the morning," she said, singling the ignition key out from the others and edging toward the hall that would take her back around to the office.

"You can go out the main entryway. I'll lock the office," he volunteered.

"Thanks." She followed as he led her through the living room to the front of the house. "I'll be careful with your truck."

He held the door as she went out, bade her good-night and watched her drive away. Then he locked up and went to do the same in the office. But when he passed the copier room, he couldn't help stopping in and opening the file drawers. Sure enough, every folder was now clearly labeled and perfectly organized. He'd been wrong to assume the worst.

"I'll be damned," he muttered, closing the last drawer. "And she did it on her first day."

Maybe hiring her hadn't been so stupid. Maybe she was just what Perrini Homes needed.

Maybe she was just what *he* needed.

No. Laura, or someone like her, suited him better, he told himself. But he couldn't explain why he wasn't more disappointed that his ex-girlfriend hadn't contacted him. Neither could he say why it wasn't her lips he imagined kissing as he climbed back into bed.

LEATHER INTERIOR. Nothing smelled better, Jaclyn decided as she drove the ten miles to her house, coveting Cole's smooth-riding Navigator. Once she got her real-estate license and started selling homes, she'd be able to buy herself a new SUV. She used to drive expensive cars and trucks all the time when she was with Terry, but it wasn't the same. Like everything else, their vehicles had belonged to Burt.

Jaclyn grimaced as she pictured Burt's face. If she disliked anyone, she disliked him. He ruled his house with an iron fist, had Terry's mother, Dolores, completely cowed, and thought Terry should have been able to exert the same kind of control over Jaclyn. When Jaclyn had sued for divorce, it was Burt who headed up the opposition. First he tried to shame her into staying, then he tried to bribe her with a new house and a larger monthly allowance. At last he waged a smear campaign against her on the basis of her parenting skills and tried to take away her children. Fortunately, the judge hadn't allowed him to take them completely—he'd given her and Terry joint custody. But the courts had cooperated more fully with the Wentworths in the financial realm. The smile on Burt's face the last time she'd seen him told her the court battles might finally be over, but nothing was set in stone. He thought poverty would eventually drive her back to Terry. But thanks to a little help from Cole and a whole lot of determination on her part, the great Burt Wentworth wasn't going to get what he wanted. Not this time.

Signaling, Jaclyn pulled into the 7-Eleven only a few blocks from her house. It was late and she was tired, but she was enjoying driving Cole's SUV, listening to his CDs and smelling the lingering scent of his cologne. When they were in high school, she'd never really let herself think about him—her heart had always belonged to Terry, and Cole had seemed too…sensual, too dangerous somehow—but she had to admit he was attractive. She could definitely see how Rochelle had fallen for him.

Jaclyn browsed through the store, eventually buying an iced mocha and a microwave burrito for dinner, along with a couple of candy bars for dessert. How long had it been since she'd felt this good? she wondered as she carried it all back to Cole's truck. Ages. Since before the divorce—years before, when her parents were alive, and she was still hopeful that her marriage had a chance.

She sat in the lot and ate her meal to a Santana CD, then tossed her garbage into the trash and headed home. Maybe her life was about to get easier, she thought. But then she pulled into her drive and saw Terry's truck parked at the house, and knew, for tonight, it was only going to get worse.

"What's he doing here a day early?" she muttered, parking to the side so he could still get his truck out.

The door to the house opened before Jaclyn ever reached the porch, and Terry emerged, wearing his usual Wrangler jeans, T-shirt and cowboy hat.

"Where the hell have you been?" he demanded, taking one look at her dress, and the high heels she carried in her left hand.

"At work," she said.

"Like hell. We went by Joanna's. They said you don't work there anymore. They said you were fired."

Jaclyn would rather Terry not know about the firing, but

now that the truth was out… "I was," she admitted. "There was a misunderstanding. But I've got a new job now."

He glanced beyond her to Cole's truck, and his lips twisted into a sneer. "Looks like it pays a whole lot better than waitressing."

Jaclyn's stomach started to hurt. Maybe she'd eaten too fast. Or too much. Or maybe she felt another argument coming on. "It does. But the Navigator's not mine."

"Whose is it?"

Remembering his reaction the last time she mentioned Cole, Jaclyn decided to keep him out of it. "A friend's. What are you doing here today, anyway? You weren't supposed to come until tomorrow."

"What's the matter? Now that the kids are back, you afraid you're not going to be able to run around anymore?"

"Why are you acting as though you're doing me some kind of favor taking the children?" she asked. "You're the one who sued for custody!"

"That doesn't mean I'm going to let you use me to baby-sit while you go out on the town looking for another meal ticket."

Anger made Jaclyn's hands shake. "I'm not looking for a meal ticket," she said. "The children are welcome to stay with me all the time. You just say the word and sign them over."

"You'd like that, wouldn't you. To cut me completely out of the picture?"

"You can't have it both ways, Terry. Either you take them, which means I'll have some free time, or you don't, which means you won't see them. It's your decision."

"You don't care either way."

"I care. I wouldn't want them to miss their father, but you don't seem to be too concerned about their welfare."

"Oh yeah? Who was watching them tonight while you

were out doing God knows what with the man who owns that truck?''

Jaclyn clenched her jaw against the desire to tell him to go to hell. It had already been a long day. But the last thing she needed was to poison the neighborhood against her by having a knock-down drag-out with her ex. ''Keep your voice down,'' she hissed. ''I don't want to wake the children or the neighbors, especially because I wasn't doing anything with the man who owns that truck. I work for him.''

''As what? His personal call girl?''

''I do his filing, answer his phones, that sort of thing.''

''Right,'' Terry scoffed. ''You expect me to believe you were doing office work? This late?''

''It's true.''

Brushing past her, he strode to Cole's Navigator and tried to open the driver's door, but Jaclyn had locked it. When he couldn't get in, he whirled to face her. ''Give me the keys.''

Jaclyn was holding them in her right hand. Instinctively she made a fist around them and tucked it behind her back. ''No.''

''I want to know who owns this truck, dammit.''

''It's none of your business, Terry. I'm home now. You can leave.''

''I said, give me the keys.'' Grabbing her arm, he twisted, forcing her to let go of them. Then he unlocked the Navigator and checked the registration.

''I'll be a son of a bitch. It's Cole Perrini's,'' he said. ''You're screwing that trailer trash we went to high school with.''

''I'm not screwing anyone. And he's not trailer trash,'' she said.

Terry shoved his cowboy hat back to smirk at her. ''Coulda fooled me. As I remember it, most days he didn't even show up for school. Ran around in that beater truck of his drinkin' and fightin' and causin' trouble—at least, until he knocked up Rochelle.''

The way Jaclyn remembered it, Terry and his friends had done less fighting, but they'd certainly done more drinking. ''I don't care what Cole was like in high school. It's in the past. It doesn't matter.''

''It doesn't matter? It doesn't matter that he left Rochelle only a few months after she lost their baby? That she was so broken up by how he'd treated her that she tried to commit suicide? What kinda man would leave his wife on the heels of a tragedy like that?''

''We don't know what happened. It's none of our business, anyway.''

Terry acted as though she hadn't spoken. ''And you think he was true to her while they were married?'' he went on. ''Hell, no. That boy don't know what it's like to be true to anyone, except maybe those no-good brothers he was always fighting for.''

''You're one to talk about fidelity,'' Jaclyn said, so disgusted she couldn't hold back any longer.

''At least I always loved you, took care of you. Cole didn't give a shit about Rochelle.''

''You're repeating small-town gossip,'' she said. ''That's all.''

''You can think that if you want, but there ain't no secrets in Feld.''

God, didn't she know! Every time Terry had stepped out on her, the whole town knew—usually before she did. She'd walked through the grocery store or post office in the wake of whispers and nods, even chuckling, more times than she could count. It had been downright humiliating.

''Regardless, Cole's cleaned up his act,'' she said. ''You should see him now. He got out of Feld and he's made something of himself.''

''He has?'' Terry spat on the Navigator. ''Anyone can finance a damn car. Don't let this baby fool you.''

"At least he owns something that doesn't belong to his daddy," she replied.

He stared at her, his jaw sagging, and for a moment Jaclyn thought she'd pushed him too far. Her nails dug into her palms as she waited for his shouted response, but when he spoke, his voice was soft, almost pained.

"I know where you're comin' from, Jackie. I should have fought my father, got us our own place, like you said. He's just so..." He shook his head. "I don't know. I love the crusty old bastard, but I hate him, too. And I want you to know that the divorce stuff and all that, well, that was more him than me. You know I'm not a bad guy. I've made my mistakes, but I've loved you since high school, and I'll love you for the rest of our lives, if you'll let me. That's really why I brought the kids home early. I wanted to talk to you about putting all this behind us and starting fresh, somewhere far away from my father. That's what you always wanted, isn't it?"

Jaclyn squeezed her eyes closed. She'd downright pleaded for Terry to take her away from his parents' ranch more times than she could count. She'd always believed that if they had just struck out on their own, they might have had a chance. But Terry hadn't been strong enough then. And she doubted he was strong enough now. In either case, it was too late. As much as she wished they could get back together for the children's sake, something had changed inside her. She didn't know if she'd ever even *want* to marry again, to leave herself so vulnerable to another's mistakes and decisions....

Even if she did get married again, it wouldn't be to Terry. "I'm sorry," she whispered. "It's too late."

Head bowed, he spat in the dirt and adjusted his hat to sit lower on his brow. "Then, do me one favor," he said.

"What's that?"

"Don't get involved with the likes of Cole Perrini. He's bad news, Jackie, probably more than you know."

"There's nothing going on between me and Cole," she replied. "I work for him. That's it."

With a nod, he indicated the Navigator. "I suppose that's a company car, and that you get off at midnight every day?"

"I worked late on a project, my battery died, and Cole didn't have any cables. He was nice enough to lend me his vehicle so I could get home tonight."

Terry studied her, looking skeptical. "Just don't let him do you too many favors. You might not like what he expects in return."

He turned and left, and Jaclyn stood in the drive staring after him until the sound of his engine died away. Cole might have his problems, but they were personal problems that had nothing to do with professional relationships. What he'd done to Rochelle had nothing to do with her. How he treated his love interests had nothing to do with her, either, because she wasn't one of them.

Taking a long look at his Navigator, she tried telling herself that once more, more forcibly: *I have no romantic interest in Cole Perrini. He might be as handsome as the devil, and as charismatic, too, but I'm not interested in any man. At least, right now.*

But there was still a small rebellious voice in the back of her mind that called her a liar and dared put forth the thought that she wasn't interested in any man *but* him.

She might have pondered that notion, weighed it for veracity, but out of the corner of her eye she saw a curtain move in the bedroom window of Mr. Alder's house. Had he been watching her? Had he heard her and Terry's whole argument?

If he was awake, he probably had. The night was warm and all his windows were open.

"Just my luck," she grumbled, wincing at how bad some of Terry's comments had made her look. Then, exhausted, she headed into the house.

CHAPTER SIX

"WHERE'S DADDY?"

Jaclyn blinked, struggling to reach full consciousness. It was light outside, but the alarm hadn't gone off yet. What had awakened Alex so early?

"He went home," she mumbled.

"What?"

"He went home," she clarified, trying not to slur her words this time. "Did you have fun at Grandma and Grandpa's?"

Alex stood at the side of her bed, scowling, his sandy-colored hair mussed, and didn't respond.

"Aren't you going to answer me?" she asked, shoving both pillows behind her back and propping herself up so she could see him better. "Come give me a hug, sweetheart. I missed you. A lot happened while you were gone that I want to tell you about."

Such a statement would normally have elicited a storm of enthusiastic and curious questions. Today her son merely stuck his lip out farther.

"What's wrong?" she asked.

"Is Daddy coming back?"

Jaclyn hesitated. After her and Terry's conversation the night before, she wasn't sure if he was going to continue to take the children as regularly as he had in the past. "I'm sure he'll be back sometime, but I don't know when. We haven't discussed it yet."

"What does that mean?" Alex demanded.

''Just that we need to coordinate our schedules.''

''No, it doesn't. It means you and Daddy aren't getting back together.''

Jaclyn caught her breath. Evidently Alex hadn't been asking when he was going to see his father again. He was talking about something else entirely. ''Did someone say we were going to reconcile?'' she asked.

''That's why we came back early. Daddy said it was time we were a family again.''

''I'm sorry he told you that,'' she murmured. ''I wish we could've remained a family, too.''

''Then, why did we leave? Why can't we just go back?''

Was it only last night that she'd thought her life was getting easier? She'd never given Terry any indication that she'd changed her mind about the divorce, so why would he suddenly assume she'd take him back? ''Because there are some issues between Mommy and Daddy that can't be resolved.''

''He told me he's sorry for whatever it is you're mad about.''

Mackenzie and Alyssa appeared at the door, rubbing their eyes and yawning. ''I heard Daddy say it, too, Mommy,'' Mackenzie volunteered.

Jaclyn held her arms out to her daughters, and they came forward to give her a hug. Fortunately they were too young to hold a grudge. Alex was the one who worried Jaclyn. At ten, he was old enough to understand what the Wentworths were telling him but not emotionally mature enough to qualify it.

''I'm not angry at Daddy anymore,'' she said. ''I just can't live with him.''

''That doesn't make any sense,'' Alex insisted.

''I'm sorry, honey. Come here.'' Jaclyn slid over, trying to entice her son to join them in the comfortable bed, but he wouldn't budge.

"Grandpa said if you really loved us, you'd move back home," he said.

What wouldn't Burt say to make her look bad? Jaclyn wanted to tell Alex that if their *grandfather* really loved them, he'd stop filling their ears with things that were only going to hurt them—but she refused to say it. She wouldn't use her children as emotional pawns the way Burt and Terry did.

"Grandpa is wrong," she said firmly. "He's getting old, and sometimes he gets a little confused."

"You always say that. I told him, too."

"What was his response?"

"He choked on something and got all red in the face."

"And Grandma had to smack him on the back," Mackenzie added.

Jaclyn bit her cheeks to hide a fleeting smile.

"Then he left the room and didn't come back," Alex added.

The urge to smile disappeared when she saw the hurt and resentment in her son's hazel eyes. "Listen to me, Alex. If I didn't love you, I wouldn't have fought so hard to take you with me when I left."

"Maybe you shouldn't have taken us. Maybe you should have just left us there!" he cried, and stomped away.

Jaclyn felt tears prick the back of her eyelids, felt one roll across her temple and into her hair. She wanted her son to be happy again, as he was before the divorce. Sometimes she blamed herself as much as Terry for destroying that, but when she considered her options, she knew too much had happened to go back.

"Mommy, why you crying?" Alyssa asked, her brows knitting worriedly above her wide blue eyes.

Jaclyn forced a smile and kissed her round cheek. "I'm okay, baby. It's just that I love you kids so much."

"I love you, too," she said, slipping her small arms around Jaclyn's neck.

Mackenzie shoved her light brown hair out of her eyes and snuggled closer. "So do I," she whispered.

Jaclyn enjoyed a whole five minutes with the warmth of their little bodies pressed close to her own. Then the alarm went off.

COLE WAS IN HIS OFFICE when Jaclyn arrived at work, but he heard her out front talking to Rick. She was explaining why she'd taken the Navigator home. Rick recommended an auto-parts store, not far from the office, where she could buy a battery at lunchtime. Then the conversation turned to how impressed Rick was with the files.

Cole fidgeted with his pen and thought about going out to greet Jackie. He'd been half listening for her since 7:45, feeling an odd sort of anticipation. But he doubted he would have dashed out front to say hello if she was any other employee, so he closed his door to keep from being distracted again, and finished signing the payroll checks.

Fifteen minutes later, Cole pinched the bridge of his nose and swiveled away from the letter he'd been writing on his computer. He could no longer hear what Jackie and Rick were saying, but the hum of their voices filtered into the room and made it impossible for him to concentrate. When Jaclyn laughed, he felt he was missing something. When Rick laughed, he grew irritable. Rick and Chad and half the construction crew could have been standing out front, shouting at the top of their lungs, and it wouldn't have affected his ability to work. But add one Jaclyn Wentworth to the office and suddenly he couldn't think of a blasted thing, except her smile and whether or not she found herself attracted to Rick and whether or not he should go out and say good morning...

Damn. Evidently, I was *stupid for hiring her.*

Jaclyn's laugh reached him again, and Cole frowned. What was so darn funny? Rick wasn't exactly a comedian.

He rarely flirted, had a formidable temper, could be down-right cynical...and charming as hell, if he wanted to be.

Shuffling through the papers on his desk, Cole quickly gathered a handful of items he could discuss with his brother and strode out of the room. Jaclyn was *his* friend, *his* secretary. There were plenty of other women in the world. Rick didn't need to turn his attention on the only girl Cole had ever idolized. Ten years might have passed since Feld, but Cole felt a little proprietary toward Jaclyn all the same.

When he reached the front office, he tried to slow his step but seemed to charge into the room, anyway. Both Jaclyn and Rick looked up.

"Good morning," Jaclyn said, welcoming him with a smile that hit him like a knockout punch.

He nodded and said hello, but couldn't manage a smile. He was too troubled by his reaction to her and the fact that ten years suddenly seemed like nothing. "I have a few things I need to discuss with you," he said to Rick, in-stantly regretting the terseness in his voice because it lent his words too much gravity.

Rick shot a glance at Jackie, then blinked at him. "You want me to come into your office?" he asked in surprise.

Cole knew Rick was wondering what they had to talk about that Jackie couldn't hear—Cole was wondering the same thing. But he couldn't very well explain that he'd actually intended to join them, to casually become part of their conversation so he could talk and laugh with Jackie, too. Because he'd screwed it up. There hadn't been any-thing casual about his sudden appearance or his brisk man-ner.

"If you've got a minute," he said, managing to temper his voice this time.

"Sure." Rick scooted his chair back and stood. "Jaclyn, I'll be right back. Would you mind picking up the phones while I'm gone?"

"Sure thing."

Cole led the way to his office, wondering what the hell he was going to say once Rick closed the door behind them. The papers he held in his hand were actually business items they'd discussed before, sometimes more than once. He had nothing new and certainly nothing secret to go over with his brother. And he feared Rick would see right through him—Rick possessed an uncanny ability to do exactly that—if he didn't come up with something legitimate, fast.

"What is it?" Rick asked, leaning against the wall near the door once they were safely ensconced in his office.

Cole hadn't decided what he was going to say, at least consciously, so what came out of his mouth surprised him. "I want you to tell me what's going on with you."

Rick scowled. "What are you talking about?"

"Last night. I want to know where you were."

"That's none of your business and you know it," he said, shoving away from the wall to approach his desk.

Of all his brothers, Rick was the most unpredictable. He was often angry, always strong-willed and sometimes resentful. Cole knew he shouldn't push him—they'd been careful to respect each other's boundaries for years, ever since their mother died—but now that the subject had been broached, Cole's curiosity compelled him to finish what he'd started. "You're my brother. That makes it my business. You're different lately. Preoccupied. Vague. Are you in some sort of trouble?"

"Trouble. You *would* think that," Rick said, chuckling mirthlessly. "I forgot—you're the only one smart enough to amount to anything. The rest of us should be damn grateful to ride on the coattails of your success. Is that it, Cole? Tell me, don't you think that's just a little arrogant?"

Cole dropped his voice to warning level. "Watch it, Rick. I don't think you've earned the right to judge me. I've always said you could do anything you put your mind to. I sat on you through high school, tried to make you finish when you wanted to drop out. I—''

''Beat the hell out of me every time the school called to say I had another unexcused absence. How could I forget?''

The bitterness in Rick's voice was unmistakable now, triggering a tide of memories and emotion Cole was helpless to suppress. Did Rick still hold those years in Feld against him? Did his brother think he'd done what he had back then out of arrogance—because he figured he had all the answers? Hell, no! He'd been lucky to survive. At times he'd been so tempted to run away that he'd buried his face in his pillow at night and sobbed, despite the self-loathing such weakness had caused. But he'd stayed. He might not have done a perfect job of raising Rick, but at least he'd stayed. He'd dug in his heels and fought harder than he'd ever fought for anything in his life—even Perrini Homes— because he loved his brothers, because they *were* his brothers, dammit!

''It was the only way I knew, Rick,'' Cole said. ''It was all I *could* do. I'm only three years older than you. You wouldn't cooperate, listen to anything I had to say. Force seemed to be the only thing that had an effect on you, and to be honest, you ungrateful bastard, sometimes I resent it as much as you do.''

Rick's chest was rising and falling fast; his fists were clenched at his sides. ''Then, maybe it's time we gave each other some room. Maybe it's time we started down our own separate paths, Cole. You've been taking care of me long enough, don't you think?''

Rick's words cut Cole to the quick. After everything he'd done to keep them together, Rick wanted a separate path?

''Is that what you want?''

Rick nodded. ''I think it is.''

God, he couldn't lose one of his brothers now. Surely they could overcome the past. They'd made it so far....

For a fleeting moment, Cole contemplated apologizing.

He couldn't imagine his life, or Perrini Homes, without Rick. His brothers were the reason he'd built the business in the first place, to give them something to fall back on, to keep them from ending up like their father, who'd died a poor broken man. But something in Rick's eyes told him an apology would never be enough. The pain Rick carried inside him was too big for "I'm sorry."

"Do you honestly think there's something better out there?" Cole asked softly.

Rick stared at him for several seconds. "I don't know," he said, his Adam's apple bobbing as he swallowed, "but I think that's something I need to find out for myself."

He turned to the door, and Cole got up, wanting to stop him. If it had been Chad or one of the younger two who was about to walk out on him, Cole wouldn't have been half as worried. Like all siblings, they had their disagreements, but his relationship with each of them was basically sound.

Rick was different. If Rick walked out the door, he might never come back.

"Rick, think about what you're doing...."

His brother glanced over his shoulder, one hand on the doorknob. "I knew this was coming, Cole. It had to happen eventually, because I can't respect myself if I never risk life out from under the safety of your protective wing. And this is as good a time as any to venture forth."

Suddenly filled with a horrible sense of loss, Cole grasped for anything that might hold Rick until they could work things out. "But you have a job here—"

"You built this business from nothing, Cole. You know enough about what I do to get by until you can hire someone to replace me. Maybe Jaclyn can even do my job. It will be tough at first, and I'm sorry for that, but I think we both know it's better this way." He opened the door. "I'll see you around,'' he said, but it came off a lot like *Have a nice life*.

Then his purposeful tread sounded in the hall. The front door slammed, an engine roared to life, tires squealed.

He was gone.

CHAPTER SEVEN

JACLYN SAT AT HER DESK, staring after Rick Perrini's truck long after it had disappeared down the street. She'd been able to tell by the look on his face as he'd stormed out of the office that something was terribly wrong, but he hadn't spoken a word to her. Neither had she heard anything in the past fifteen minutes from Cole. Had he fired Rick? Had Rick quit? Was it just a brotherly spat that would mend itself before noon?

Somehow she doubted it. The silence was too heavy, the screech of Rick's tires too final for this incident to be anything less than serious. So what should she do now? Let it go as if nothing had happened and finish the index she was working on for the filing system? Or see if there was something she could do for Cole?

Smoothing the wrinkles out of her dress, Jaclyn rounded her desk and walked slowly down the hall, trying to muffle the sound of her approach so she could get a look at Cole before deciding whether or not to interrupt him. Would he rather not be bothered?

The door to his office stood open, probably just the way Rick had left it, and Cole was sitting behind his desk, staring off into space. His profile was grim, hard. He certainly didn't look like a man who needed or wanted anyone. But then he turned, and Jaclyn saw the emotion in his eyes.

He was hurt. Evidently, Cole Perrini was as vulnerable as any other man.

Hesitantly, she crossed the room, wondering what she was going to do or say once she reached him. She had no idea what was wrong between him and his brother. And she didn't know them well enough to guess. But Cole had been there for her a few days earlier when she'd been at the end of her rope, and she wanted to return the favor.

As she drew near, she expected the tough facade he normally wore to snap back into place. She thought he'd stand up and in his most professional voice ask her what she needed. Instead, he rolled his chair back and simply looked at her.

Stepping closer, Jaclyn tentatively put her hands on his forearm. "Are you okay?" she asked. His skin was warm beneath her fingers and she felt a sudden need to hold him, to comfort him.

He didn't answer. Nor did he move. He looked at her as though he was experiencing the same desire to touch as she was. Jaclyn thought he might pull her to him, maybe lay his cheek against her stomach, but the sound of Chad's voice intruded, and she moved away. "Where the heck is everyone?" he called from the front office.

Jaclyn took another step back right before he appeared in the doorway. "Here you guys are. What's going on?"

When they didn't answer immediately, he grinned, catching on to the fact that he'd just interrupted something significant. "Doing a little dictation?" he asked, winking at her.

Jaclyn cleared her throat and glanced at Cole, who was watching her with a shuttered expression, the pain she'd seen in his eyes just a few moments earlier now hidden, if it still existed. "I was just, um, checking on something," she said, when a more specific reason for being in Cole's office—and for standing so close to him—eluded her.

"How was it?" Chad asked.

"How was what?" she replied, edging toward the door.

"Whatever you were checking on."

"Good," she admitted. "It was good." Then she slipped from the room and fled to her desk.

"WHAT'S UP WITH RICK?" Chad asked, as soon as Jackie disappeared down the hall. "He told me yesterday he'd have the checks I need to pay the cement subs for Phase II waiting on his desk, but they're not there. When I called him on his cell to ask him why, he said I needed to talk to you."

Cole forced his attention away from Jackie and the longing she'd evoked when she touched him, and focused on his younger brother. "He quit," he said simply.

"He what?"

"He's going out on his own."

"To do what?"

"He didn't say."

"Is he going to build houses?"

Cole shrugged. "I don't know."

Chad propped a callused hand on his hip and frowned. "That's crazy, man. We can make a lot more together than we can apart."

"I don't think it's about money," Cole said.

"Then, what's the problem?"

The problem was the past, the things he and Rick did, the things they couldn't forget, the things they couldn't forgive. It was the love and the hate between two brothers, but Cole wasn't about to explain that. Deep down, Chad already knew.

"He'll come around," he said, hoping it was true.

"I'm sure he will. Rick was with you from the start, when the rest of us were still in school. I can't imagine him walking away now."

"Except, he's changed," Cole said. "Something's up."

Chad's eyebrows lifted. "What do you mean by that?"

"Do you spend much time with him at night?"

"No. We used to go out every now and then to hit a few nightclubs or maybe a movie. We'd even double-date on occasion. You know how it was—you used to go with us sometimes until you got too busy. But he never calls anymore, and when I call him, he tells me he's already got plans. I just assumed he's met a woman and will introduce us to her when he's ready.''

"He claims he's not seeing anyone. You don't think he's gambling or losing his shorts in the stock market, do you?''

"Wouldn't that motivate him to keep his job, instead of quitting it?''

"I don't know. Rick's not an easy person to second-guess.''

"Are you saying he might be in some sort of trouble?''

Cole shook his head. "I wish I knew.''

BORED. BORED. BORED. God, she was bored. She'd been working for Cole more than two weeks, and every day she had less to do.

Covering a yawn, Jaclyn checked the clock on the wall and counted the hours and minutes until five: three hours and eight minutes—six minutes less than the last time she'd looked. She synchronized her watch and straightened the few items on her desk, then stared at the phone, silently pleading for it to ring. She'd already interviewed all those who had called about the sales position and had made her recommendations to Cole. He was planning to meet with the final three candidates tomorrow, but she hated to see him hire someone so soon.

Then the only task she'd been given of any consequence, besides the filing system index, which she'd finished long ago, would come to an end. Cole had promised to train her at some point, but ever since Rick had quit, he hadn't had the time. He was doing his job and his brother's, too, and was either gone on appointments or shut away in his private office until late at night. Which left Jaclyn with nothing to do but answer the phone and hope the opportunity to do another interview would break the tedium, despite all the things piling up on Rick's desk. If only she had a few minutes of Cole's time, or the permission to dig through the stack of work and see what she could do to help, she might be able to accomplish some of the items that needed attention, but most days Cole was too engrossed to even speak to her.

The phone rang, and Jaclyn snatched it up. "Perrini Homes, Oak Ranch Estates."

It was Margaret Huntley, one of the real-estate agents she'd recommended to Cole, returning her call. Jaclyn set up a time for her to come in tomorrow and meet with him, then hung up and wondered what she was going to do until the phone rang again. Finally she picked up the receiver and called the kids.

"Mommy, we're fine. Why do you keep calling?" Mackenzie asked when their sitter, Holly Smith, brought her to the phone.

"I'm just missing you," Jaclyn said. "How's Alyssa?"

"She's fine."

"How's Alex?"

"Good."

"Does he want to talk to me?"

Mackenzie didn't answer directly, but her voice nearly broke Jaclyn's eardrum when she yelled for her brother. In the interim that followed, Jaclyn heard Holly encouraging Alex to come to the phone, but he must have refused, because Mackenzie spoke to her again instead. "He's playing Nintendo," she said. "He wants to know when you're going to get to drive your boss's car again."

"Probably never. Our car is working fine since I bought the new battery. There's no need to borrow anyone else's. Does Alyssa want to say hello?"

"She's outside on the patio riding her trike with Travis." Travis was Holly's son, an only child just six months older than Alyssa and one of two other children in the neighborhood.

"Okay. No need to bother her. I'll see you in a few hours."

Mackenzie said goodbye, and Jaclyn hung up. So much for talking to the kids. They were beginning to get annoyed by the number of times she'd called. After working at

Joanna's, where she'd been running every minute, the sudden standstill was driving her nuts. She'd wanted this job so she could learn real estate and build a future for herself and her children. She didn't want Cole paying her twenty-five hundred a month just because she was an old friend he couldn't refuse. If only she knew more about office work, she'd start to dig through the things on Rick's desk the way she had the filing. But she was afraid she'd mess something up or overstep her bounds.

Unfortunately the only thing she was really good at was running a household. She could cook and sew with the best of them. She could can and bake and decorate. And she could clean. Not that any of it was very useful in her current situation. Or was it?

Suddenly Jaclyn had an idea. If Cole didn't have time to teach her the business and preferred to let Rick's job go undone, maybe she could help him in other areas. Judging from the bare cupboards in his kitchen, the few meals he actually took the time to eat and the thick layer of dust covering almost everything in his part of the house, he didn't need a secretary half as badly as he needed a housekeeper and cook.

And she was a darn good cook.

SOMETHING SMELLED like heaven.

Only half listening to what Larry Schneider from the bank was saying over the phone, Cole pushed away from his desk and sniffed the air. Pot roast, with onions. Or maybe it was steak and onions, but it sure smelled like pot roast....

"Cole?"

"Hmm?"

"What do you have to say?"

"About what?"

"About the interest rate. Are you willing to go up half a percent? Otherwise, I doubt I'm going to be able to sell this loan to the board. I mean, if I were the only one who had to approve it, that'd be different. But on a project this size…"

Where was that aroma coming from? A barbecue outside? No, a few of the homes in the first phase of Oak Ranch had already sold due to drive-by traffic, but they hadn't closed escrow yet. The closest neighborhood to his development was more than a mile away. Even with every window in the house open—and there weren't any because the air conditioner was running—he wouldn't be able to smell someone's dinner cooking from that far away—

"Cole? Are you there?" Larry demanded.

"Yeah, I'm here. What was that again?"

"What was what? I need an answer."

Cole couldn't give him an answer because he couldn't remember the question. He couldn't think of anything except dinner. He'd been holed up in his office for nearly eight hours without breaking for lunch. He was famished and tired and annoyed about the amount of work Rick's absence had caused, and worried about everything that wasn't getting done—and he couldn't figure out why his house suddenly smelled like a winter holiday in late August.

"I'm sorry. I have to go, Larry. I think someone's cooking pot roast in my kitchen."

"You *think?* You don't know?"

"It could be something else."

"I meant—"

"I'll call you in the morning."

After hanging up, Cole followed his nose out of his office and down the hall to the kitchen, where he found Jaclyn lifting a roasting pan out of the oven.

"Hello," she said, smiling when she saw him.

"What are you doing?" he asked. "It's four-thirty in the afternoon. You're supposed to be in the office."

Her expression grew uncertain. "There wasn't anything to do in the office. There hasn't been for over two weeks. And I can't imagine that you appreciate paying me twenty-five hundred a month to sit behind my desk and answer five or six calls an hour. So I brought the cordless phone in here with me and decided to make better use of myself.''

Cole eyed the steam coming off the meat and cut-up carrots, potatoes and onions she'd just uncovered. ''I knew it was pot roast.''

She glanced up at him as she set the lid aside. ''It was the only thing I could find without running to the store. I was going to ask if I could defrost the meat, but you've been on the phone for hours. So I called Chad on his cell, and he said to do whatever I thought would be the most helpful.''

''And that was making dinner?''

She shrugged. ''You've got to eat. Restaurant food has to be getting old for you, and at least this way you're getting something for the money you're paying me. Hope you don't mind.''

Did he mind? Cole jammed a hand through his hair as he tried to decide. If his secretary had been anyone else, someone old and gray, perhaps, he wouldn't have thought twice about it. He would have thanked her and enjoyed the meal. But seeing the girl he'd dreamed about all through high school standing in his kitchen wearing oven mitts and serving him dinner seemed to cross the ''too personal'' line. Ever since the day Rick left, when she seemed to know just what he needed and had reached out to him in his office, he'd been careful to keep his distance. If he didn't, he could end up raising another family, and he just didn't have it in him for a repeat performance, especially after raising a child as difficult as Rick.

''I don't mind, but neither do I expect it,'' he said, rounding the island to find coleslaw, an apple-nut salad and what looked like breakfast biscuits waiting in separate bowls for him on the table.

''I know it probably seems like an odd medley,'' she said, glancing at the food. ''But you didn't have any fruit aside from apples, and you had very little produce. I'll go to the grocery store tonight. Tomorrow's dinner will be better.''

Tomorrow's dinner? Was she going to make a habit of this? Cole opened his mouth to explain that he had no intention of having her cook for him on a regular basis. But the food smelled so good, and she seemed so pleased with her efforts, that he decided to save the ''never again'' until later.

''It looks great.''

''Good.'' She put a single place setting on the table and started serving up his plate.

''Am I eating alone?'' he asked. Considering the amount of food, he'd expected her to join him.

She checked her watch. ''Unless you'd like to invite someone over. I have just enough time to clean up the dishes. Then I'm off to pick up my kids.''

The single setting and her brisk, matter-of-fact manner quickly dispelled the intimacy of her having cooked for him. He even felt embarrassed about the way his mind had jumped to the conclusion that she was probably trying to shackle him. But instead of bringing Cole the relief he expected, the thought made him feel…slightly disappointed. Apparently the pot roast didn't mean anything.

''Are you saying you're willing to cook as part of your job?'' he asked.

''Just until I can learn more about real estate. I've signed up for some home-study classes to get the mandatory school credits out of the way and to help me prepare for my state test. And I'm hoping you'll still train me around here when you get the time. Meanwhile, I thought I could do some cleaning, maybe take over the laundry, pick up your dry cleaning, that sort of thing. I know this is a…difficult time, with Rick gone, and I want to help. You're paying me too much to just answer the phone.''

She seemed in earnest. Cole couldn't help but admire her work ethic. He couldn't see how he stood to lose, either. As long as Jackie could manage what he needed her to do in the office, she could fill in around the house. Why would he want to say no to home-cooked meals, to having his shirts cleaned and pressed? It was like getting the benefits of a wife without the liabilities. She wasn't even planning to eat with him. Certainly she had no designs on him as her children's new daddy.

He cut a piece off the slice of roast she'd given him and took his first bite. Delicious. Every bit as good as the smell had promised.

"How is it?" she asked, above the water running in the sink.

"Excellent." He smiled for the first time since discovering her in his kitchen. "I'll give you some money so you can go to the grocery store and get whatever you like."

"Any special requests?"

He sampled the salads and was surprised to find them almost as good as the roast and potatoes and gravy. If she could do this well with what he'd had in his cupboards, the situation might definitely be taking a turn for the better.

"Meat loaf," he said decisively. "It's been fifteen years or more since I've had meat loaf."

RICK WAS EXHAUSTED. It had been three weeks since he'd quit Perrini Homes, but the last person he wanted to see, other than Cole, was Chad, standing on his front doorstep when he returned home after a long day.

"Did Cole send you?" he asked, braking in his driveway with his car window down so he could speak to his brother, who'd stepped off the porch and started toward him.

"Does it matter if he did?" Chad responded, shoving his hands in the pockets of his jeans as he walked.

Letting his engine idle, Rick stared at the two white holes his headlights seemed to bore into the garage as his brother came alongside his car. "It's after midnight on a Wednesday night, and I know you have to get up early," he said. "I was just going to save you the trouble of staying out any later if Cole's behind your visit. Because if he sent you, I don't have anything to say.''

Chad left his hands in his pockets but stood straighter, obviously surprised and probably offended by the statement, but Rick wasn't about to back off. He had to draw a hard line with Cole, with all his brothers, or he'd soon find himself working at Perrini Homes again. And he didn't want to go back.

"What's going on?" Chad demanded. "Cole's been good to you. He's been good to all of us. Aren't you being a little ungrateful?"

"Ungrateful?" Rick shook his head. It was gratitude and grudging respect that had tethered him to Cole in the first place. He'd spent the past ten years of his life helping to build Cole's business, trying to repay his older brother for the sacrifices he'd made when they were growing up. But Rick had finally realized that what he owed Cole was a debt he could never satisfy. Nothing he did now would change what had happened when they were kids. Nothing could make up for it.

"It's just time for something new," he said to keep things simple, knowing that Chad would never understand how he truly felt. His younger brother was satisfied to be Cole's contractor, would probably be happy with the position for the rest of his life. Chad wanted nothing more than to put in a good week's work and collect his pay, all the while knowing Cole was behind him with a safety net should something go wrong. Why Rick couldn't be more like him, or Brian or Andrew, he didn't know. But for some reason, he had to prove, if only to himself, that he could make it without big brother's help.

"Weren't you making enough money?" Chad asked.

Rick glanced beyond Chad to the home he'd bought just a few months earlier. Set on a big lot in an upper-class neighborhood, it was a nice place. He hadn't yet finished the landscaping in back or furnished all the rooms, but he'd bought it more as an investment, anyway. He planned to sell it in a few years, take his equity, and upgrade to a larger place. Maybe by then, he'd have a family and need the space.

"It wasn't the money. I just have some things I want to do on my own."

Chad leaned against the side of the car and kicked a small stone off the driveway. "I'm not going to get in the middle of it," he said at last.

"I don't think it's possible to remain neutral and still feel like you're being loyal to Cole. I understood and accepted that when I left. I know how you feel about him."

"I owe Cole a lot, but I'm not going to give up one brother because of another," he said.

Rick smiled. He'd thought he'd have to walk away from the whole family to gain his freedom, but Chad seemed to be offering him an alternative, at least where he was concerned. "Thanks, man. I appreciate it."

"No problem." Chad shoved away from the car. "Want to go out tomorrow night? Have a couple drinks?"

"I can't," Rick said. "I've already got plans."

Chad squinted through the darkness, studying him, and Rick expected him to start in where Cole had left off, drilling him about how he was spending his nights. But he didn't.

After a moment he simply nodded and said, "Okay. You've got my number."

Then he left.

CHAPTER EIGHT

COLE HAD NEVER hated weekends before, but as he walked around his empty house on a Saturday afternoon in mid-September, he had to admit he was beginning to dread them. Without Laura to occupy his nights and Rick to talk to whenever he felt like calling, he had little to stop him from closing himself in his office and working like he did every day, which was exactly what he'd been doing since dawn. But he was tired of work, tired of being alone. A man needed some social interaction.

He poked around his kitchen, wondering what to eat for supper, considered some of the leftovers in his fridge, then decided he'd go out, instead. The still, silent house was getting to him. He needed to be with people, needed something to distract him from his usual thoughts about escrows and loans and land.

What if he called Laura? They'd always had a good time together. They could go to dinner, catch a movie, maybe come back to the house later. Three months without female companionship was starting to feel like a long time.

But if he contacted Laura and she agreed to see him, he'd be putting the two of them right back where they'd been before—with her wanting a more permanent relationship and him unable to give her one. Now that they'd made the split, he didn't really want to put them through that again, did he?

No, he cared enough about Laura to let her move on.

He could always hang out with one of his brothers, he

decided. Except that Chad was in Sacramento looking at some lots, Andrew and Brian were at school six hours away and he didn't feel like making the drive, and he wasn't about to contact Rick. He and Rick hadn't spoken for nearly a month, ever since Rick had walked out on him, and now was not the time to try to mend that fence. Neither did he think, after what Chad had told him, that Rick wanted to hear from him. Whatever Rick was doing with his life, he wanted to do it on his own, and Cole was determined to respect that.

Which whittled his options down for the evening to the possibilities contained in his little black book. He could go through the names and numbers in his day-planner and call one or two of the women he'd dated in the past. Or he could call Jackie Wentworth. He'd been tempted to do so before and had ultimately decided not to, but he couldn't see any harm in calling her now. He saw her almost every day, anyway. She'd been cooking and cleaning for him for nearly two weeks, and her efforts had made a significant difference. His cupboards were stocked with homemade pickle relish, strawberry jam and bottled peaches and pears. A lemon bundt cake sat under cover on his counter, and homemade white bread—his favorite item so far—stocked the bread box. But that wasn't all. Things he'd never even thought about cleaning had been scrubbed—the blinds and light fixtures and baseboards. There wasn't a cobweb or dust bunny in sight, and the whole place smelled like chocolate-chip cookies. Cole had never had anyone take care of him before and was beginning to think he'd made a real bargain when he hired her.

A man could get used to having someone see to such comforts, he decided. The only problem was the hours she was gone. She left him with plenty of food in the refrigerator to get him through the weekend, and the house generally survived his neglect until she returned. After all, he'd managed for years before she came. But there was still something missing when she wasn't around. He felt it more and more strongly as time went on, and he was beginning to fear it was her physical presence.

That's crazy. I'm just bored—or maybe I'm lonely—but either way she's an old friend. It can't hurt to call her.

He picked up the phone, then hung up again. She'd be surprised to hear from him on a weekend, and he'd be put on the spot and wouldn't know how to break the ice. He had to come up with some reason, some excuse....

He could tell her he dropped a cup and the vacuum wouldn't work so he could clean up the glass, ask to borrow hers.

No, then he'd have to break his own vacuum.

What if he called to see how she thought Margaret, their new real-estate agent, was working out? He could do that, but it would seem pretty obvious. Jaclyn had interviewed and recommended Margaret in the first place, and Margaret had already sold four houses in her first week. She was doing great, and everyone knew it. Besides, Cole could ask Jaclyn about Margaret at work. Since she was going to start working Saturday mornings in October, Margaret left at four o'clock, which meant he and Jaclyn had an hour at the office alone together every day.

What if he told Jaclyn he wanted to entertain friends tomorrow and was hoping to hire her services as caterer?

Cole rubbed his whisker-roughened chin. That was a possibility. He was just thinking about embellishing the story with a list of those who were supposedly coming when he saw something out of the corner of his eye that told him he wouldn't need to lie.

"WHEN'S DADDY GOING to pick us up?" Mackenzie asked, standing on a chair beside Jaclyn at the counter, handing her the bowl of zucchini they'd just grated for the bread they were baking. Alex was setting the table for dinner, and

Alyssa was pretending to wash the dishes piled high in the sink.

"It's been nearly a month," Alex complained, his tone as sulky as ever. "Now that we're in school, we can only go to Feld on weekends, and it's Saturday. Why doesn't he come? Did you tell him not to?"

"No, I didn't," she said, refusing to let Alex's accusatory tone goad her into an angry response.

"Then, what's happened?"

Jaclyn raised her voice above the whine of the mixer she'd just turned on. "I don't know. He's called a few times," she said, trying to be positive. But she didn't really know how to explain her ex-husband's sudden neglect. He'd promised the kids he was coming to get them on two different occasions, then called and canceled at the last minute. Had he met someone? He wasn't happy she was working for Cole. Had he decided to punish her by making sure he didn't provide baby-sitting, in case she and Cole wanted to socialize? With Terry, anything was possible. "Maybe he's just been busy."

"Too busy to come get us?" Mackenzie demanded.

Jaclyn turned off the mixer. "I'm sure he'll come soon. You can call him after supper if you like."

"I don't want to talk to him," Alex grumbled amidst the clink of the silverware he was desultorily plunking down beside each plate.

"Alex is always in a bad mood," Mackenzie complained, making a face at her brother. Fortunately he didn't see her. "*I* want to talk to Daddy."

"Me, too!" Alyssa echoed.

Jaclyn rinsed and dried her hands, then tucked a strand of Alyssa's fine blond hair behind her daughter's ear and kissed her soft cheek. "As soon as we finish supper, we'll give him a call, and those who want to talk can, okay?"

The doorbell rang just as Jaclyn was taking out the enchiladas she'd made for supper. She quickly loaded the zucchini bread into the oven and headed to the front door, but Alex beat her to it.

"Is your mother home?"

Jaclyn instantly recognized the voice and wished she'd cleaned up. On Saturdays she rarely bothered to do her hair or makeup, and today wasn't any different. She'd pulled her hair into a ponytail and spent her time playing Four Square with the kids, an outdoor game that had eventually turned into a water fight—until Mr. Alder had come out to scold them for hitting his bedroom window with the spray from the hose. Since then they'd been inside, where Jaclyn had been busy making salsa, baking zucchini bread and cooking dinner.

"Cole, I didn't expect to see you today," she said. He was standing in her doorway wearing a pair of shorts and a T-shirt, instead of the usual suit and tie, and he looked younger and more carefree than she'd ever seen him, at least since high school.

Jaclyn glanced down at her own shorts and tank top, hoping, by some miracle, that they were at least clean. Fortunately she didn't notice any blobs of batter or red streaks of tomato juice, but she doubted her clothes could withstand a close inspection.

"What brings you here?"

"I was in the area and thought I'd drop by and give you this—"

He lifted one hand to reveal the jacket that went over her lavender dress. She'd left it at the office several days earlier and kept forgetting to bring it home. But the jacket certainly wasn't important enough to require a special trip.

"Thanks," she said, taking it from him and wondering if he had another reason for driving over.

"No problem." His gaze returned to Alex, who was standing between them, staring up at him with frank curiosity. "So this is your son?"

"Yes. This is Alex. He's ten."

"Was it your car my mother drove home a few weeks ago?" Alex asked.

"If it was that one right there, yes." Cole indicated the black Navigator parked at the curb.

"That is *so* hot," Alex said. "When I get big, I'm going to drive one of those."

"By then there'll be something on the market you'll want a lot more," Cole said. "I guarantee it."

Mackenzie and Alyssa had trailed Jaclyn to the door and were now crowding around her and Alex to peek at their visitor, so Jaclyn introduced them, as well. "This is Alyssa, my youngest, and Mackenzie, who's nearly six. This is my boss," she told the children. "His name is Mr. Perrini."

"They can call me Cole," he said.

An awkward moment ensued while she tried to decide whether to invite him in. She longed for adult companionship, someone to talk to and to laugh with, but Cole hardly fit the mold of a platonic friend. He was too charismatic, too handsome, and she knew too much about his past.

Still, that day in his office had shown her that he possessed a sensitive side. At night, somewhere between sleep and wakefulness, she often relived the moment she'd touched his arm and he'd looked at her with such longing.

Cole cleared his throat. "I guess I'd better be going."

"Have you had any dinner?" she asked, the manners her parents had instilled in her as a child overtaking her better judgment. "We were just about to sit down to eat, and there's plenty if you'd like to join us."

She thought he'd decline. She actually hoped he would. Considering their professional relationship and her dependence on it, she'd be stupid to become too friendly with him. What if he made advances and she had to rebuff him, like Rudy? She couldn't afford to lose her job again.

"Are you sure I wouldn't be imposing?"

Jaclyn cringed. According to everyone she'd ever known

in Feld, Cole had a taste for illicit affairs, and she'd just invited him to dinner.

"It's no imposition," she heard herself say. "Alex, why don't you set an extra place?"

For once Alex obeyed without complaint, saving Jaclyn from any embarrassment in that area, so she took heart. As long as Cole was going to join them, the least she could do was pretend to want him there. "Can I get you drink?" she asked, holding the door while he stepped inside. "A glass of wine? Some soda?"

"I'll have a cola if you've got one. Is there anything I can do to help with dinner?"

"No. It's just about ready. Why don't you sit down and make yourself comfortable?" She gestured toward the living room.

He did as she suggested, and Jaclyn dashed into the kitchen to pour his drink. She called Mackenzie to come and take it to him, then finished the salad she'd started before mixing the zucchini bread. Her dinner looked pretty sparse with only a main dish and a salad. It certainly wasn't something she was proud to feed to company, but Cole was here whether she liked it or not, and she had no time to improve the fare—or her appearance.

She glanced quickly at her reflection in the window above the sink and tried to fix her falling ponytail. Without a brush, her efforts proved futile.

It doesn't matter, she told herself, giving up. She wasn't trying to impress Cole. She couldn't afford to get too close to him, anyway.

While she bustled around making the salad dressing, Jaclyn could hear Alex in the living room telling Cole all about his soccer team. From the sounds of it, her son was dragging out photos of the previous years, along with all his trophies. Then the girls started bringing their dolls and accessories to show him, and by the time dinner was on the table, Cole was surrounded by toys, trophies and stuffed animals.

Chuckling to herself, Jaclyn realized her children would probably scare Cole away long before she had to say anything.

"I hope you weren't overwhelmed by the kids," she said, while Alex and the girls washed up. "We don't have company very often."

"I practically raised my younger brothers. Kids are nothing new."

He smiled as he stepped over the clutter, and Jaclyn grudgingly admitted to herself that she liked it when he smiled. He had great teeth, a strong chin and high cheekbones, but his appeal extended to more than his good looks. The Cole she'd known in high school had been bold and flirtatious, downright cocky. The mature Cole had confidence that ran deeper—and he was all the sexier for it.

He was quite a package, she decided. Tough, renegade boy turned self-made man. It was no wonder Rochelle had fallen so hard for him, poor thing.

"What are you thinking?" he asked, catching her looking at him as they seated themselves at the table.

"I was just remembering you as the boy I knew in school," she said, telling him only a portion of the truth and hoping the warmth that infused her cheeks wouldn't give away the fact that she'd actually been admiring him—and feeling sorry for his ex-wife at the same time.

"Have I changed?"

"I think so."

He studied her for a moment. "What about you?"

"What *about* me?"

"Is Jaclyn Wentworth a different person from Jackie Rasmussen?"

"Probably not entirely."

"Sometimes I look at you and I see Feld High's carefree prom queen."

Jaclyn smiled, remembering her moment in the sun, too, but her smile wilted when he continued.

"At other times, I see a sadness in your face that I never saw before, and I wonder who or what put it there. I'm guessing it was Terry."

His expression was so intense, Jaclyn couldn't break eye contact. She hadn't expected him to be so direct. At work they kept their conversations to simple greetings, good wishes and the weather. Half the time he acted as though he'd rather she not be around. But the one thing consistent from the beginning was the impression he gave that he didn't want to talk about Feld, didn't want to revisit the old days. Which was perfectly fine by Jaclyn. So why was he suddenly bringing up the past?

He looked as if he was about to say something more, but the kids came flooding back, jabbering at the top of their lungs, and he seemed to think better of it. He turned his attention to passing her their plates so she could dish up the food, then listened attentively to Alex and the girls, who talked throughout dinner about school, the toys they wanted for Christmas and how mean Mr. Alder had ruined their great water fight.

When the girls left the table to play with their Barbies, Alex stayed to tell Cole about the fun he'd had during the summer going to Sand Mountain with his father.

"I used to go out there when I was a kid, too," Cole told him. "My brothers and I didn't have a Quad runner or sand rail, but we used to climb the mountain in my truck. One time the engine stalled at the worst possible moment, and I was sure we were going to roll."

"Did you?" Alex asked, his eyes wide with interest as he pushed his plate away.

"No, I managed to get it started again, and we slowly backed down."

"Did your dad get mad at you when he found out how close you'd come?"

"He didn't find out," Cole said.

"What about your mother?"

Cole hesitated long enough to make Jaclyn wonder if Alex's questions were bothering him. She couldn't remember Cole's mother, or his father, for that matter. She doubted she'd ever seen either of them. They didn't get involved in community activities, didn't come out to the high-school football games the way her parents and Terry's had. Cole was sometimes there, with one or two of his brothers in tow, but he didn't play on the team. He teased the girls, and winked at Jaclyn, even though he knew everyone around her would tell Terry. And he heckled the cheerleaders and usually left with one of them afterward.

Jaclyn knew Cole and his family had been poor, guessed they were proud, but that was about it.

"She was sick. We tried not to tell her things that would upset her," he said.

"What was wrong with her—?"

"Alex," Jaclyn interrupted, "why don't you go in and turn on the television? It's seven o'clock. There might be something good on."

"No, that's okay," Cole said. "She had multiple sclerosis."

"What's that?"

"It's a disease that does different things to different people. For some reason, my mother went downhill pretty fast. Only five years after they diagnosed it, she couldn't walk or use her hands. In another five years, she couldn't see or talk."

Alex looked horrified. "What *could* she do?"

Jaclyn cleared her throat, wishing her son could read the clues in Cole's body language. They were saying, loud and clear, that his mother was a sensitive subject. But Alex was just a child, and his curiosity blotted out all else.

"She could only hear," Cole told him. "And sometimes she'd try to laugh."

Trailer trash. In light of his mother's illness, the epithet Terry's crowd had reserved for Cole and his family seemed particularly cruel. That Jaclyn hadn't taken a stand against it made her feel ashamed.

"Where is she now?" Alex asked.

"She died a year after I graduated high school."

"What about your father—?"

"That's enough questions," Jaclyn said, and she knew the firmness in her voice had finally gotten through to her son, because he scowled at her. "Go watch some television."

"Aw, Mom. I was just talking to him."

"Do as I say," she insisted.

When Alex finally left the room, Jaclyn turned back to Cole. "I'm sorry to hear about your mother," she said. "I didn't know. That must have been very difficult for a boy your age."

"It wasn't my *age* that made it difficult," he said, but when she pressed him for his meaning, he added, "It's ancient history. I'd rather not go into it."

Jaclyn stood and started clearing away the plates. "Then, what would you like to talk about?" she asked. Now that she'd let him in and fed him dinner, she found herself strangely reluctant to see him leave. He'd been kind to the kids and was easy to have around, and it had been so long since she'd had dinner with a man.

He helped her carry the plates into the kitchen. "What about the days since then?"

"What about them?" she asked, rinsing off the food.

"What happened to you and Terry? You were head-over-heels in love in high school."

"We had a lot of problems," she answered. "His father was one of them."

Cole finished clearing the table while she took the zucchini bread out of the oven. "So, Burt was a problem, huh?" he said when they were both in the kitchen again.

Jaclyn wasn't surprised Cole remembered him. The whole town knew Burt Wentworth. The whole town revered him. "Yeah. He was so controlling, so blind when it came to Terry. He refused to let him grow up, and Terry didn't have the confidence he needed to make his own decisions. I tried to convince him that we'd be better off on our own. I was sure Terry would take responsibility as a husband and father if we could just get away. And I felt like a guest living at his parents' place. I know it's tough for others to understand, because I had everything I needed—materially. But I hated it. We had no privacy. His parents knew about every argument we had and silently disapproved of me saying anything when..." Jaclyn let her words trail off. She'd been about to blurt out the whole story of Terry's many affairs. She'd had so few chances to talk, to really explain what she'd been through, that she'd nearly forgotten Cole would have no sympathy for her in that regard—at least, not if he'd done the same thing to Rochelle.

"When what?" he prompted.

"Never mind."

He looked at her, obviously curious about her sudden retreat, but Alyssa and Mackenzie entered the kitchen at that moment and saved Jaclyn from having to confront the question in his eyes.

"You said we could call Daddy tonight," Mackenzie said.

Ordinarily Jaclyn would have asked the girls to wait a few minutes until she'd finished the dishes. But she needed the distraction, so she picked up the phone and dialed. "Did you see if Alex wants to talk?" she asked.

Mackenzie nudged her sister. "Go tell Alex we're calling Daddy."

Alyssa headed to the living room. Mackenzie took the phone, and Jaclyn and Cole returned to the dishes. After a minute, Mackenzie came into the dining room, where

Jaclyn was balling up the tablecloth so she could take it to the laundry, and announced that her daddy wasn't home.

"Can we call Grandpa and Grandma?" she asked. "They might come get us."

Jaclyn doubted they would. They hadn't been to Reno yet, and she didn't really want them to start coming now. Her life was much more pleasant since she didn't have to deal with them directly, but she hated to disappoint the children. "They go to bed pretty early," she said, stalling while she tried to make up her mind.

"Not this early," Alex said, coming around the corner with Alyssa.

Evidently Alex had changed his mind about calling Feld. Since the divorce, his moods shifted quite often. One minute he was angry with Terry, the next he was upset at her. "You want to talk to Grandpa?" she asked.

He shrugged. "I guess so."

Hoping it might do him some good to touch base with his grandfather and receive whatever reassurance Burt might offer, she swallowed a sigh and agreed. "Okay. Come here."

This time when she dialed, she handed the phone to Alex and waited to hear what Burt would say. Cole stood at the entrance to the kitchen, looking mildly curious, one shoulder propped against the doorway. The girls wiggled expectantly at her side.

"Hi, Grandpa, it's Alex…I know, it's been a long time. I miss you, too. Where's Daddy? How come he doesn't come get us… What?"

Alex looked at her, and Jaclyn knew her name had been mentioned. She doubted it was in a positive light. With Burt, it never was.

"I don't know. She just never has. Dad always comes to get us…I guess I could ask, but…I know…maybe she will…hang on."

Pulling his ear away from the phone, Alex turned to her. "He wants to see us," he said.

A trickle of unease crept down Jaclyn's spine. "Great. When's he coming?"

"He says it's your turn to drive us out there."

Her turn? Alex made it sound as though she was under some sort of obligation, but it had always been up to Terry to do the driving if he wanted to see the kids. She glanced at Cole, wishing for a moment of privacy, and he seemed to understand because he stepped into the dining room.

"Honey, I would if I could," Jaclyn said, lowering her voice. "But my car is old and not very reliable. I don't think it would be wise to drive so far out of town. We could get stranded in the desert."

"You drive your car to work every day."

"Right, but work is only fifteen minutes away. If I break down, I can always call someone. Out in the desert, there won't be anyone to call. I don't have a cell phone, and I'm not sure there's coverage out there even if I did."

"So?"

"It's too dangerous, Alex. Aren't you listening to me? We'd have the girls with us. The tires on the car are nearly bald, and it's been running hot—"

"You always have some excuse. I haven't seen Dad for a month, but you don't care!"

Jaclyn was conscious of Cole standing in the other room. He'd given her some space, but she seriously doubted he was out of earshot. Her house wasn't big enough to avoid his hearing Alex's high-pitched voice.

Why did this have to come up tonight?

"It's not my fault that you haven't seen him, Alex, and you know it," she said.

"Then, whose fault is it? Dad's?"

Yes! Jaclyn wanted to scream the word, but she was the adult in this situation and was determined to act like one.

Tempering her response to something kinder, she said, "I don't want to place blame. It just hasn't worked out."

"Come on, Mom. The car will make it," Alex pleaded.

"I promise you, honey, I'd take you to Feld if I could, but I can't. What if something went wrong? We'd be in real trouble."

Alex narrowed his eyes at her and spoke into the phone. "You were right. She won't do it. She won't ever let us see our dad!"

Jaclyn opened her mouth to refute the unfair claim, just as Cole stepped back into the kitchen.

"Tell your grandpa to wait up," he said. "You'll be there in a couple of hours."

"What?" Jaclyn gaped at Cole.

"We'd better start out before it gets too late," he told her.

"You're driving us there? To Feld?"

He shrugged. "Why not? My car will make it."

"But it's a long drive. We won't get back until late tonight, and then there's the problem of getting the kids home tomorrow."

"Won't Terry bring them?"

"I don't know. He's not even home so we can ask him."

Alex put on his "please, please, please" face. "Can't you guys just stay?"

"Where?" Jaclyn asked.

"With Grandma and Grandpa," Mackenzie supplied, as though the answer should be obvious to everyone.

Jaclyn tried not to blanch openly. "No, guys, listen. Staying overnight is too much to ask of Cole."

She expected Cole to concur by claiming he had something to do come morning, but he didn't. He studied one child's hopeful face, then each of the others before turning to Jaclyn and cocking an eyebrow in challenge. "Feld has a motel or two, if I remember right. I'm sure we can manage a couple of rooms for the night, if you're up to it."

"Are you serious?" she asked, knowing everything rested on his answer. She couldn't say no now, not without adding credibility to Alex's charge that she was being less than cooperative when it came to letting them see their father.

Cole grinned and mussed Alex's hair. "Go pack your bags," he said. "All of you. I'll run by my place and be back to pick you up in twenty minutes."

CHAPTER NINE

FELD.

God, he was going back. Cole couldn't believe it. When he'd left, he swore he'd never return, yet here he was, driving through the desert, the lights of Feld just ahead. Worse, he had his high-school prom queen and her children in the car and was taking them to see a family that had always treated him and his brothers with scorn. And he was staying the night. What on earth had possessed him to volunteer for this assignment?

He could have let Jaclyn take his truck, he thought. Then he'd be sleeping in his bed right now, comfortable in the world he'd created, safe from the part of his life he'd rather forget. But she could have gotten a blowout or something, even in his vehicle. No, he'd had to take them. He was caught the moment he'd heard the tears in her son's voice.

Or maybe he was caught long before that. Maybe he was caught the moment he'd run into Jackie at Joanna's. He'd known instinctively that someday she'd stir up old painful memories, make him confront Feld one more time.

Cole stifled a groan and glanced at her out of the corner of his eye. She'd dozed off twenty minutes ago, her face serene in the amber glow of his instrument panel. The children slept, too, while he hurtled ever closer to the demons of his past.

The lay of the land, the streetlights and the buildings on the outskirts of town instantly brought back his senior year and the year after—the year his mother died. But it was the smell that made the memories crowd so close he could scarcely breathe. Sagebrush and dust and fried chicken from the takeout diner combined to create a scent that was uniquely Feld, a scent that hadn't changed in ten years.

Briefly Cole squeezed his eyes closed against the echo of his mother trying to call to him after she'd lost the ability to speak, and gripped the steering wheel more tightly. Feld was just a place, not so different from a thousand other small American towns, he told himself. What had been painful here was gone. Feld couldn't hurt him anymore.

"Are we there?" Waking when he slowed for the first traffic signal, Jaclyn blinked and stared out the window. Russ Groves's small real-estate office was still on Main Street next to One-Two-Three Burgers and Shakes and across from the 7-Eleven on the corner. A handful of new businesses had sprung up since he'd left, and a few had changed hands or been modernized, Cole noticed, but for the most part, returning to Feld was like taking a step back in time.

"Just about," Cole answered. "The Wentworth ranch is on the other side of town, right?"

"Yeah. Turn left at the last light."

Cole remembered. Terry's place had been the weekend party haunt for almost everyone in his graduating class, except Cole. He'd never been invited, but being left out hadn't bothered him. He'd been too busy wishing for other things—his mother's improved health, his father's continued strength, his brothers' safety and well-being. What he'd hated in those days was the way Terry had taken his father's money and power, and all it afforded him, for granted, and the way he'd strutted through school looking down his nose at anyone less fortunate.

He wondered if Terry had changed.

"How long has it been since you've visited here?" she asked.

Not long enough, he wanted to say. Instead, he responded, "I left about eighteen months after my divorce. I haven't been back since."

"I didn't think so. The last time I saw you was when I was pregnant with Alex."

"At the grocery store."

They came to the light and made a left.

"Do you ever talk to Rochelle?" Jaclyn asked, when they passed the small florist shop owned by Rochelle's parents.

"No. Is she still in town?"

"Probably. She was here when I left a year ago."

Great. If he was really lucky, he could run into his ex while he was in town, end up facing every person he'd never wanted to see again.

"Has she remarried?" he asked.

"Not that I know of. She—" Jaclyn glanced over at him. "She had a hard time getting over you."

"Somehow that doesn't surprise me," he said.

A faint grin lit Jaclyn's face. "Are you saying you're unforgettable?"

"I'm saying Rochelle has problems." *And for a while, those problems were my problems. If things had gone any differently, if I hadn't found out…*

Cole shook his head in an attempt to clear his mind. He *had* found out. That was the important thing.

"What's wrong with her?" Jaclyn asked.

Starting with Rochelle's mental instability, Cole could have given her a pretty long list. But Jaclyn knew too many people in Feld. Regardless of what had transpired between him and his ex-wife, their marriage was over now, and it was enough for Cole that he'd gotten out. He wouldn't divulge what Rochelle had done because it served no purpose except to make her look bad. "It doesn't matter anymore."

Jaclyn adjusted her shoulder strap and checked on her

sleeping children. "What time do you want to head back tomorrow?" she asked, changing the subject.

"I thought we'd let the kids spend the day, then leave around seven. That should get them in bed by nine or nine-thirty, early enough for school the following morning. Sound okay?"

"That's fine, but you don't mind? Staying so long, I mean?"

It wasn't a matter of whether he minded, Cole realized. It was a matter of commitment. He had said he'd bring them; he'd see it through. Certainly he could survive a single day in the town of his old alma mater if it meant Burt couldn't accuse Jaclyn of trying to keep her kids from their father.

"Tomorrow's Sunday. I won't be missing anything."

"Do you have family or friends here you'd like to visit?"

There were a few teachers who'd been kind to him and his family, including one who'd actually come out to the house and tutored Rick—but Cole didn't know where they lived or whether they were still in town. He thought he might look up Wild Bill, the crusty geezer who'd given him the trucking job when he'd married Rochelle, and he might swing by and say hello to their old neighbor, Granny Fanny. Other than that, the only people he wanted to see were buried in the cemetery.

"Not really. I lived here less than three years and didn't make many long-term friends," he said. "My parents came from Kansas. My extended family on both sides is back there."

"Do you ever go to Kansas to visit them?"

"No. I didn't grow up knowing any of my cousins, and I've been too busy since I got older."

"Here it is," she said, pointing through the window at two white brick posts topped with lion sentries.

Slowing, he turned down the long, tree-lined drive he'd

passed hundreds of times when he was a kid. Under the light of the moon, the Wentworth ranch looked exactly the same as it had in high school. The house was a long rambling affair with a big barn in back and cows lowing off in the distance. Hay piles covered with black plastic sat in a field to one side, and at least a dozen vehicles, from tractors to trucks, were parked at various points along the circular drive.

"Where did you and Terry live?" Cole asked above the grind of tires on gravel. "Is there a smaller house in the back?"

"No, we shared the big house with his parents. Technically, we were supposed to have the south wing to ourselves. We had a separate kitchen and everything, but his mother did the accounting and payroll for the ranch, and I pretty much took over as cook and housekeeper, so we usually ate together. It just didn't make sense to have two people cook each night when we were all living under the same roof, you know?"

"Sounds like you spent a lot of time with your in-laws." Cole couldn't imagine what it must've been like, living with the arrogant Wentworths, but then, he couldn't imagine what had attracted her to Terry in the first place. Cole had never cared for him.

With a sigh, she blew a strand of hair out of her face. "It wasn't so bad at first. I thought they were very supportive and good to us. His father was paying for everything we had, everything we did. But we were working for it, too. Both of us. I might never have been directly involved in the business, but Terry spent nearly twelve hours a day out on the ranch, and I wasn't exactly sitting around. I was doing things that enabled Terry's mother to stay in the office."

She shook her head, staring out the front window at the house where she'd spent all her married years. "Burt never seemed to credit us for what we did, though. He acted like he was God and we were living on his good graces, that we were ungrateful wretches if we ever talked about leaving the ranch.''

"Golden handcuffs."

She chuckled without humor. "No kidding. Burt even threatened to disinherit Terry one time, when he brought up the subject of our moving. Terry kept telling me we'd leave eventually, and I kept trying to be patient, to compromise, to get along, but..." Her eyes grew troubled. "There were some...other issues that came into play, and pretty soon I just couldn't take it anymore."

Cole put the transmission in Park and cut the engine. "Do you like living by yourself better?" he asked.

Jaclyn paused, seeming to choose her words carefully. "Living alone has been difficult. I won't lie about that. It's something I never pictured myself doing. But I'm getting by, and I certainly don't regret leaving Terry. If it weren't for the kids—" she glanced at them again as if to reassure herself that they were still sleeping, peacefully oblivious to her words "—I would never look back."

So, it appeared he and Jaclyn had more in common than he had thought. They might have come from opposite sides of the tracks. She might have been Miss Popularity and he a two-bit punk trying to scrape enough together to buy a new pair of jeans when his others wore out, but neither of them held any love for Feld or the Wentworths.

"Let's get this over with, then." He started to open his door, but Jaclyn stopped him with a hand on his arm.

"There's something you should know before we go in."

"What's that?"

"Terry and his family may not be...friendly. He's been trying to talk me into coming back to him, and I won't."

"I don't expect them to roll out the red carpet. They never liked me to begin with." He started to climb out again, but she pulled him back.

"It's more than that now. He might blame you that I won't take him back," she clarified.

"Me? How?"

"You gave me a job."

Cole scowled. "What does that have to do with your relationship?"

"It gives me the ability to support myself. He and his father made sure I didn't get much when we divorced. They were hoping desperation would drive me back."

So that was the answer to the child support riddle. Cole had wondered, but he also knew the Wentworths had plenty of money. Why would they be so stingy with Terry's children? "What about the kids?"

"I don't know how they justify their behavior where the kids are concerned. I know they love them, so it doesn't make sense that they wouldn't be more worried that they have heat in the winter and food in the fridge. The only thing I can figure is that they don't really understand how hurting me hurts them."

Disgusted, Cole shook his head. The Wentworths had all the odds in their favor, and they were still playing dirty. "They know. They're counting on the fact that you'd never let anything hurt your kids. You'd come back first."

Jaclyn thought about that for a minute. "I probably would. If it came down to them having what they needed, I'd do anything. But I'd sacrifice a lot of things before turning tail and running back to Feld. Anyway—" she grinned at him, a hint of triumph in her expression "—I don't have to worry about that now that an old friend has given me a decent job."

If Cole had ever been glad he hired Jaclyn, and lately he was—every time he smelled dinner cooking or found a freshly ironed shirt in his closet—he was happy now. He loved that he was the one who'd given her exactly what she needed to fight the Wentworths. Burt might think he could get away with pushing his ex-daughter-in-law around, that he could use her own children against her—and maybe in Feld he could. But Jackie wasn't in Feld anymore.

"Anyway," she was saying, "you were so nice to bring us out here, I wanted to warn you. I thought if you understood what to expect, you wouldn't be hurt."

Cole chuckled. "The Wentworths can't hurt me, Jackie. You don't ever have to worry about that."

"I'm glad *someone* is safe from them," she said, her smile sincere but her expression skeptical. "Still, maybe you'd better stay here while I take the kids to the door."

"If you don't mind, I'll help you carry their bags. Suddenly I'd like to see Burt and Terry one more time."

Jaclyn seemed unsure of how to take his words, but Alex roused at that moment and cried, "Hey, we're here!" which woke the girls.

"Fine, let's go," she said, and Cole spent the next few minutes helping Jaclyn get their overnight bags out of the back of the truck and bringing them to the door. Then he waited on the doorstep beside her, the three children standing in front of them, while Alex rang the bell.

"Hi, Burt," Jaclyn said, when Terry's father answered the door.

Even though he hadn't seen her since their last day in court, Burt Wentworth didn't respond directly to her. He spoke to the children, instead, trying to make the snub as obvious as possible.

"Here they are, all safe and sound," he announced to Dolores, who stood behind him, wearing what she called a housedress, a cotton print number that fell to just below the knee and snapped up the front. As always, she looked like a sweet, gray-haired grandma. But Jaclyn had done the unforgivable when she'd divorced Terry, and couldn't count on any kindness coming from Dolores.

Jaclyn greeted her, but Terry's mother followed her husband's lead and spoke only to the children.

"Come give Grandma a hug. We've missed you. Seems like we never get to see you anymore. Why did you have to go and move so far away?"

Alex cast Jaclyn a blame-filled look, and Jaclyn's false smile faltered. But Cole put a hand on the small of her back, a silent communication of support, and she became more determined than ever to finesse her way through this uncomfortable meeting.

"Where's Dad?" Alex asked, as the children burst into the house babbling excitedly.

"He went out with some friends tonight," Dolores said.

"Where?" Mackenzie pressed.

"I want to see him," Alyssa said.

"I don't know, dears. He'll be home shortly, though, I'm sure."

Jaclyn thought she could guess where Terry and his friends were. They hadn't changed how they spent their weekends in the past twelve years. She doubted they'd change in the next. They were all going nowhere fast, and that more than anything had fueled her disappointment in Terry when he was her husband.

But she didn't have to worry about Terry anymore. She was steering her own ship now. Being in control was a little scary, but it was also unbelievably liberating.

"Here's their stuff," Jaclyn said to no one in particular, when Burt and Dolores left the door standing open and allowed the children to press them back into the house. No one had acknowledged Cole. No one had invited them in or thanked them for bringing the children to Feld. But Jaclyn hadn't expected any great show of gratitude. She hadn't come to town as a favor for the Wentworths, anyway. She'd done it for her children.

"We'll pick them up tomorrow at six o'clock, grab a burger and head out. We don't want to get home too late."

At first Jaclyn thought Burt and Dolores were going to ignore this statement, as well, but finally Dolores glanced up long enough to respond with a clipped "That's fine."

Eager to be gone, Jaclyn put her hand on Cole's forearm to draw him away, but just as they reached the outer glow of the porch light, her ex-father-in-law addressed her.

"Terry said you had a new man. This him?"

"I beg your pardon?"

Burt angled his gray, buzz-cut toward Cole and shoved his hands in his pockets to rattle his change. He wasn't a particularly tall man, but his shoulders were wide and his hands big, the effect of which gave him a square solid look. "This your boyfriend?"

Jaclyn let go of Cole's arm, only now realizing, amid her preoccupation, that she was still hanging on to him. "Um, no, Cole's my boss and an old friend. You might remember him. He went to high school with Terry and me. He's the oldest of the Perrini boys."

"Perrini boys, huh?" Burt squinted at Cole, obviously sizing him up. "I remember him, all right. Caught him and his brothers out here ruining my lawn with their truck tires one night."

If she'd heard about that incident, Jaclyn didn't remember it, but she didn't put it past Cole. Everyone did that kind of thing in high school. It was how the teenagers of Feld created their own fun in a town that had one theater and no mall. And Cole had been as wild as they came. He was always in trouble, unpredictable in every regard, except one—if anyone messed with his brothers, there'd be hell to pay from Cole.

"I guess we all did a few stupid things like that," she said, hoping to mediate so the conversation wouldn't turn ugly.

But Cole clearly wasn't interested in her help. "That must have been someone else," he said flatly.

Burt rocked up onto the balls of his feet and jingled his change again. "Oh, yeah? Seems to me it was you."

"No, I was at the 7-Eleven that night. I remember because Terry got busted for stealing beer, right after he threw up at the front door." Cole smiled. "But maybe that incident slipped your mind, since nothing ever came of it. You knew the police officers involved and fixed things with the store clerk, too, I guess, because Terry got off, just like he always did."

Burt clamped his mouth shut. He'd been trying to put Cole down, to insinuate something about his background and poor upbringing, but Cole had quickly and easily turned the tables on him. Peeling out on someone's lawn was one thing. Stealing beer from a store was something else, and Terry had been underage, though Jaclyn knew his father cared more about the embarrassment Terry had caused him than any moral implications.

"I guess boys will be boys, huh?" Cole said. "See you tomorrow at six." Slinging an arm around Jaclyn, he walked her to his Navigator and opened the door for her to climb in. To the casual observer, she knew his actions made them appear closer than they were, but she didn't care. Cole was putting Burt on notice that she wasn't alone anymore. He was lending her his support, and it felt...well, wonderful. Having Cole with her was like putting the wind at her back. She hadn't realized just how tough it was to weather Terry and his family's ill will alone.

"Thanks," she said, as soon as he'd climbed in and started the truck.

"You don't have to thank me. I didn't do anything," he said, but he took her hand, and Jaclyn gladly entwined her fingers with his. The last few minutes had united them somehow, made them allies against the Wentworths and Terry—even Feld.

"Where should we stay for the night?" he asked.

There were only three motels in town, mom-and-pop establishments with small, cabin-like rooms. None was very expensive. None was very nice. But they were good enough for Jaclyn. She was just glad to put some distance between her and the ranch.

"Let's see if the Starlight Motel still has its Jacuzzi," she suggested.

He hesitated before pulling out of the circular drive and onto the road. "I didn't bring a suit."

Jaclyn smiled, feeling wild and free and on top of the world for the first time in what seemed like an eternity. It was as though all the responsibility she'd shouldered for so long had suddenly disappeared, allowing her to be young again. "Neither did I."

CHAPTER TEN

COLE GAVE JACLYN an incredulous look. When they were in high school, the Starlight Motel was known popular for its private Jacuzzi, which couples used in half-hour increments. Cole had taken Rochelle there on their honeymoon—he hadn't been able to afford anything better—but strangely enough, he could scarcely remember that night now. All he could think about was Jaclyn, the girl he'd wanted from the beginning.

"You must be joking," he said. "You'd never go skinny-dipping."

"Why not?"

"You're not the type."

"Oh, yeah? From what I heard, you went skinny-dipping often enough when we were in high school. Why am I so different?"

With the engine still idling, he propped one arm over the steering wheel and turned so he could see her better. "A lot of people went skinny-dipping in high school. You weren't one of them."

She frowned, and glanced away. "Maybe I'm tired of being so straitlaced. Maybe I want to do something daring and fun for a change. It's not like I'm suggesting we share a room. I'd never get involved with you. We work together."

Cole might have thought the same thing at least a million times, but somehow he didn't like the sound of those sentiments coming from her. Maybe it was an ego issue, because she hadn't wanted him before, when he'd wanted her. Or maybe it was because a part of him still hoped to change her mind.

No, that couldn't be the case. He wasn't interested in taking on the responsibility of a woman with children. He'd raised his share of kids, knew how tough it was. And stepparenting would be even worse, what with Terry and his family still in the picture.

He put the truck in gear and pulled onto the road. "You're too—" he looked at her "—shy," he finished, but he was trying to talk her out of the idea for *his* sake, not hers. She might be able to strip, climb into a hot tub with him and dress again without feeling the slightest desire for anything more to happen between them, but he doubted he'd be so...hormonally removed.

"I'm not shy," she protested.

"Has any man seen you naked besides Terry?"

She shrugged and said sheepishly, "No."

"See? You won't go through with it."

"Fine. Forget it. Don't go to the Starlight. It was just a passing impulse."

He gave her a knowing smile. "That's what I thought."

"What?"

"That you'd back out before we ever reached the hot tub."

"I wouldn't have backed out if you hadn't...never mind." She folded her arms and turned toward the window, giving Cole the opportunity to admire her profile. He was with Jackie Rasmussen, his high-school heartthrob. After ten years, she was finally in *his* truck and not with Terry. He thought of her in his English class, drinking a cola at the football game, sitting in an assembly with her friends. How many times had he dreamed of having her as his girl? In Reno, those dreams felt like ancient history, another chapter in his life. But in Feld, they seemed like only yesterday. If he wasn't careful, he could feel the same longing for her right now....

The Starlight was coming up on their right. Cole saw the sign lit up with shooting stars and the words Private Jacuzzi, and determined to drive past in favor of the Sand Mountain Inn down the street. But when they reached the entrance, he found himself turning in and parking the Navigator in a slot marked Office.

"I thought we were going someplace else," she said, her eyes widening.

He grinned. For a moment there, he'd almost done the safe, sensible thing and played it straight. But Jaclyn was the only person he'd ever consistently wanted and, despite the risks, he wasn't about to miss out on something this good.

"I think you're right," he said. "I think it's time you did something a little wild and crazy. And I'm just the man to do it with."

WHAT HAD SHE GOTTEN INTO? Suddenly as shy as Cole had accused her of being, and more than a little embarrassed, Jaclyn folded her arms over her shirt, inhaling the smell of the chlorine in the hot tub, while Cole hung the Occupied sign on the gate. When she'd suggested it, her idea of skinny-dipping had seemed tantalizingly dangerous and incredibly exciting—something impulsive and entirely out-of-character for her normally conservative self. She'd wanted to feel young and attractive again, probably because she'd felt old and tired for too long. And skinny-dipping hadn't seemed like such a big deal. Teenagers did it all the time, right?

Then, why did taking off her shorts and tank top seem so terrifying now?

Probably because she had a couple of stretch marks no one but Terry had seen, while Cole's body was perfect. At least, he looked perfect in his clothes—tall and muscular and as darkly handsome as ever.

Cole seemed to sense her sudden reluctance; he caught her eye and smiled reassuringly. His manner said, *Trust me, I'll take care of everything,* and she wanted to believe him. She did believe him. So far, he'd never let her down. But...

"Having second thoughts?" he asked before removing his T-shirt.

Jaclyn glanced at the steam curling off the small, round hot tub, and was tempted to rise to the challenge in Cole's voice. He didn't believe she'd go through with it, and she wanted to surprise him by peeling off her tank top as though she was as confident and brazen as she sometimes wished.

But she couldn't do it. He was her boss. Regardless of what had happened at the Wentworth ranch, she was suddenly very aware of their true relationship. And she was also afraid of the attraction she felt toward him. Getting naked would hardly help douse that.

She bit her lip and curled her nails into her palms. "I guess I'm all talk, huh? Still a Goody Two-shoes."

He grinned. "There's nothing wrong with that, Jackie. I'm surprised you came this far. You want to go back to our rooms?"

Jaclyn wasn't quite ready to turn in for the night. Despite her hesitancy to disrobe, she still wanted to be with Cole. He generally avoided or ignored her at the office, but she had his full attention now. And it was a heady experience.

"Can we sit out here and put our feet in the water?"

"Why not?" He kicked off his sandals and, rolling up the legs of his knee-length shorts situated himself on the edge of the hot tub.

"The water feels good, doesn't it," he said as she joined him.

The hot water did feel good, but sitting next to Cole felt even better. Jaclyn smiled and nodded. She knew she should keep her distance from this man, even with her clothes on, but he was so...alluring. Certainly it couldn't hurt to sit close enough to enjoy the masculine smell of him.

"How long did you say you've been divorced?" he asked after a few seconds of silence.

"A year," she told him.

"Have you started dating again?"

"No."

"Don't your weekends get lonely?"

"Are you kidding? I've got three kids and some old neighbors to keep me company," she said flippantly. "What more could a woman want?"

"A love life." He dipped his hand in the water and ran it through his black hair, causing water droplets to roll down his face. "Aren't you interested in getting married again? Or did the divorce burn you too badly?"

Jaclyn didn't want to think about her love life. Otherwise, she might be tempted to improve it tonight, with Cole. She wasn't completely sure he'd be game, but he *had* pulled into the Starlight, instead of going somewhere else.

"Maybe someday. Not soon," she said, staring at the pink polish on her toenails, as the water bubbled around her calves.

He nodded and leaned back to look at the star-filled sky. "What type of man would you look for next time?" he asked.

"I don't exactly have a job description. I know it would take someone willing to love my children, and someone willing to put up with my ex and his parents, for my children's sake. That's a pretty tall order."

"I don't think you need someone who is willing to put up with your ex and his family. I think you need someone to keep them honest."

She chuckled and kicked her feet gently back and forth.

"They're not used to running up against any resistance. The divorce itself came as a pretty big shock to them."

"I can tell. You don't ever worry about them taking the children and not bringing them back, do you?"

"No. For that to happen, Terry would have to take off with them and stay in hiding, and he's not about to leave Feld and his parents and the ranch. It's his future. He's planned on taking over for his father his whole life. He did try to gain full custody while we were getting the divorce, though, by claiming I'm an unfit mother. Fortunately that didn't work. We wound up with joint custody, so unless they want to risk kidnapping charges, the Wentworths are stuck with sharing."

Closing her eyes, Jaclyn reveled in the heat that was working its way up her legs and relaxing every muscle. "How come you've never remarried?" she asked.

"I'm not husband or father material."

"Really? How long were you with Rochelle?"

"Nine months."

"And nine months taught you that?"

"Believe me, nine months has never seemed so long."

"Why?"

He sighed. "I don't know. I was young, I was stupid. Take your pick."

"Did you love her?" Jaclyn asked. She felt awkward posing the question, wondered if it was too personal—but sitting alone together with their feet in the steamy tub seemed kind of intimate, and she'd always wanted to know.

"No."

His unqualified answer surprised her. "Ever?"

"There was a time, right at first, when I thought I might be able to love her and make the marriage work. But then things changed."

Jaclyn waited, hoping he'd elaborate, but he didn't. "Were you still trying to take care of your brothers?"

"Yeah. My mother was dying. My father had had his

first heart attack. Things were pretty much going to hell in a handbasket. Maybe I could have figured something out if the situation had been different.''

"I'm starting to realize how rough life was for you back then, Cole,'' she said. ''Teenagers can be so selfish and oblivious to the rest of the world. I had no idea at the time.''

He shrugged. ''I'm through it now.''

"You did a good job with your brothers. I've never seen anyone more fiercely protective.''

"I was the oldest,'' he said simply.

He was the oldest, so he assumed responsibility and looked out for them. She was an old friend of his, so he took care of her, too. Did he feel the need to care for everyone he knew? ''Have you made a habit of that?''

"Of what?''

"Of taking responsibility for other people's problems?''

"God, I hope not.'' He started searching the water for a jet, and by the time he found one, he'd moved a little closer. For a moment Jaclyn thought he might slip his arm around her, but he didn't.

"What was your dad like?'' she asked.

"My dad didn't say much. He was a quiet man who worked too hard.''

"Has he passed away, then?''

"Yeah. Had a second heart attack a couple of years after my mother died. What about your parents? They still around?''

His arm brushed hers, leaving Jaclyn's skin tingling. His close proximity and the warmth of the rising steam—or was the heat Jaclyn was feeling coming from an internal source?—made her want to melt into him, to let his body support hers.

"They moved to Los Angeles right after I married Terry,'' she said, scooping up some water and dribbling it on her thighs, just below the hem of her shorts. ''They wanted to be near my aunt, who was getting old, so they could take care of her. They were planning to move back once she died, but they never did. They were killed in a car crash three years later.''

''I'm sorry,'' he said.

She missed her parents, especially while she was going through the divorce, but after six years, she'd grown somewhat accustomed to being without them. Still, she smiled because she appreciated Cole's sympathy—and liked the way their shoulders were touching.

''What did you think of Burt?'' Jaclyn asked. She braved a glance at his face, now just a few inches from her own, and thought she could drown in his eyes. Thick lashes framed chocolate-brown eyes that were looking at her mouth. She let her own gaze drop to his lips and felt her stomach flutter. The only man she'd ever kissed was Terry, and she couldn't help but wonder what it would feel like to have Cole's lips pressed to hers.

''I think he hasn't improved with time,'' he said.

''No kidding.'' She forced herself to look away. ''Try living with him.''

''I can see why you couldn't.''

''Burt wasn't the reason I left. Terry was.''

His face glistened with moisture from the heat of the water as he gazed down at her. His eyes were heavy-lidded, and seemed even more preoccupied with her mouth.

''Are you ready to tell me why?''

''I told you tonight after dinner that he wouldn't stand up to his father and get us out—''

''But that wasn't all of it, was it.''

''No.''

''What's the rest?''

Jaclyn hesitated. She felt a wonderful sense of security sitting here with Cole, the bubbles from the jets perking around their knees, the steam blocking out everything more than a few feet away. But Terry's infidelity was something she didn't particularly want to discuss with her boss. She thought he might try to justify Terry's actions, tell her the affairs meant nothing. And she had another reason for keeping it a secret. Something she'd never admitted to anyone.

"It's okay if you'd rather not tell me," he said, returning his attention to the water.

She thought she was going to nod and take the out he'd given her, but instead, tears filled her eyes, and she could only blink helplessly. Maybe she *did* want to say what was really bothering her, what had bothered her all along. Maybe she had to get it off her chest.

"What is it, Jackie?" he murmured.

"He was unfaithful," she said, one tear slipping down her cheek. "But jealousy wasn't the worst of it. The worst of it was knowing I wasn't woman enough to keep him from straying." *There. She'd said it.*

He tilted her chin up so she couldn't avoid his eyes, which were more intense than usual. "How can you blame yourself for that?" he asked. "What Terry did probably had nothing to do with you and everything to do with him. He's not exactly used to denying himself."

"If I'd been enough to satisfy him, he wouldn't have felt the need to go elsewhere, right? I mean, he wouldn't have had any desire for other women. It's only logical."

"Logic doesn't necessarily apply when things like ego are involved," Cole said, using his thumb to wipe away the second tear that fell down her cheek. "You're woman enough for any man, Jackie. You're the only woman *I've* ever wanted." Then he lowered his head and kissed her, a kiss so warm and tender it nearly melted Jaclyn's bones. His mouth moved slowly on hers, as the hot water swirled around their legs, making her feel giddy, almost weightless. She could have pushed him away if she'd wanted to, but the thought never entered her mind. Letting her eyes drift closed as his arm came around her, she tried to take in every sensation separately so she wouldn't miss one, starting with Cole's mouth and how he tasted. One hand cradled her jaw and lightly caressed her cheek....

Suddenly he broke away. "It's getting too hot in here. We'd better go," he said, leaving Jaclyn to wonder if he was as unaffected by what had just happened as he seemed, or if the world had stopped turning for him, too.

IT WAS TOO MUCH, her sitting there, her big eyes staring up at him, filling with tears. No man could have resisted kissing her, right? A kiss wasn't anything, not really. It certainly wasn't any kind of commitment.

We're just friends, he assured himself as they crossed the parking lot to the motel entrance. *I didn't cross any lines. I was only comforting her.* But the heat in his groin attested to exactly the opposite. He wanted to do a lot more than comfort Jaclyn. He wanted to take her to his room and—

Suddenly Jaclyn stopped.

Surprised, Cole looked up to see Terry, and three of the guys Terry had hung out with in high school, leaning against his Navigator, watching them.

"Look, boys, it's Cole Perrini. Quite an upgrade since high school, huh?" Terry angled his head toward Cole's SUV. "What'd you do with the old rattletrap, Cole? That hunk of junk finally die?"

Cole ignored him. He was too busy taking stock of the odds. He could tell immediately that this wasn't a friendly meeting, and he wanted to have a plan in case a fight broke out.

"Terry, what are you guys doing here?" Jaclyn asked.

"Just thought we'd drop by to say hello. It's been a long time since we've seen Cole. The boys and I have missed him, haven't we, guys?"

"Oh, yeah, we've missed him, all right," someone muttered. Cole thought it was the kid they used to call Rocket.

"Haven't you missed your children?" she countered. "Why aren't you home with them?"

"They're fine with Grandma and Grandpa. You saw to that so you and your new boyfriend here could do your thing in the hot tub."

"We didn't do anything in the hot tub."

"Don't look to me like you're carrying any swimsuits."

Jaclyn felt a blush rise to her cheeks. "Cole's my boss, Terry."

"Right. Why would I think anything else? It's perfectly natural for a woman to get naked with her boss, don't you think, Jimmy?"

Jimmy Hansen, who looked, more than any of the others, like the stereotypical redneck, grinned and nodded. He used to play center for the high-school football team, Cole remembered, and wasn't surprised to see he'd only gotten larger with the passing years. "I like it when my secretary gets naked with me," Hansen said.

"What Jaclyn and I do or don't do is our business," Cole said.

"That's where you're wrong, Perrini. Everything Jaclyn does is my business," Terry countered. "She's the mother of my children. And they're not going to have any father but me. You understand that, we can avoid a lot of problems."

"You should have thought about being their father long before now," Cole said. "Maybe she'd be more than the mother of your children. Maybe she'd still be your wife."

Terry stepped away from the car to stand directly in their path. The others moved forward, too, congregating behind Terry and smirking.

"What about you, asshole? What about all the times you screwed around on Rochelle? You think we don't know about that? You think we don't know why she tried to kill herself?"

The unfairness of Terry's accusation caused Cole to clench his teeth against an instantaneous flood of anger. It was Rochelle's twisted thinking that had caused her to attempt suicide. He wasn't about to take responsibility for that. And he refused to let Terry taunt him about it. Especially when Feld's spoiled rich kid and his friends didn't really care about Rochelle. This was about Jaclyn.

"Your daddy must not be keeping you busy enough kissing his ass, Terry, because you've had plenty of time to stick your nose where it doesn't belong," Cole said. "You don't know what happened between me and Rochelle, so don't pretend you do. Looks to me like you've got enough of your own problems."

Terry's face purpled, and Cole fully expected him to take a swing. He knew he shouldn't have provoked Terry, that even now he should take Jaclyn and walk away, but he couldn't. He had too much emotional baggage left over from those years in Feld, and these people and how they'd treated him. He didn't think they'd let him go peacefully, anyway.

"You spoiling for a fight, trailer trash?" Terry taunted.

"Terry, please. This is so unnecessary," Jaclyn interrupted.

Cole put a hand on her arm and pulled her slightly behind him, just in case. "You fellas been out drinking and now you're looking for trouble. But you don't want to look here."

"Oh, yeah? Why not?" Terry demanded. "A few of the guys have a bone to pick with you. You broke Jason's nose thirteen years ago, remember?"

Cole let his gaze flick toward the man on Terry's left. "I remember the day he stole my brother's lunch for the last time, if that's what you mean. He want to fight about that again?"

Jason's eyes lowered, but Terry's remained hard and glittery and eager for violence. "Maybe it's time we settled the score between us once and for all."

"You've got to be kidding!" Jaclyn said, outraged. "Haven't any of you boys grown up since high school?

My God, Terry. Cole was nice enough to drive the kids out to see you, and you bring your friends here to start a fight with him? When are you going to stop being a child and start being a man?''

Her words stung. Cole could tell by the way Terry reared back.

''I'm more man than you can handle, sweetheart,'' he said. ''I think we've already established that.''

''Then, prove it and walk away,'' she said.

''Come on, she's right,'' Jason said. ''I'd rather drink than fight.'' He started to leave, and Rocket followed.

Jimmy and Terry remained, but Cole was starting to feel a little better about the odds. At least he had a chance of surviving a fight now, if one broke out.

''You guys leaving, too?'' he asked.

Jimmy glanced at Terry, then back at Cole. ''He's not worth it, Terry,'' he said at last. ''You want to spend the night in jail?''

''Old LeRoy's not gonna throw our butts in jail.''

''He might not put *your* butt in jail, but my daddy doesn't own half the town, and Georgia would probably leave me if I got into trouble again. Come on, let's go,'' he said, clasping Terry's shoulder. ''Come on, man.''

Terry gave Jaclyn a cold, hard look. ''I used to think you were too good for trailer trash like him, but maybe you two deserve each other,'' he said, then let Jimmy pull him away. They got into the truck parked next to the Navigator and peeled out of the lot.

It took a few seconds for the adrenaline pumping through Cole to subside. When he felt calm again, he reached for Jaclyn's hand.

''I'm sorry about that,'' she said.

''There's nothing for you to be sorry for. What happened was Terry's doing, not yours.''

''I didn't mean the pissing contest,'' she said. ''I'm sorry about what he called you. You're not trailer trash. You never have been.''

Cole made an effort to shrug it off. ''Don't worry about it.'' He started walking to their rooms—which were on the ground floor, next door to each other—but she pulled him back.

''I do worry about it. I feel badly because I let that go on when we were in high school.''

''Jaclyn, you couldn't have saved me from anything.''

She smiled, remembering that he'd handled things pretty well on his own. ''I could have tried,'' she said. ''I wish I had.''

Cole studied her face, tempted to tell her how crazy about her he'd been back then. But he decided it would only make her feel worse. ''It didn't bother me,'' he lied.

At their rooms, Jaclyn unlocked her door and stepped inside, then hesitated when he said good-night. ''Are you tired? Or do you want to come over in half an hour or so and watch a movie on Pay Per View?'' she asked.

All Cole's warning bells were going off. After everything that had happened tonight—dinner at her place, the confrontation with Burt at the ranch, the…kiss by the hot tub and the showdown in the parking lot, he'd be smarter to call it a night. But since when had he been one to do the sensible thing? He'd proved that by being willing to go skinny-dipping with Jaclyn in the first place. Now he was going to her room at ten o'clock where they'd be alone for hours….

Hell, why not? he asked himself. Life was a series of risks. He'd just have to be smart enough not to let this one get the best of him. ''Sure. I'll be over in a few minutes.''

''Give me thirty,'' she said. ''I'd really like to shower.''

CHAPTER ELEVEN

JACLYN QUICKLY SHAVED her legs and rinsed the shampoo out of her hair before turning off the water. Then she stood in front of the mirror and tried to see herself as Cole would have seen her, had she been willing to disrobe at the hot tub. She'd lost weight since the divorce—that was one positive thing that had come from it. She'd had trouble shedding the last ten pounds of pregnancy weight after having Alyssa, but it was gone now.

She turned sideways to be sure, checking the flatness of her stomach and the shape of her breasts—something she hadn't done in ages—and was encouraged. For thirty-one, she didn't look bad. But she wondered, if Cole *were* to see her, would he notice the three stretch marks below her navel? Drawing closer to her reflection, she fingered the marks of her last pregnancy and frowned. Cole had no doubt dated some very beautiful women. There was no way she could ever compare.

Which made no difference to her, she told herself firmly. He wasn't interested in her romantically. He scarcely talked to her at the office, and it was only this weekend that he'd shown any inclination to become better friends. Her sudden interest in how appealing or unappealing she was simply indicated that it was time to get out and start dating.

After putting on some makeup and blow-drying her hair, she pulled on the denim skirt and sweater top she'd brought for the next day, then surveyed herself again. Her hair was getting long and could use a trim, but it had plenty of body.

It fell past her shoulders in a curly mass. She was contemplating whether to pull it up, when Cole's knock came at the door.

"Jaclyn, it's me."

A stutter in her pulse told Jaclyn she was more excited to see him than she wanted to be, but she shoved that thought out of her mind. She didn't have the kids tonight and was determined to enjoy herself. Even if inviting Cole over to watch a movie did feel as though she was crossing a boundary between them, she knew better than to let things get out of hand.

If only she could stop picturing Cole's face just before he kissed her....

She wondered if she'd ever banish the image, then decided she'd be stupid to do so. It was already one of her favorite memories.

"Coming." She flipped off the bathroom light, checked to make sure she hadn't left any clothes lying around, then answered the door.

"Hi." He was carrying a bottle of wine and two glasses, and was wearing a snug-fitting pair of faded jeans and a gray sweatshirt—plain, casual clothes, but he looked great in them. Jaclyn doubted he could look bad in anything.

Smiling, she stepped back to let him in. "Hi."

"Did you have a chance to check the movie listings?" he asked, angling his shoulders to fit past her.

She hadn't thought about movies since she'd extended him the invitation. She'd been too preoccupied with trying to decide whether or not her breasts were beginning to sag. "Not yet. I just showered."

He put the wine and the glasses on the table, then sat on the bed closest to the television before facing her. "I was thinking maybe we should forgo the movie and just talk."

"Okay." Jaclyn got the impression this evening wasn't going to be the "fun without the kids" she'd been looking for. She took the seat next to the television, hoping he wouldn't read her disappointment. "What do you want to talk about?"

He hesitated, glanced at the wine, then back at her. "I'm not a good bet for you, Jackie. I'm not saying I don't want to take our relationship to…a more intimate level, but I'm not the marrying kind."

Jaclyn tucked her hair behind her ears. "So you're just putting me on notice?"

"I didn't want to disappoint you."

"Okay."

Their eyes met for a long minute, then Jaclyn said, "Does that mean you don't want to see a movie?"

"It means I don't know if I should stay."

"Because you think I'll want to marry you if something happens?" She grinned. "You must be even better than I thought."

He scowled at her teasing. "Come on, Jaclyn. I'm just trying to be up-front and honest here. You know where what happened at the hot tub could lead."

"It could lead a lot of places. We could become lovers. We could also become the best of friends. Or we might decide we don't really like each other at all. You don't have to take responsibility for decisions we haven't made yet, Cole. And you don't have to go around posting Consumer Beware notices for me—'Caution, I may have sex with you but that doesn't mean I'll want to marry you.' Jeez, I may be naive, but I know sex and love aren't necessarily the same thing. And if I ever make the decision to get involved with you on those terms, I'll know better than to hold you to anything deeper, okay?"

"So what's the bottom line?" he asked.

"Exactly what I said. That I'm perfectly capable of deciding whether or not to invite you over for a movie, even if we did kiss."

"Do you want anything from our relationship, besides a job?"

"I want to be friends."

"That's it?"

"Are you asking if I'm interested in something physical between us?"

He studied her for a moment, then said, "I guess I am."

"No." Jaclyn's answer was quick and firm, even though on one level she knew it was a lie. She did want to kiss Cole again, wanted to do more than kiss him. She was attracted to him, and she was lonely—a dangerous combination. But she wasn't the type to have sex with a man, then smile and wave goodbye in the morning. Which meant they weren't right for each other, something Jaclyn had known all along.

He didn't respond right away, making Jaclyn wonder what he was thinking. His face was so shuttered, she couldn't tell whether he was disappointed. "I understand. What do you want to watch?"

The conversation turned to a discussion of the available movies. They chose *Proof of Life,* and Cole ordered it. Then he poured them each a glass of wine, Jaclyn turned off the lights, and they settled on separate beds to watch Meg Ryan and Russell Crowe.

The next thing she knew, it was morning, and Cole was gone.

FELD HADN'T CHANGED MUCH. Cole drove around the town in the early dawn, wondering how different he'd be if his family hadn't moved here. His mother would still have died of multiple sclerosis, his father would have had to work night and day to keep a roof over their heads, and Cole would have had to look out for his younger brothers. Those things would not have changed. But he might have retained a certain amount of anonymity and not felt the need to cover the pain and fear inside him by acting out. And he wouldn't have met Rochelle.

He thought about Jaclyn and the conversation they'd had

last night, and felt his mood darken. They'd had a good time at the hot tub. Why he couldn't go to her room and simply enjoy a movie was beyond him. Instead, he'd brought up the subject of their relationship, forced her to commit herself, and now he wasn't sure he was happy with the outcome. He didn't know what he'd been trying to achieve, except to stop what had happened with Rochelle from happening again.

Rochelle. All roads in Feld seemed to lead back to her. Terry had accused him of cheating on her, and he had— once. But that was at the very end, when it was all over, anyway. The secretary who worked for the same trucking outfit he did came over to console him the day Rochelle tried to kill herself, and she was very warm and friendly and forward. Things got out of hand, but his marriage had been destroyed long before that. The reason had nothing to do with fidelity and everything to do with obsession.

Slowing at the entrance to the old trailer park where he used to live, Cole turned in and crept down the main road, studying the beatup trailers he passed. Even the Desert Mirage Trailer Park was the same, he decided. Same people. Same poverty.

He took a right at the first turnoff and pulled to the side of the road to sit and stare at the trailer his family had once rented. It had been a piece of junk all those years ago. It was worse now. Cole couldn't believe it was still standing.

"Aha! I thought you'd come back one day!" A hand smacked his passenger window, and Cole dipped his head to see the old, wrinkled face of Granny Fanny, the widow who'd lived next to them.

He rolled down the window. "Don't you ever change, Fanny? I swear you don't look a day older than you did ten years ago."

"That's 'cause I was old and ugly then, boy. Ain't no-place to go from there."

"I've always liked the way you look," he said.

"That why you keep sendin' me money?"

Cole raised his brows in surprise. "What makes you think I'm sending you money?"

She smiled, revealing some gaps in her teeth that hadn't been there before. "No one else would do it."

"It's not me," he said, lying so she wouldn't feel beholden to him. To salvage her pride and release her from any sense of obligation, he'd never included a return address or a note. He only wanted to help her out, since her own kids never did. She lived pretty lean; it didn't take much.

"Bullshit," she said.

Cole chuckled. Evidently her propensity for swearing hadn't changed, either. "Why would I send you anything?" he teased. "You've always done a good job looking out for yourself."

"Damn right. But I guess you send it, anyway, 'cause you got a heart the size of Texas. That you'd bother with an old lady like me after all these years might come as a surprise to some, but not to me. You were a good boy."

"Come on. I was a hell-raiser."

"No one could ever convince me of that. You movin' back, Coley? Lookin' for a place?"

"No." Cole took a deep breath and returned his gaze to the trailer where he used to live. "Just taking a walk down memory lane."

"Well, I got something for you, then." She stepped away from the truck, moved the sprinkler that was watering a small green patch of lawn and disappeared inside her narrow home, while Cole climbed out of the truck to wait. When she returned, she was carrying a bottle of pickled beets in one hand and an envelope in the other.

"I haven't bottled for a few years," she said, giving him the beets. "Arthritis is finally getting the best of old Fanny. But I saved this for you. Knew you always liked 'em."

A knot in Cole's throat suddenly threatened to choke

him, and he glanced quickly away so she wouldn't see how her gesture affected him. She'd always been kind to him. In her gruff way, she'd stood by him at a time when there was no one else.

"Thanks," he said. "There's nothing better than your beets."

"And there's this—" she added. "I hate to even give it to you, but here it is."

The envelope she handed him had his name on the front—and Rochelle's return address in the upper left-hand corner. Cole tensed automatically.

"She came by here," Granny explained, "'bout a year ago, cryin' and claimin' she needed to find you. She was up to no good, that girl, if you ask me. But I said I'd keep the letter and give it to you if I ever saw you again."

Cole opened the passenger door and shoved the envelope in his glove box. He didn't want to touch it, let alone read it. "She tell you anything about what was wrong?"

"No. Just blubbered like a damn crybaby, trying to win my sympathies. But I could see right through her. I'd be ashamed of her if she was a kid of mine."

Cole nodded. He could have written a book on Rochelle's manipulative tactics. "Thanks," he said. "Someone's expecting me in town. I'd better go."

"Sure. It was good to see you, Coley. You turned into something to be proud of. I knew you would."

The lump in Cole's throat threatened to return. He swallowed hard. "You take care, Fanny."

"I'm doin' just fine," she said. "Don't you worry none about me."

IT WAS ONLY EIGHT O'CLOCK when Cole returned to the Starlight. He was planning to let Jaclyn sleep in, but when he pulled into the lot, she opened her door, and he could see that she was showered and ready to go for the day.

"What are you doing up so early?" he asked, getting out.

"You were up earlier than me. I thought maybe you'd abandoned me."

He smiled. If he could have abandoned her, he would have done it the day she'd shown up at his office and asked for work. "I'm not going anywhere. I just didn't sleep very well last night. Decided to take a drive."

"I guess the wine put me right out. I slept like a log."

He remembered. She'd fallen asleep during the first thirty minutes of the movie, and he'd spent the next hour-and-a-half telling himself he shouldn't move over to her bed and try to change her mind about wanting something physical between them.

"You hungry?" he asked.

"Yeah, but I can grab a doughnut or something, if you've already eaten."

"I haven't. I was waiting for you. Where do you want to go?"

"I guess the Skillet is still about the best place for breakfast, unless there's a new restaurant I don't know about."

"The Skillet's fine." Anywhere they went, they were going to draw attention, Cole thought. He was used to it, at least in Feld. Jaclyn, on the other hand, had always been Terry's girl and the town darling. He wondered if she was going to mind damaging her image by being seen with him.

"Hop in." Cole had been planning to shower and shave, but he didn't want to make Jaclyn wait. He adjusted the ball cap he'd pulled on when he left earlier, figuring he might look a little rough around the edges, but he'd have to do.

Jaclyn climbed into the truck, and Cole pulled out onto Main Street.

The Skillet was an old greasy spoon located right in the center of town. It served breakfast all day, every day, and had always been a popular place, even when Cole lived in

Feld. Today, probably because it was Sunday, it was packed.

"You mind waiting?" he asked Jaclyn, when they entered and he saw several parties ahead of them.

"No. We don't have anything else to do."

The smell of hash browns, eggs and coffee roused Cole's appetite as Jaclyn handed him a section of the *Feld Independent* she'd found spread out on the vending machine next to the door. They stood to the side so others could get by. Cole was reading about Burt Wentworth's plans to open a car dealership west of town, when one of the waitresses who'd been rushing past them recognized him.

"Cole! What are you doing in town? I swear it's been— what?—ten years?"

It was a short plump brunette. Cole had known her in school, but she'd been downright skinny then. "Hi, Mary-Jean. It's been at least that long. You still with Ducky?"

"No. We broke up just after graduation, but you were a couple years older than me and were gone by then, I guess. I married his older brother, Clint. We have four kids," she said proudly. Then she saw Jaclyn and her eyes widened. "Are you two together now?"

"No. I work for Cole," Jaclyn said, "in Reno."

Cole could tell Mary-Jean didn't buy Jaclyn's denial for a second. She smiled as though she'd been trying to get a peek at someone's underwear and had just hit pay dirt.

"You're kidding," she said. "I heard you moved away, Jackie, but I wouldn't believe it for the longest time. I couldn't imagine you and Terry breaking up. You were always the perfect couple. And now look at you! You've hooked up with the town bad boy!"

"It's not what—" Jaclyn started, but Mary-Jean, lowering her voice conspiratorially, cut her off.

"Don't worry. I don't blame you. I'd choose looks over money any day."

"I didn't leave Terry for Cole," Jaclyn said, but Mary-Jean's incredulous smile lingered as she turned to Cole.

"Rochelle know you're in town?"

If she didn't, Cole knew she soon would. Mary-Jean's mind was obviously working at a frantic pace, probably running through the list of people she couldn't wait to tell that Cole Perrini and Jaclyn Wentworth had come in to the restaurant together. "I don't think so. We just got in last night."

"Where did you stay?"

Cole hesitated. Even though they'd had separate rooms, mention of the honeymoon haven known as the Starlight would definitely raise Mary-Jean's eyebrows. For Jaclyn's sake, he didn't want to add any more fodder to the gossip mill. She still had ties to Feld, ties Cole didn't have.

"A motel here in town," he said.

Mary-Jean looked as if she might try to pin him down, but a cook barked at her from the kitchen to get some food delivered, and she muttered, "I'm coming. Jeez, give me a freakin' break," and turned away. "Good to see you, Jackie," she said over her shoulder. "I always had a crush on you, Cole Perrini," she added with a giggle.

Cole managed a polite smile that disappeared the instant she was gone. Then he cleared his throat and looked at Jackie, hoping to get a read on what she was feeling. "I guess it's my turn to apologize," he said.

"For what?" She acted calm, poised, but she glanced around the restaurant as though she expected to be accosted again.

"For my reputation. Everyone's going to think you went over to the dark side."

She smiled. "Who says it's the dark side?"

WAKING TO FIND he'd fallen asleep over his textbooks again, Rick yawned and rubbed the imprint on his cheek. The other students seemed to spend a fraction of the time he spent studying, but he wasn't cut out for book learning, never had been. He hated anything that involved sitting on his ass for too long. But he wasn't bad at practical applications—at least he'd taught himself quite a bit about accounting while working for Cole—and he wasn't about to let his past beat him.

He'd already gotten his G.E.D., over the summer. Now he was going to put in a few years at Reno Community College, then transfer to the university and get his degree. Since he'd quit Perrini Homes, he was able to go full time, which meant he could graduate a year after Andrew, if everything went well. And when that happened, he'd move to California and start his career in computers—a little late, perhaps, but better late than never.

He pictured himself breezing into Cole's office with an invitation to his graduation, anticipated Cole's surprise. And he imagined, as he always did, that Cole would be proud of him. Finally.

That's pathetic.

Refusing to think any more about his older brother, refusing to acknowledge how badly he missed him, Rick slammed his books closed. He'd joined a study group that was meeting at the school library this morning. If he didn't get moving, he'd miss it entirely.

CHAPTER TWELVE

"JACKIE. JACKIE WENTWORTH, is that you?"

Not again, Jaclyn thought as she spotted Mrs. Kirby, her old piano teacher, trotting down the street toward them. Five different people had interrupted their breakfast to say hello and catch up. Jaclyn would have been flattered by the attention, except that the conversation always centered on her divorce, and the fact that she and Cole were together. Even Mary-Jean had stopped by their table to say that if Jaclyn *wasn't* with Cole, she knew plenty of women who'd be happy to have him.

Jaclyn suspected she was talking about herself, despite the husband and four kids.

"Pretend you didn't hear her," she told Cole, staring at the ground and starting for the truck.

"Jackie! Wait! It's me, Mrs. Kirby!" The woman's voice rang louder in the warm, still air, and Jaclyn paused. She couldn't do it. Mrs. Kirby was an old busybody, but Jaclyn couldn't purposely ignore her.

"Too late. She's got me," she muttered. "But I'll try to make it short."

Cole stopped and turned when she did, only a brief frown telling Jaclyn that he was as tired of providing the town's entertainment as she was, and waited while Mrs. Kirby caught up.

"Jackie Wentworth. Where have you been? I haven't seen you for ages."

Jaclyn felt her eye twitch but managed a smile. "I live in Reno now. I'm just visiting."

"Really? Do you *like* the big city?"

"I do."

She wrinkled her nose in distaste. "With all those casinos? I don't think I could live there."

Jaclyn took a steadying breath. Maybe she liked Reno because it wasn't Feld. "Well, it's not for everyone, I suppose."

"And who is this?" she asked, eyeing Cole.

"You don't know Cole Perrini? He used to live here, too, but only for a few years."

"I guess we've never met."

Thank goodness, Jaclyn thought. At least they'd be spared another mention of Rochelle.

Cole said hello, and Mrs. Kirby dipped her head in his direction before speaking to Jaclyn again. "Are you still playing the piano?"

"No, I'm afraid not lately."

"What happened? You were one of my best students. You have real talent."

Talent did her no good without a piano to practice on. "Pianos are expensive instruments. I'll get one someday."

"What about that baby grand Terry gave you for Christmas? It was beautiful."

It was also still at the ranch, along with everything else they'd acquired during their marriage. "Terry has it."

"I didn't know he played."

"He doesn't." No one at the ranch knew how to play, but that, of course, didn't matter.

"Divorce is a terrible thing," Mrs. Kirby said.

The mourning in her voice made Jaclyn's smile real. She missed her piano, but Mrs. Kirby was acting as though she'd had to leave a child behind. "I'm afraid we've got to go," she said, "but it was wonderful to see you again."

"Save up for that piano, now. I don't want you to forget everything I taught you."

"I will. It's at the top of my list." If she ever made it to her list. She had to take care of the children's needs first.

Slipping her hand into the crook of Cole's arm, Jaclyn walked with him to the Navigator. "Can we get out of town?" she asked, when they reached it.

"Where do you want to go?"

"What are our options?"

Cole thought for a moment. "That depends on how much fun you want to have."

"What if I want to have the time of my life?"

He grinned. "Don't tempt me," he said.

"I mean the best time a girl could have with her clothes *on*," she clarified.

His smile didn't fade, proof that he'd been teasing her, as he tapped the newspaper he'd carried out of the restaurant. "Leave it to me."

SHE WAS GOING TO DIE!

Jaclyn screamed and squeezed Cole's arm as he steered the sand rail up the huge mountain of sand. He gave it plenty of gas, and they shot straight to the top, going so fast it made her eyes water. Her stomach lifted as they sailed over the peak and hung suspended for a split second before landing with a solid *thump*. Then they hurtled down the other side.

"My face hurts from smiling," she complained, wiping the moisture from her eyes when they reached the bottom. A fine layer of dirt covered her shirt, her shorts, her legs, everything, even her teeth, and her hair was completely windblown. But Cole wasn't any cleaner. He was wearing a pair of jeans and a T-shirt that was no longer white. His ball cap was on backward, and he had a streak of dirt across his forehead and even more clinging to the smile lines of his face.

"You were screaming like a banshee," he said, laughing.

Jaclyn tried to look indignant. "No, I wasn't. I was trying to tell you something."

"What? 'Let me out'?"

For a second there, right as they'd reached the peak and looked as if they'd roll down the other side, Jaclyn *had* wanted out. Cole had been taking it easy on her before that, letting her get used to the machine he'd just bought second-hand from an ad in the paper. But this last ride was wild and frightening, and the most fun yet. "No, I was saying it's my turn to drive."

He nudged her playfully. "Liar. I tried to get you to drive before and you wouldn't."

"Well, I'm new at this."

"I can't believe Terry never brought you out here."

Jaclyn's eye followed a cloud of dust up the mountain. It was a Quadrunner, a low, four-wheeled motorcycle with wide knobby tires. "He did bring me out here. I just wouldn't take a ride with him."

"Why not?"

"I was too scared."

Cole blinked at her in surprise. "So what made you get in with me?"

She wasn't sure she had a good answer to that question. There was something about Cole that made her feel safe, as if he had everything under control, as if he could do anything. Probably because he'd done so much. When he'd left Feld, he had nothing. Now he was back and could write a check for a couple thousand dollars to buy a used sand rail out of the paper as though he were buying nothing more expensive than a pair of shoes. And when Jaclyn had asked him what he planned to do with it after today, he shrugged and said he'd take it home, like it was no big deal to part with so much money even though he didn't know if he'd ever use the rail again.

"I guess I felt confident you wouldn't kill me," she said. "And I've had a blast. I'm glad I trusted you."

He smiled. "So am I. Did you guys come out here often?"

"Not me. Terry did. It was kind of a guy thing. He'd hang out with his friends or take Alex. And I really didn't mind." She sighed. "It was the after-hours stuff that upset me."

Cole turned off the sand rail to let the engine cool. "Who'd he mess around with, Jackie? Did you know her?"

"You mean *them?*" She leaned her head against the black pad that was supposed to cushion her neck and stared through the metal cage to the clear sky above. "No. They were prostitutes mostly. He and the guys liked to frequent strip joints and whorehouses. He thought he was doing me a favor having sex only with women who were routinely tested for STDs. But he did have a brief affair with someone who worked at the hair salon." She grimaced. "That was pretty embarrassing. Do you know how much those girls talk?"

"The affair got back to you?"

"In bits and pieces. He'd bought her a necklace, and she was showing it off to everyone who came in."

"What did you do?"

"I confronted him. He called her a bitch and a liar. By the time it was all over, I actually felt kind of sorry for *her.*"

"Did you ever prove it one way or another?"

"No. I didn't need to. I'd already found enough souvenirs in his truck to know what was going on. I could smell perfume on him some nights, too." The memories nearly turned Jaclyn's stomach, even now. There'd been so many nights when she'd nearly paced a hole in the carpet waiting for Terry to come home, wondering where he was, suspecting the worst. Then there were the times she'd found cigarettes in his truck even though he didn't smoke, or a strange brand of chewing gum in his ashtray—or something more telling. To this day she couldn't smell certain brands of perfume without feeling sick.

Cole turned his hat around to the front, a frown etched in the rugged lines of his face. "He wouldn't stop?"

Jaclyn closed her eyes against the pictures in her mind—pictures of herself pleading with Terry, summoning enough trust to give him one more chance, coming face-to-face with his failure when he blew it again. "He kept promising he would. We'd get counseling, decide to try again. I didn't want my children to grow up without a father. I was willing to put up with living at the ranch, even though I didn't like it. What I couldn't endure was the constant humiliation. My self-esteem was completely destroyed."

She tried to brush the sand off her shorts and wished she could brush the past away, as well, but it was no use.

"I'm sorry, Jackie. That must have been hell," Cole said.

Rochelle's face flashed in Jaclyn's mind, but she didn't say anything. Knowing Cole's background, it was probably better to avoid fidelity as a topic of conversation. She wasn't sure what had made her open up to him in the first place. Probably sheer loneliness.

"Let's not ruin the day by talking about Terry. Let's talk about something else," she said.

"Like what?"

She thought for a minute. "Like Margaret Huntley. She's great, don't you think? She really knows what she's doing."

"She seems to. I'm pretty happy with her so far. You picked a winner, there."

"She definitely stood out from all the rest. She was warm, friendly, direct and goal-oriented. I think she's going to sell a lot of houses."

"She's already sold four. Did she tell you?"

"Yeah. How many would you like her to sell every week?"

"Five would sell us out in three months. That would be ideal."

"Then what would we do?"

"Move to the next construction site."

He seemed to have it all figured out, huge development projects that he ran with ease. Jaclyn wanted to tell everyone in Feld, just so they'd know that they'd been wrong about Cole Perrini. "How did you get your start in the business?" she asked.

"When I left Feld for Reno, I decided I wanted to be in real estate. I didn't have any schooling. It didn't require a degree. And it had great upside potential." He grinned. "A perfect fit. So I talked an old couple into selling me their house and holding the mortgage. They wanted to travel and didn't really need the money. They'd already bought their motor home, so they went for it. My brothers and me moved in there and fixed up the place. We tore out the kitchen, put in a tile floor, nice oak cabinets, new appliances. We put on a new roof and painted and did a lot to the yard. Then we put it up for sale and made twenty-thousand dollars, which I used as a down payment on my next project. I did that over and over again for the next few years, then started splitting my money between two and three homes. Pretty soon I had some net worth and could get financing, which enabled me to do even bigger projects, and here I am. I owe my soul to the bank, but my business is thriving and I'm enjoying what I do."

"You make it sound easy."

"It wasn't easy, but so far it's working—providing the market holds. A man named Ed Bly helped me in the early days with short-term loans for the remodeling and other stuff. I wouldn't have done so well without him."

"Where did you meet him?"

"At a lumberyard, believe it or not. We struck up a conversation, I told him what I was doing, he came and looked at a few of my projects, and we went from there.''

''Where is he now?''

''His wife forced him into retirement, and they're living in Oregon. We call each other occasionally, enough to stay in touch. There will always be a bond there.'' He got out of the sand rail. ''You ready to eat?''

Jaclyn glanced at her watch. It was nearly three. This morning she'd wondered what they were going to do until six o'clock when they picked up the kids, but the day had gone quickly. By the time they'd bought the sand rail, the food for their picnic and the clothes she'd needed—since she hadn't brought anything appropriate—it was one o'clock. They'd been riding the sand ever since.

''Yeah, I'm hungry.''

''Let's go.''

They walked back to the truck, moved it to create some shade—since there wasn't a tree for miles—and spread out the blanket they'd borrowed from the motel.

''It's not the most scenic picnic you'll ever have,'' Cole said, gazing around at the barren desert, while Jaclyn dug through their sack of food, ''but you get used to the surroundings here, huh?''

She *was* used to Feld. She'd been raised here and had liked it well enough when she was a girl. She hadn't wanted to get away until after she'd married Terry and the town had become synonymous with the Wentworths and their power. She wondered how she would have liked Feld if she'd married someone else, like Cole.

Then she remembered the rumors about him and Rochelle, and decided she probably wouldn't have liked it any better.

''It has sort of a stark beauty, don't you think?'' she asked, giving him a soda before getting comfortable on the blanket next to her own plate.

Cole cocked an eyebrow at her. "No. It has a lot of stark memories, maybe."

She laughed. "Okay, you've got me there. But not all my memories are bad. Are yours?"

He seemed to consider the question. "Not my memories of you."

Jaclyn felt a stab of surprise. She and Cole didn't have many memories together. They'd never talked much, never gone out. "What do you remember about me?" she asked. "And don't say anything about prom night. Lula Jenson should have been queen. I just won because I was Terry's girl."

"*Why* were you Terry's girl?" he asked. "I've never been able to figure that out. For a while I told myself it was the money, but you're not like that."

Jaclyn chewed slowly so she'd have more time to think. She'd gone over those years in her mind again and again, wondering how she could have avoided her disastrous marriage. But even in retrospect, she couldn't find an easy out. "It wasn't the money so much as it was the promise of security, I guess. Terry's…well, he's bright. And he can be sensitive, when he's not around his friends. I don't know. We just got together so young, created so many ties, and I never questioned what was happening. When we graduated, marriage seemed like the next logical step. Everyone expected it, even our parents. Everyone thought we were lucky to have each other. I guess I just trusted that fate had dealt me the hand I was to hold." She ate one of her chips. "Why were you with Rochelle?"

He took a drink of his soda, then swiveled the can in the sand. "Because I couldn't escape her. She followed me everywhere, called me night and day, came to the house. I swear, if Margaret turns out to be as dogged as she is, I'll be a multimillionaire by this time next year."

Jaclyn remembered the lovesick Rochelle. The girl had been pretty aggressive, and completely smitten by Cole.

Still, Jaclyn had always pictured Cole as someone who could take the heat. He was strong, determined. But then she remembered that Rochelle had something over him. "You married her because of the baby, didn't you."

He scowled.

"Most guys wouldn't have married her, not if they didn't love her, and not with the way she chased you. But you had a weakness most boys your age didn't have—a strong sense of responsibility."

"I thought we were talking about pleasant memories," he grumbled.

"You haven't mentioned any."

"Okay, here's one. The first time I saw you, you were sitting in English class. I'd just enrolled, and someone in the office brought me into class. Everyone was busy doing some sort of writing assignment. Then you looked up."

"And?"

"And you smiled," he said.

Jaclyn got the feeling this moment held some sort of significance for him, but she had a hard time believing it could. Every girl in the class had probably looked up and smiled. Cole had always been wickedly handsome and drawn more than his share of female attention. He still did. What was so special about a girl smiling at him in English class?

"I'm sure I wasn't the only one."

"You were the only one I thought I was going to marry."

Jaclyn nearly choked on her soda. "Are you kidding?"

"No."

"But you said marriage isn't for you."

"I was too young to know better at the time."

"Now I understand why you never liked Terry."

He laughed ruefully. "He never liked me, either."

"He was jealous of you," Jaclyn said. "That was the reason he put you down so badly. You had none of the advantages he had—the name, the money, the history—but you had something else he couldn't compete with. I still can't name exactly what it is. Confidence or charisma, I suppose. Maybe both.''

''If I have charisma, how come it's never affected you?'' he asked, emptying out the rest of his bag of chips.

Was now a good time to admit that it had? Several times? ''I found you attractive, but I was convinced you'd treat me as casually as you did all the other girls who threw themselves at your feet. I thought they were foolish for even trying to hold your attention. Trying to catch you was like trying to catch a moonbeam—impossible.''

''And now?''

Jaclyn took a long drink of her soda. And now? She was completely infatuated with him, but her opinion hadn't changed. Neither had her commitment to avoid the heartache another unfaithful man would bring. ''Now we work together,'' she said simply.

''I could always fire you,'' he said.

She gave him a pointed look. ''That's exactly what I'm trying to avoid.''

''You think I'd let you go at the office if we got together?''

''You don't want to get together,'' she said. ''You're older and wiser now, and you know you're not the marrying type, remember?''

''God, is there no other type of together for you?''

She finished her sandwich and wadded up the trash. ''No.''

COLE SAT IN HIS MOTEL room while Jaclyn showered, staring at the envelope he'd brought in from the truck, the one that contained a letter from Rochelle. He hadn't spoken to his ex-wife for nearly ten years. He had no desire to hear from her now. But his curiosity, and the old guilt—for being unable to love her, for things between them ending so badly—was getting the best of him. He'd never wanted to hurt Rochelle. He'd just been a dumb kid when he'd gotten involved with her, a kid who already had too many problems.

But if it was money she needed, he could probably help her...if he could step back into her life without starting everything all over again.

He ran a hand through his hair, still wet from his shower, and sighed. What could it hurt to read her letter? She'd once been his wife. He owed her that much.

Opening the envelope, he pulled out a single sheet of lined paper, covered in writing on both sides. Then he unfolded it, smoothed it out and, despite his sense of dread, began to read.

Dear Cole,
If you ever get this, I know it will come as quite a surprise. After everything we've been through, you may not even want to hear it. But I have to tell you I'm sorry, for me, if not for you. You were right. I did lie about the baby. There was never any pregnancy. I was so in love with you and so desperate not to lose you, that I made it up so you'd marry me. I didn't think what I was doing was so bad. I told myself that I'd make you happy—that we'd make each other happy—and I planned to get pregnant right away and start a family. You would have made such a great father. The way you always looked after your brothers was truly amazing. But fate can be cruel, huh? When the fifth month passed and I wasn't pregnant, I had to do something. I wasn't gaining the usual weight or showing, which is why I faked the miscarriage. I was afraid you'd hate me if you found out. But you found out anyway. I remember when you confronted me. I lied again. Lies to cover lies to cover more lies. All because I loved you, Cole. Was I so hard to love in

return? I guess I was. I don't think you ever felt the same way about me. In any case, I thought you should finally hear the truth. I'm tired of kicking myself for what I've done. The only thing I want now is your forgiveness. Can you give me that much, Cole? Please? Or is it too late?

Love always,
Rochelle

Cole tossed the letter on the bed and dropped his head in his hands to rub his temples. Finally she was admitting there had never been a baby. He'd suspected, of course. The doctor had no record of her visits, no pregnancy tests or anything. But she'd claimed she was afraid of doctors and simply hadn't gone. Cole hadn't known for sure what to believe, only that something wasn't right. Then, when she miscarried, there'd been very little blood, no fetus, no real mourning, nothing—other than Rochelle's desperate desire to get pregnant again. She begged him for another baby, but at that point he couldn't trust her anymore. He was seeing his young wife in a whole new light, believed deep down she'd purposely trapped him, and was getting to where he could scarcely tolerate being in the same room with her. And every time he tried to tell her their marriage wasn't working for him, she'd cry, then threaten to kill herself if he ever left her.

He remembered the time she actually made good on her threats. He'd come home to find her sprawled on the bathroom floor, an empty bottle of aspirin lying next to her.

God, Rochelle. What you did to yourself? What you did to both of us!

Shaking his head to banish the memory, Cole picked up the envelope the letter had come in and stared at the return address. Maybe if he told her he forgave her, she'd be able to put the past behind her and make a fresh start. Maybe doing that much for her would finally erase the guilt he felt for those years, too.

Picking up the telephone, he called Jaclyn's room and told her he had to go out for an hour or so. Then he shoved the letter in his back pocket and left.

CHAPTER THIRTEEN

ROCHELLE WAS LIVING at her parents' house just behind the florist shop. Cole recognized the address on the envelope, remembered coming here for Christmas and Thanksgiving when he and Rochelle were together and living in a trailer next to his father and brothers, but he cringed at the thought of facing his ex-in-laws again. He doubted they'd be very thrilled to see him. They'd never been close, probably because he was gone a lot when he was driving a truck and hadn't even been close to his wife.

He glanced around the yard as he approached the door, finding a few modest changes. Someone had attempted to overhaul the flower beds in the front. Someone had hung an American flag beside the door. And someone had painted the trim bright red, which wasn't particularly becoming but was definitely noticeable.

"Hello?" Mrs. Stewart answered his knock, speaking before she really saw him. When she recognized him her jaw dropped, and she paused as though she didn't know what to say.

"Is Rochelle living here?" he asked. He thought maybe Rochelle would be covering for her mother at the flower shop, since her mother was obviously home. But then he remembered that it was Sunday and the Stewarts closed the shop on Sunday.

"Uh, yes, yes, she is."

"Can I speak with her?"

"Um...just a minute. I'll see."

The smell of cooked cabbage crept through the crack Mrs. Stewart left in the front door, making Cole wonder if he was interrupting their dinner. He almost had himself convinced that he shouldn't have come and was about to leave, when Rochelle appeared. Wearing a pair of jeans, a button-up shirt and no shoes, she looked much the same as when he'd last seen her, right down to the black eyeliner above her blue eyes. Only her white-blond hair was different. It had been long when they were married. Now it was short and wispy.

"It *is* you," she said, licking her lips and looking nervous. "I...I didn't think I'd ever see you again."

"Mary-Jean hasn't called yet?"

"Who?"

"Never mind. Granny Fanny gave me your letter."

She stepped outside and closed the door, then wiped her palms on her pants. "I'm glad. I—I really wanted you to have it. I would have mailed it, but no one around here knew where to find you."

"I live in Reno now."

"Really?"

"Yeah."

"What are you doing there? Still driving a truck?"

"No. I build homes."

"That sounds great. Do you like doing construction work?"

Cole smiled to himself. Even Rochelle assumed he'd always work for a day wage. He didn't bother to correct her. "Yeah. What about you? What are you doing now?"

She shrugged. "The same, you know, helping out at the shop, living here. I'll probably die in Feld," she said on a short laugh.

"You always liked it here."

"But I would have gone anywhere. With you," she added softly.

Cole cleared his throat, feeling uncomfortable at the reminder of her devotion. Rochelle might have done some horrible things, but she'd only wanted him to love her. Why couldn't he have loved her?

"How're your folks?"

"Dad's wanting to sell the shop and retire. Mom doesn't want to give it up. I think we'll keep the status quo for a few more years."

"And your sister?"

"She married and moved to California. Can you imagine? My younger sister has a family, and I'm still stuck at home."

"You're an adult. Move away, get a job, go to school, something. Make a change, if you want to."

"I wouldn't know where to go." She sighed. "And I wouldn't want to go alone."

They stood in awkward silence for a few minutes, then Rochelle shoved her hands in her pockets and dropped her gaze to the ground. "You ever remarry?"

"No."

"Me neither."

"I'm sure you'll find someone eventually." She seemed so downcast, Cole reached out to squeeze her shoulder in a formal offer of comfort, if not a tender one, but when he touched her, she closed her eyes and stepped quickly away.

"Don't," she said. "It...I still...all you've ever felt for me is pity. I hate that."

"I wish things could have been different."

Her smiled quivered, but she kept it bravely in place. "How are your brothers?"

"Fine." Cole told her a little about what each of his brothers was doing, glossing over his rift with Rick, then started hedging away. "I'd better get going," he said. "I just wanted to stop by and tell you that I...that I don't hold anything against you. I know what you did, but that was years ago. Forget it and move on and be happy, okay?"

A tear trickled down her cheek, running her eyeliner and

mascara. "You were always a kind man, Cole. I have to give you that. And you were generous. You never told anyone what I did, did you. You took the brunt of it all."

"I was leaving. I didn't mind letting you paint me as the bad guy." Cole smiled to lighten the moment, but she remained serious.

"I shouldn't have done it," she said. "It was wrong, just like everything else I did to you. I wanted to punish you for rejecting me—but you tried. You did your best." She shook her head. "God, I loved you. I will always love you."

Cole felt a tremendous sadness for what she'd suffered because of that love. "I'm sorry, Rochelle."

"Me, too," she said, and disappeared inside the house.

"YOU BOUGHT A SAND RAIL?" Alex asked, his voice filled with awe, as he and the other kids circled the trailer Cole had hitched to the Navigator so they could transport his new rail to Reno.

"We needed to have something to do while we were waiting for you," Cole said.

"So you went to Sand Mountain? Without us?" Mackenzie whined.

Jaclyn noticed Terry's scowl darken. He and his parents were standing in the drive with them, seeing the kids off, and it was another one of those awkward moments in which she didn't know quite how to behave—friendly, despite the hostility that crackled through the air? Indifferent? Offended that the Wentworth's couldn't be bigger about the divorce? Terry's family used to be her family, too, but now they were enemies, despite her desire for peace.

"We knew you wanted to spend time with your dad and Grandpa and Grandma Wentworth," she said. "That's why we brought you out here. But now we have to get going. Hop in the truck. You kids have school in the morning."

"Will you take me to Sand Mountain sometime?" Alex asked Cole.

Cole glanced at Terry, then shrugged. "Maybe someday, if you want."

"I have a sand rail, son. You don't need anyone else to take you," Terry said. "I'll come get you next weekend. We'll go there together."

"What about me?" Mackenzie demanded.

"And me?" Alyssa added.

"You girls are still too young," Jaclyn said. "Daddy will take you when you're older."

The girls moaned about being left out as Jaclyn helped them into the car and buckled them in. "So you're coming next Friday?" she asked Terry, pausing before climbing into the passenger's seat.

"Yeah. I'll be there in the afternoon sometime."

Jaclyn hesitated. Next Friday was her thirty-second birthday. She didn't expect Terry or anyone else to remember that, but she wanted the children with her. She didn't exactly relish the idea of spending her birthday alone. But after what the children had been through the past few weeks, not getting to see their father, she decided to grin and bear it the best she could. She could always celebrate on Sunday, when they returned.

"I don't get off until five," she said.

"It'll be around then."

"Okay." She closed her door and waited for Cole to start the car, then rolled down her window. "See you next Friday."

Burt and Dolores waved to the children as the truck pulled away. Mackenzie and Alyssa responded enthusiastically, but Alex sat in silence until the ranch was well behind them.

"My dad said he knew you in high school," he suddenly said to Cole.

"Feld's a small town," Cole said. "For the most part, everybody knows everybody else."

"He said he didn't like you then and he doesn't like you now."

"Alex, you know better than to repeat something like that!" Jaclyn cried, but she could tell by the look on her son's face that he didn't intend to offend Cole. He was working something out in his mind, probably trying to decide, after hearing all that the Wentworths had said, what Cole signified in their lives—so he'd know where to place his loyalties.

"Did you like my dad?" Alex asked.

"I had a lot of things going on in high school. I didn't pay much attention to your dad," Cole replied. His answer was both diplomatic and kind, considering what he could have said, but Alex immediately saw through it.

"That's a no."

Cole didn't attempt to correct him. He didn't say anything.

"Why not?" Alex pressed.

"Honey, it's not polite to put someone on the spot like that," Jaclyn said, hoping to bring the conversation to a close. "He and your dad might not have been the best of friends, but we're all adults now and capable of looking past our differences. What happened in high school doesn't matter anymore."

"It does to Dad," Alex countered. "He said Cole wanted to marry you in high school, but he didn't get you then, and he won't get you now."

Jaclyn struggled to stem her outrage. "Your dad has no right to say that," she replied.

"He said if Cole married you, it would be over his dead body. That's what Dad said," Mackenzie added.

Embarrassed, Jaclyn closed her eyes for a brief second and pinched the bridge of her nose. "Thank you for sharing, kids."

Mackenzie beamed proudly, obviously taking her words at face value, but Alex ignored her. His eyes were still fastened intently on Cole. "So are you gonna? Marry her, I mean?"

Cole smiled. "We wouldn't want to upset your father, now, would we?"

"WHAT is that?"

At the sound of Chad's voice, Cole turned to see his brother walking up the driveway behind him, staring at the sand rail he'd just parked in the garage of one of the houses still under construction.

"What do you think it is?" Cole asked.

His brother's puzzled expression was barely discernible in the dark. None of the streetlights had been put in at Oak Ranch yet, and it was nearly ten o'clock.

"Looks like a sand rail to me. But I can't imagine what my workaholic big brother would be doing with a toy like that."

"I took Jaclyn and her kids to Feld last night," Cole said.

Chad's eyebrows lifted. "You did?"

"Yeah. The kids wanted to see their dad."

"That was good of you."

Cole ignored the undercurrent in his words. "I saw Granny Fanny."

"How is she?"

"Same as always. Still cussin' like a sailor."

Chad shook his head and chuckled. "She's somethin'."

"When did you get back from Sacramento?"

"Just a few hours ago. Thought I'd stop by and tell you about the lots."

"Are we going to want 'em?"

"They're looking pretty good. I think we can get into the project for a good price, too."

Chad went on to describe the location of the subdivision,

the lay of the land, how much it would cost to bring in the utilities, and how much more he thought it would cost to build in California as opposed to Nevada, but Cole was having a difficult time concentrating. He kept seeing Jaclyn in his mind's eye.

Jaclyn sitting next to him at the hot tub. Jaclyn riding asleep in his truck. Jaclyn's eyelids closing as he kissed her. Jaclyn laughing in the sand rail.

"Cole? You want me to come back tomorrow?" Chad asked.

"Hmm?"

"Your mind's a million miles away. I thought maybe you'd rather go over this stuff later."

Cole sighed. "Sorry, I'm just tired."

"You know what I think?"

"Do I want to know?"

"I think your new secretary has baked bread in your house one too many times," Chad said.

"What's that supposed to mean?"

His brother grinned. "You're falling, buddy, big time."

Remembering the day he'd found Rochelle on the bathroom floor, Cole felt a sudden wave of panic, not because he was afraid of falling for Jaclyn but because he was afraid of *her* falling for *him*. What if she set her heart on him the way Rochelle had? And what if he didn't return her feelings? He couldn't deal with the guilt associated with those kinds of problems again. And he couldn't face raising more kids, not after failing Rick so miserably.

"You're wrong," Cole insisted, scowling.

"Am I?"

"Yeah. Jaclyn has three kids and too many ties to Feld. I'm not getting involved with her."

Chad glanced at the sand rail and laughed openly at this statement. "Oh, yeah? Well, I have news for you, then. You already are."

RICK HELD HIS BREATH in anticipation as he crowded in with the other students to check the list of grades Professor Hernandez had just posted on his office window. English was his worst subject, and this latest essay had been particularly difficult. It was on Homer's *The Odyssey,* a story he found painfully boring and pointless despite what the critics said. How could he expect to do well when this was the first formal writing he'd ever done, and he hated what he was writing about, besides? He thought Telemachus should have taken a firm stand at the very beginning and kicked out the men who were loitering at his house waiting to take his father's place. So what if he was young? Rick and Cole had been young when they'd had to take charge of their house, too.

But Rick doubted his sentiments would go over very well with his soft-spoken, poetry-loving professor. So he'd pretended to see the masterpiece everyone else saw and forgot about Telemachus as he muddled through an essay delineating Odysseus's heroic qualities.

Parish, Perego, Perrini… Rick's eyes trailed along the dotted line, then followed his name to find a *C* in the grade column—and let his breath out. He'd passed. He hadn't exactly excelled, but it was early in the semester yet, and he'd passed.

"So how'd you do, Perrini?"

Rick turned to find a young woman who'd asked him out the first week of school standing behind him with one of her girlfriends. A trim brunette with stylish glasses, a quirky smile and a knockout figure, she was certainly attractive, but she was too young for him. That was one of the problems with going back to school at twenty-eight, especially at a community college. Everyone else was almost a decade younger. "I passed," he said simply. "What about you?"

"I passed, too."

Her blond friend made a strangled sound and rolled her

eyes. "You passed? You *passed*, Abby?" she echoed, then she looked at him. "Abby got an *A*. Abby always gets an *A*. If you ask me, it's pretty sickening."

Abby's face colored, and she glared at her friend. "Stop it, Caitlin. I have to get an *A*. I wasn't serious about high school and blew my chance to get a scholarship. I'm trying to make up for lost time."

"I understand you're properly motivated," Caitlin replied. "That's not the sickening part. The sickening part is how *easy* getting good grades is for you."

Rick had turned Abby down when she'd asked him to dinner a week ago, but he felt his interest level rising now. The study group he'd joined wasn't really working out. They spent more time talking than they did studying, and he wasn't attending school for its social aspects. He wanted a study partner who was dependable and serious, and if he had his guess, Abby was both. Age wasn't an issue when it came to learning.

"Do you belong to a study group?" he asked.

"No."

"Would you be interested in studying with me?"

She hitched her backpack higher on one shoulder. "No," she said and walked away, leaving her friend gaping after her.

"I guess she hasn't forgiven you for turning her down," Caitlin explained with a helpless shrug, then hurried to catch up.

HER BIRTHDAY WAS TOMORROW. If she didn't do something about it, she was going to spend the evening alone.

Jaclyn glanced nervously at Cole, then tossed the fettuccine she was making for his dinner in her special pesto, sun-dried tomatoes and grilled chicken sauce, and dumped it onto a plate. He liked pasta, and he looked relaxed sitting there at the table, reading the Preliminary Title Report on the Sparks project. They'd just received loan approval from

Larry at Reno Bank & Trust, so he was in a great mood. Now was probably a good time to ask him to spend the evening with her tomorrow night, but she'd been wanting to do it all week and hadn't managed to find the nerve. What made her think today would be any different?

"I'm taking off," Margaret said, poking her head into the kitchen.

"You're getting out of here late tonight. It's almost five," Cole said.

"I had some calls to make. I think I've got another buyer on the hook for Little Acorn Court. Nice family, two kids. They're going to let me know tomorrow."

"That's great. You're selling houses like crazy."

"You're giving me nice houses to sell. Anyway, I've changed the sign out front to Closed."

"Thanks." Cole buried his nose in his reports again.

"Smells great in here, Jaclyn," Margaret said.

"It's pasta with garlic and sun-dried tomatoes," she said. "Would you like to try some?"

"No, I'm meeting a friend for dinner. Save me some, though. I'll have it for lunch tomorrow."

"Okay."

Margaret trudged away, leaving Jaclyn to stew some more about her birthday. Last year she'd turned thirty-one only a few months after leaving Feld, and it had been one of the loneliest days of her life. She didn't want to repeat the experience. She wanted to go out to dinner and see a movie or go dancing, and she wanted to do it with a man, preferably Cole. Which meant she had to ask him, right? But how?

If she mentioned it was her birthday, he might think she was hinting for a gift or a card or something. If she didn't mention that it was a special occasion, he might think she was pursuing him.

"Ouch!" she cried, burning her hand on the hot pan she'd stuck in the sink.

Cole looked up in surprise. "You okay?"

"Yeah, fine. Just a little burn," she said, taking an ice cube from the freezer and holding it on the red mark until the pain went away.

"You've been pretty quiet today," he said. "What's going on?"

"Nothing."

"Terry still coming to get the kids tomorrow night?"

"Yeah, last I heard." *Now,* her mind prompted. *Ask him now.* He'd just brought up tomorrow night, giving her the perfect opportunity. But she couldn't bring herself to say any of the lines she'd rehearsed. They all sounded too much as though she was asking him out, probably because that was exactly what she'd be doing.

"Jackie?"

"Yeah?"

"Is something else burning?"

"Oh! The garlic bread!"

Roiling smoke filled the kitchen as Jaclyn opened the oven door. She grabbed a hot pad and quickly removed the bread, but it was already too charred to eat.

"It's ruined," she said in disgust, slamming the pan down on the counter. What the heck was wrong with her, anyway? Why wasn't she keeping her mind on her work, where it belonged, instead of daydreaming about a night out on the town with her boss?

"Jackie, are you going to tell me what's going on?" Cole asked, coming to stand behind her. "You seem...I don't know—preoccupied."

Jaclyn could feel his warm breath on her neck and knew he was close. It was all she could do not to fling herself into his arms. "I'm sorry," she said, fighting tears.

"For what?"

"For ruining your dinner and wasting your food."

"It's only bread, okay?"

It was only her birthday. What did it matter if she sat home alone? "Okay."

"Is something else wrong?"

Other than the fact that she couldn't quit thinking about him? That she knew he wasn't good for her, that marriage wasn't part of his life's plan, and she wanted him, anyway?

God, was she turning into another Rochelle?

"No." She ran some cool water into the sink to ease the sting of her burn so she could finish the dishes and go, but he slid his arms around her waist and pulled her back against him.

"Tell me what you're thinking," he said.

For a moment Jaclyn closed her eyes and let him hold her. She wanted to forget about the dishes, her job, her birthday—especially her birthday—and simply turn in his arms and lift her face for his kiss.

But Rochelle's words, that day Jaclyn had run into her in Feld four years ago, kept echoing in her head: *He cheated on me…cheated on me…cheated…and it broke my heart.*

Jaclyn knew about broken hearts. She'd experienced the same kind of betrayal and devastation. Which meant she'd be a fool to ask for more of the same, right?

Right.

"I'll see you tomorrow," she said softly, slipping out of his arms. Then she grabbed her purse and left, not allowing herself to look back.

CHAPTER FOURTEEN

COLE ROLLED OVER and punched his pillow down so he could see the time. *Damn.* It was three in the morning. What was wrong with him? Why was he having such a difficult time sleeping? Work used to keep him up. He'd plan his next project for Perrini Homes, go over profit-and-loss statements in his head, or get up to make a note on something he didn't want to forget. But he couldn't blame tonight's insomnia on business. Jaclyn was the only thing on his mind. He kept reliving the moment he'd pulled her into his arms at the sink. She'd felt like heaven and smelled so good. He'd nearly slipped his hands up under her shirt. He'd wanted to caress her soft, creamy skin and had been almost positive she'd allow it. But then she'd changed. She'd stiffened, pulled away, left.

Why the turnaround? Was it Terry? Was she still in love with her ex-husband? Was it the divorce? Had she been hurt too badly to get involved in another relationship?

Or was it him?

Trailer trash. The crowd she'd hung out with in high school hadn't thought much of him. Maybe, deep down, Jaclyn had a problem with his poor background, too. Or maybe she just didn't find him appealing, for whatever reason. In any case, she'd made it clear that she wasn't interested in a physical relationship without the possibility of marriage. And he wasn't interested in anything that included the expectation of it.

So they were at a standoff and needed to forget about

each other. Simple. Except that they worked together and couldn't avoid contact, which meant it wasn't going to be easy. Especially when there were times marriage didn't seem like such a bad trade for spending the rest of his nights in Jaclyn's arms. Who else would he rather be with? No one. No one had ever affected him the way she did. And her kids were good kids, not nearly as difficult as Rick had been. Surely he could grow to love them....

Cole groaned. Loving them wasn't the problem. It never had been. He simply couldn't risk failing Jaclyn the way he'd failed Rochelle.

Kicking off the blankets, he went to the kitchen for a glass of water, then sat at the table in the dark, wearing nothing but his boxer-briefs. The weather had been completely clear for weeks. He couldn't remember the last rain, it had been so long ago, but a storm was definitely brewing now. Clouds scuttled across the face of the moon, the wind whipped at the young trees in the yard, and it was a little chilly, even in the house.

He wondered what it would feel like to crawl into Jaclyn's warm bed and make love to her while lightning flashed outside and thunder rumbled in the distance, and knew immediately that he had to start thinking of something else or he was going to drive himself crazy.

Maybe he should call someone. Laura. An old friend. Rick.

Cole eyed the phone. He'd purposely left his brother alone for more than a month now, hoping he'd return on his own. But he hadn't heard from Rick, and Cole felt as if he was drifting away from everything he'd always known. He needed an anchor to remind him of the decisions he'd made before meeting Jaclyn. He'd wanted to build Perrini Homes into something so big his brothers would never again suffer the kind of want they'd known growing up. And he'd wanted to reclaim his life and live it free from the challenges and failures associated with marriage and raising children, right?

It had all seemed crystal clear. So why was he confused now?

He just needed to talk to Rick. Rick was the missing piece of the puzzle. Cole had ignored his absence and tried not to dwell on it, but nothing was quite right without his brother.

Picking up the cordless phone, Cole dialed Rick's number. It was the middle of the night, but he didn't care. He'd waited too long to make this call already.

"Hello?"

"Rick?"

Rick seemed to pull himself out of sleep immediately. "Cole? Are you okay?"

"Fine. You?"

A tired sigh. "I'm hangin' in there."

Silence fell, and Cole knew Rick was waiting for him to explain why he'd called. He had to say something, but now that he had Rick on the phone, he didn't know where to start.

"You see the football game last Sunday?"

"Yeah. Shame about the Forty-niners, huh? They're not what they used to be."

"I was gone last Sunday so I recorded it, but I could hardly bear to watch the fourth quarter."

"It was pretty painful."

Another silence. Cole searched his brain for other events in the world of sports, but drew a blank. He hadn't been keeping up as well as he usually did. And it wasn't exactly easy to segue from football into emotional matters.

"Well, I'll let you go," he said at last.

"Why'd you call?"

Cole hesitated. Here was his chance to say all the things he'd never said. It was time to tell Rick how much he meant to him.

Closing his eyes, he took a deep breath, but the words wouldn't come. On separate occasions, he'd told Andrew and Brian, even Chad, that he loved them, but he couldn't tell Rick. Maybe it was because they were so close in age. Maybe it was sibling rivalry. Or maybe Cole still resented how difficult Rick had been growing up. Cole couldn't say for sure. He just knew he couldn't express his feelings, even though he loved Rick just as much, maybe more, than the others.

"No reason. Just wondered if you'd caught the game," he said. *And if you're coming back.*

"You called at three o'clock in the morning to ask if I saw the Forty-niners lose nearly a week ago?"

"Yeah." *And to tell you things aren't the same around here without you.*

"Okay…"

"Maybe I'll see you around sometime," Cole said, silently praying that day would be sooner rather than later. *Come back, Rick. We're brothers, man. We're brothers. Nothing else matters.*

"Maybe," Rick said. He sounded hesitant, confused, but Cole couldn't help him understand. They'd established their patterns of behavior years ago, and, as fatalistic as it sounded, Cole thought it was too late to change them now.

"Goodbye," he said, and hung up. Then he sat staring out the window, listening to the wind howl outside.

JACLYN TOOK A BOLSTERING breath when she heard Terry's truck pull into her driveway. At least he was on time today, she thought, zipping the duffel bag she'd just packed for Alyssa. He'd pick up the children and leave, then she'd be free to…to do anything, really. She could watch television or grab a bite to eat. Or maybe she'd call Margaret to see if she wanted to go to a movie. They'd never done anything together outside the office before, but they seemed to get along well enough.

"Dad's here!" Alex called from the front of the house.

Mackenzie and Alyssa went running down the hall to meet their father, while Jaclyn gathered their bags and carried them to the living room. Terry was just coming into the house, dripping from the rain.

"They're all set," she said when she saw him. "Oh, wait." She handed him the bags, then dashed down the hall to retrieve Pinkie, the teddy bear Alyssa slept with at night. "You wouldn't want to forget Pinkie," she said when she returned.

Terry took the stuffed bear and put it on top of the bags he'd piled near the front door. "We'll take Pinkie when we go," he said, "but first, we have a surprise for you."

"You do?"

"We do?" Mackenzie echoed.

Terry's smile reminded Jaclyn of the man she used to know, the Terry she'd fallen in love with.

"Yep," he told the kids. "We're going to take your mother out to dinner for her birthday."

Jaclyn tucked her hair behind her ears and straightened in surprise. He remembered? He cared? After a year of hostility between them, after last Saturday at the motel, she didn't know how to respond to this sudden reversal. Where was the sullen expression he usually wore in her presence? The anger in his eyes?

"That's very nice of you," she said, "but…"

"But what?" he asked. "Don't tell me you already have plans."

He didn't mention Cole's name, but Jaclyn knew he was thinking about him. She'd been thinking about Cole, too. Only now she was glad she'd never worked up the courage to ask him to be with her tonight. Terry would have blown a gasket if she'd had to say no on Cole's account, and she wasn't up for an ugly scene. "No plans."

"Then, why not spend the evening with your family?"

He hadn't said "with your kids." He'd said "with your

family." But they weren't a family anymore. Jaclyn didn't feel good about going anywhere with Terry. She would actually prefer to stay home alone. But the kids were all speaking at once, yelling "surprise" and putting in their bid on where they should go.

"I like Chuck E. Cheese's," Alyssa said.

"No, I want to go to McDonald's," Mackenzie argued. "I'm tired of pizza."

"Dad's not going to take Mom out for fast food," Alex told them. "He's going to take her to a fancy place. Right, Dad?"

"I was thinking about the seafood buffet at the Peppermill," Terry said.

"Gross! I hate seafood!" Mackenzie cried.

Jaclyn knew Alex hated it, too. Normally he would have been the first to complain, but tonight he was throwing his support behind his father, probably hoping dinner would start something that would bring his parents back together. She didn't want to fuel those hopes, but she didn't know how to get out of something as simple as letting Terry take her and the kids to dinner for her birthday. At least, not gracefully.

"Okay," she relented. "I'll grab jackets. But I don't want to stay out long. With this storm I don't want you on the road too late."

Terry promised they'd eat quickly and head back, but once they finished dinner, he insisted on taking the whole family to Circus Circus, where they played carnival games and watched the circus acts. It was after ten o'clock by the time he let Jaclyn drag them home.

"Did we surprise you? Did you have fun, Mom?" Alex asked, as they waited beneath the overhang while she unlocked the front door to the house.

"Of course." Jaclyn put on a smile for her son's benefit as she swung the door open and they crowded past her. Terry had been the epitome of a good date—attentive, generous, fun-loving. There'd been moments she *had* enjoyed herself, but they were generally when he was preoccupied with one child while she played a game with another. She wanted things to be different between them than they'd been over the previous year. She especially wanted Terry to cooperate more fully with her when it came to the kids. But she didn't know how to respond to a loving, solicitous Terry after knowing such a bitter, sullen one for so much of the recent past.

"I had a great time," she said. "I appreciate dinner, but I'm worried about how late it's getting. You guys better hit the road."

"Oh, come on," Terry said. "It's miserable out, and it's Friday night. Why don't we put the kids to bed and watch a movie? We can always leave in the morning."

Why not? Because she wasn't interested, that was why. But once again Alex swung his support to Terry's side.

"You know how tired Dad gets at night, Mom. You wouldn't want him driving with us on these slick roads when he's like that."

Jaclyn's heart sank. Alex was right. She didn't want to risk the safety of her kids or anyone else. But neither did she want her ex-husband as a houseguest. "*Are* you tired?" she asked, still hoping for a way out.

Terry shot down that hope in a hurry. "Yeah, I got up at four-thirty this morning, and I'm starting to feel it."

He certainly hadn't felt it at Circus Circus. Each time she'd suggested they go, he'd thought of something else they should see or do. "Won't your folks be worried?" she asked.

"I could always give them a call."

She was caught. She didn't want Terry in her house, but suggesting he get a motel room wouldn't sound very nice, especially after he'd just taken her out to dinner. Besides, Alex was monitoring every nuance of her behavior, and she was tired of coming off as the bad guy. Terry was the children's father. She had put up with him for twelve years; she could certainly put up with him for one more night, couldn't she? It was bedtime already. She could feign exhaustion and turn in. Morning would come before she knew it.

"Okay," she told Terry. "You can stay, but I'm pretty tired. I'm definitely not up for a movie."

He didn't seem pleased with this response, but he took a seat in front of the television and didn't push her.

Jaclyn put the kids to bed while he watched the news. Then she made him a bed on the couch. "If you get cold, there's extra bedding in that closet," she told him.

"Don't you ever get cold?" he asked.

"What?"

"Never mind."

"What did you say?" she asked again.

"Nothing. Good night."

Jaclyn said good-night, then retreated to her room.

And I was afraid I'd be alone on my birthday!

She thought of Cole and how she'd wanted to go out with him tonight, and wished she'd had the nerve to ask him, after all. So what if it had started a fight with Terry? At least they would have stayed on familiar ground. The way Terry was behaving now…well, it was just plain odd. It made her feel as if he was setting some sort of trap.

THE DOORKNOB JIGGLED, waking Jaclyn from a sound sleep. At first she thought it was Alyssa, who sometimes climbed into bed with her in the middle of the night, but then she heard her name.

"Jackie?"

Terry! What did he want? She leaned up on her elbows to check the time, thinking it was two or later, but her alarm clock showed that it wasn't quite midnight. Evidently, Terry hadn't gone to bed yet.

"Is something wrong?" she asked.

"Can I talk to you?"

It was early October and still raining, definitely cool. Jaclyn didn't normally sleep in something so heavy, but she'd pulled on a flannel nightgown tonight, so modesty wasn't a problem.

Getting out of bed, she crossed to the door and unlocked it.

"What is it?" she asked, finding him standing in the hall wearing only his jeans.

"That couch is old and uncomfortable as hell. It's killing my back," he complained.

Jaclyn blinked at him, wondering what he expected her to do about it. She didn't have an extra bed. And it was his fault they'd stayed out so late, his suggestion that he wait until morning to leave.

"I'm sorry. Do you want to sleep in Alex's twin? You could carry him to the couch. I doubt he'd know the difference."

"Actually—" his gaze cut to her bed "—it looks like you've got plenty of room in here."

"What?" Certainly she'd heard him wrong, Jaclyn thought. After everything that had happened between them, he wouldn't be bold enough to suggest…

"Come on, Jaclyn. It's been a long time," he said. "I've missed you, babe. Don't you ever think about us? How it used to be? Remember the first time we made love?"

Jaclyn didn't want to remember. She'd been so moved, so sure she'd never be that close to another human being— until a few years passed and she realized Terry was trying to share the same experience with half the women in Feld.

"You know what I remember?" she asked. "I remember crying the first time I found out about you visiting whorehouses. I remember wondering why you wanted to go there, what I'd done to let you down."

He reached out to cup her cheek. "Oh, baby. You never let me down. There's no one like you. No one. You're the only one I've ever loved. And you're great in bed. Don't think you're not. I've never had anyone who compares.''

''You should know,'' she stated flatly, and he scowled as though realizing just how badly that line of reasoning had backfired. He was trying to play on her loneliness and the good times in the past to wiggle his way into her bed again, but his words alienated her even more. If he'd loved her *and* he'd liked the way she was in bed, why had he hurt her so terribly? Why had he destroyed their family?

''Come on. Let's not start that again,'' he said. ''It's behind us, Jackie. Let's put the past behind us and move on.'' He stepped into the room and closed the door with a quiet *click*. ''You've loved me since we were kids. I don't know what this thing with Cole is all about, but you certainly didn't care about him in high school.'' He took her by the shoulders. ''So I'm thinking you're just trying to get back at me. And that's all right. I'm willing to let bygones be bygones. But don't you think it's time to stop hurting each other and pull our family back together?''

Jaclyn gazed up at him, wondering if she was seeing him clearly for the first time. Occasionally she'd felt terrible over the past year, thinking of herself as unforgiving and fearing she was hurting him by not coming back. But he didn't know what pain was. The past fourteen months had been nothing but a big temper tantrum: he didn't know how to handle not getting what he wanted. Well, he was just going to have to learn.

''I've already told you, Terry—''

''That was before,'' he argued.

''It's still true. I'm not coming back.''

She thought he might get angry again and storm out, maybe leave the kids and go back to Feld, but he surprised her by putting his arms around her and slipping his hands down to clench her buttocks.

''Jackie, it's me. Come on, baby,'' he murmured, pressing her into his erection. "Just one more night. One last hurrah for old times' sake, huh?"

He started kissing her neck, his lips traveling up toward her mouth, but Jaclyn didn't feel the smallest flicker of desire. She knew Terry was trying to break her down any way he could. If he couldn't appeal to her heart or mind, he'd appeal to her body—anything that might help commit her to him again.

"I don't want this," she said, shoving at his chest.

Instead of moving back, Terry tightened his embrace.

"Terry, are you listening to me? I don't want this!" she said.

He lifted his head, and she recognized fury in his face. Here was the Terry she'd dealt with since she left him.

"What's wrong?" he asked. "Saving yourself for your new man? Is it Cole you want?"

Jaclyn lifted her chin and glared at him. "Maybe."

"You want to give yourself to that trailer trash? Or is that what you've already done?"

"Fortunately that's none of your business. In any case, I want you to get out. Go to a motel, go back to Feld, I don't care. Just get out of my house."

"Why? I haven't done anything. I tried to show you a good time for your birthday, that's all. And this is the thanks I get! I'm not going anywhere until the kids wake up. Then they're coming to Feld with me, just like we planned. Until then—" he walked over and plopped onto her bed "—I'm going to sleep. Right here."

He stretched out and put his hands behind his head, watching to see what she'd do. Jaclyn was tempted to one-up him by calling the police. She could force Terry out. He had no right to be here. But she didn't want to wake the kids to an all-out fight. They'd gone to bed happy. She wanted to keep their memories of the night they spent at Circus Circus pleasant. In eight hours or so, Terry would be on his way to Feld. She needed only to wait until morning.

But she wasn't going to wait here, with him.

Ignoring the smug look on his face, she left the room and walked swiftly down the hall to retrieve her coat. Then she pulled it on over her flannel nightgown, grabbed her car keys and headed out, barefoot, into the rain.

"Jackie?" She heard Terry call from her room, surprise evident in his voice.

But she didn't answer. She just closed the door behind her and dashed across the lawn.

CHAPTER FIFTEEN

HAPPY BIRTHDAY TO ME... HAPPY BIRTHDAY TO ME...

Jaclyn shifted on the office couch, trying to curl into a tight enough ball to fit beneath her coat. It was cold, and she was still wet. Why hadn't she thought to bring a blanket? Mentally she went through the contents of Cole's closets, trying to remember if he had any spare bedding, but drew a blank. He didn't buy a lot of extras because he only used his bedroom, the kitchen and his private office. The other rooms were empty.

What a miserable birthday. She hadn't thought she'd be able to top last year's, but this one *was* worse. An uncomfortable dinner where she felt as if she was being held hostage by her ex, followed by an enraging argument, then a midnight tromp through the rain to lie on a cold leather couch until morning.

She thought of Cole sleeping peacefully in his bedroom just a few feet away, his body warm beneath a knit blanket and goose-down comforter, and wondered what he'd do if she woke him. She wanted someone to talk to, wanted to pull the day out of the dumps somehow. Or at least borrow a blanket.

Abandoning her coat on the couch, she got up and padded quietly down the hall to Cole's part of the house. She'd just see how he was sleeping. If he was stirring, she'd let him know she was here. If he wasn't, she wouldn't disturb him.

His door stood slightly ajar, but Jaclyn couldn't hear anything coming from inside. Was he home? His car was outside.

She slipped into the room and tiptoed to the bed, where she had to squint to make out his form in the rumpled blankets. Bending close, she watched him for several seconds, admiring his thick dark hair and the handsome contours of his face, before realizing that he was looking back at her.

She jumped and nearly screamed when their eyes met.

"Jaclyn, is it you?"

"I'm sorry," she whispered. "I wanted to wake you, but…"

"It's okay." He paused. "What are you doing here?"

She shrugged. "It's my birthday."

"Oh." He scrubbed his face with one hand, then rolled from his stomach to his side. "Do I want to know why you're standing in my room wearing your nightgown, or does that fall under the heading of looking a gift horse in the mouth?"

Jaclyn didn't really want to go into it. She didn't want to think about Terry or real life or anything else right now. "I—I had to leave home without my clothes," she said simply.

"Is everything all right?"

"Yeah."

"Then, I definitely don't have a problem with a pajama party." A grin tugged at the corners of his lips. He came up on one elbow, and Jaclyn couldn't help but admire the muscles that bulged in his arm or the large expanse of bare chest his movements suddenly exposed to her view. "But I admit I'm afraid to ask what you want, in case it isn't what I'm hoping."

The thrill of anticipation put Jaclyn's nerves on full alert, and the song she'd been singing to herself earlier seemed to turn into a full-blown chorus, *Happy birthday to me… Happy birthday to me… Happy birthday, dear Jackie…*

"What are you hoping?" she asked, silently willing her heart to stop knocking against her chest.

"Are you tired?"

"Not really."

"Are you cold?"

She nodded.

"Do you want to get in here with me?"

Jaclyn took a deep, shaky breath. Did she want to get into bed with him? That was a two-sided question, of course. There was want. And then there was reason. She should really ask him for the blanket and head back to the couch….

When she hesitated, he pulled back the covers. He wore only a pair of boxer-briefs, and she easily imagined what his warm body would feel like wrapped around her.

"Come on, Jackie. I'll keep you warm," he said.

"My nightgown's wet from the rain."

His gaze never wavered from her face. "Take it off."

Oh boy! Jaclyn swallowed, her throat suddenly dry. This was a far cry from borrowing a blanket. But her birthday had been miserable so far. Certainly she could let her guard down long enough to enjoy some part of it. "Whatever happens, it doesn't count, though, right?" she said, wavering.

"What does that mean?"

"It's my birthday. I'm entitled to certain indulgences."

"So what happens tonight is completely off the record?"

"Yeah."

"Okay, I'll buy that."

"And you won't ever mention it again?"

"If that's the way you want it."

That *was* the way she wanted it. She wanted to wake up in the morning and pretend nothing had happened. How else could she justify what she was about to do? "You won't think things have changed between us? You won't treat me differently?"

"No. Definitely not."

His voice sounded hoarse, making Jaclyn wonder if he was to the point of saying almost anything to get what he wanted. But she was nearly at that point, too. So she closed her eyes and inched up her nightgown, then quickly pulled it over her head and slipped into the warm spot he made for her by sliding over. His arms went around her and pulled her to him, putting a quick end to her shivers, and Jaclyn thought she'd never felt anything so indescribably wonderful in her whole life.

"You feel good," he whispered, then his mouth came down on hers and she gave herself to the moment, easily forgetting every thought that wasn't centered completely on Cole Perrini. She loved the way he touched her, the way he smelled and tasted and moved. And deep down she knew she'd never experience anything to compare with the moment his body melded into hers.

Sometime later, with Cole's arm holding her possessively to him while he slept, she smiled as, in the back of her mind, she heard the rest of the song: ...*Happy birthday to me!*

COLE STRETCHED, lingering somewhere between consciousness and unconsciousness. He felt good.

No, he felt great.

With Jaclyn curled beside him, he was almost too content to move. Except that he couldn't waste the opportunity to touch her. Rolling toward her, he buried his face in her hair and breathed in her sweet scent, then kissed her neck. He was going to make love to her for the fourth—or was it the fifth?—time. Then, if they could convince themselves to get out of bed, he was going to take her to breakfast. After that he was going to buy her a birthday present. And then they were going to the drugstore for another box of condoms.

But first he was going to answer the door. Someone was banging like a madman.

Jaclyn stirred when he pulled away. "What is it?" she asked.

"It's got to be Chad," he told her. "He probably lost his key. Keep sleeping. I'll take care of it and be right back."

She murmured an assent and burrowed deeper into the covers, while he pulled on a pair of sweat pants. He lingered for a moment, watching her and promising himself he'd get rid of Chad right away, then slipped out of the bedroom and closed the door behind him.

When he reached the front office, he was especially glad he'd taken the precaution of protecting Jaclyn's privacy, because it wasn't Chad. Terry Wentworth stood on the porch. Behind him, in the street, Alex, Mackenzie and Alyssa were peering through the windshield of their father's truck.

Cole waved to the kids, purposely keeping things as pleasant as possible, then leaned against the doorjamb to bar Terry from entering. "What's up?" he asked.

"I want to talk to Jackie."

If Terry thought Cole was going to embarrass Jaclyn by dragging her to the office door wearing something of his or her own flannel nightgown, he was crazy. "I'm afraid that's not possible."

"Why not? I know she's here." He pointed to Jaclyn's Sable. "That's her car, isn't it?"

"Yes, but she's sleeping."

Terry's hands curled into fists. "In your bed?" he asked, his voice grating low.

Cole studied him for a moment, running through the possibilities of where this conversation might lead. "Do you really want to know?"

"I want to see her."

"You can leave her a message if you want."

"A message? Who the hell do you think you are? I have her kids in the car, dammit. Now let me talk to her!"

Cole stood up straight and stepped outside, closing the door behind him. He had several inches and a few pounds on Terry, and he wanted him to know it. "The way I look at it, they're your kids, too, Terry," he said, keeping his voice low. "And this is your weekend. I suggest you follow the plan and head to Feld. You can talk to Jaclyn when you get back."

Terry's eyes narrowed. "I'm going to be busy this weekend. I don't think I can take the kids."

So Terry wanted to play games, did he? "No problem. Send them in. I've been wanting to take Alex to the stock car races. Maybe we'll go tonight," he said. Then he smiled benignly as he watched Terry sift through his options. If he took the kids, Jaclyn and Cole would be alone. If he didn't take the kids, Cole would have his ex-wife *and* his children for the weekend.

Apparently Terry decided to cut his losses.

"No, I'll manage."

"That's what I thought."

"Whatever you've got going with Jaclyn, it won't last," Terry told him. "Maybe I've been stupid and chased her right into your arms, but she'll come back to me eventually. You'll see."

"Maybe," Cole said. "But until then, you need to understand something. She's not alone anymore. You mess with her, you're going to be messing with me."

Stiff with rage, his hands still bunched into fists, Terry glared at him, but Cole was no longer worried that he'd start throwing punches. Terry liked better odds. If he was going to fight, he would have done it last weekend when he had friends to help him.

"Is that some sort of threat?" Terry asked.

"Take it how you want to," Cole told him. "I've never liked a bully."

Alex honked the horn, and Terry threw an irritated glance over his shoulder. "This isn't over yet," he promised.

"Your kids are waiting," Cole said, but it wasn't until a few seconds later, when Chad pulled up, that Terry finally stalked away.

JACLYN WOKE UP SCARED. She was lying in Cole's bed alone, completely naked, with only a nightgown to wear home. And she knew she'd made a big mistake, one that would cost her dearly. What had she been thinking when she'd slipped into Cole's room? That she could handle him better than all the other women he'd known? That she could somehow escape the heartbreak loving a man like him would bring? She'd asked him for promises in the night—that what they were doing wouldn't change anything, that morning would come and everything would be just the same as it always was—and he'd given them. But already things were different. *She* was different. How could she be the same after making love to a man who could mean the whole world to her if she let him?

What am I going to do?

She listened to the hum of two male voices as Cole spoke with someone outside. She couldn't hear what was being said, but she could easily picture Cole—the way he talked, the way he stood.

What a fool I am. She'd told him she believed in no kind of togetherness short of marriage and then she'd turned around and done this! Worse, she'd allowed herself to fall in love with the wrong man—again. A man who didn't want marriage or kids. And even if she managed to change his mind, she knew his history.

She must have been completely mad.

But that didn't mean she had to let the situation get the best of her, did it? She'd gone through too much in the

past year to tumble into the same pit she'd just climbed out
of.

Scrambling from the bed, Jaclyn pulled on the flannel
nightgown she'd tossed on the floor the night before and
tiptoed to the bedroom door. She couldn't tell who was with
Cole, but she knew they were outside, probably in the front
yard. Should she simply sneak out the back, wait until the
coast was clear and drive away? She could show up for
work on Monday as usual, pretend last night hadn't happened. And why not? Cole had promised her that nothing
would change. She'd just have to hold him to it.

Only, sneaking away seemed so cowardly. Wouldn't it
be better to face him? Apologize for her mistake and move
on?

Of course. They were adults. They could handle this ma-
turely.

The front door opened and closed, and Jaclyn heard
Cole's footsteps in the hall. Throwing her shoulders back,
she told herself she could fix things, get back on track. She
had to.

"Hey, you're up," he said, smiling as soon as he saw
her. He was barefoot and bare-chested, his hair was standing up in places, he had a day's growth of beard on his
jaw—and he looked incredibly sexy.

"Chad stopped by, but I got rid of him. You hungry?"

Something about the look on Jaclyn's face must have
given her away, because his smile faltered. "Is something
wrong?" he asked.

She cleared her throat. "No, not really. Um, I've got to
get going. I've got a lot to do today."

He'd been walking toward her as though planning to put
his arms around her or kiss her good-morning or something,
but at her words, he froze several steps away. "You're
leaving? Already?"

Jaclyn licked her lips. "Yeah, you know, it's Saturday."

"That's why I thought you might be able to stay. The

kids are in Feld with Terry. I wanted to take you out to breakfast.''

"Not today."

Doubt entered his eyes, and his smile disappeared completely. "What's going on?"

"Nothing." She tried a smile of her own and prayed it looked more convincing than it felt. "It's just that it's time to get back to reality, don't you think?"

"Get back to reality? What happened last night wasn't real?"

"It was real," Jaclyn said, plucking nervously at her nightgown. "But you promised me it wouldn't change anything."

"I never dreamed you were serious about that. How could it not change anything?"

"We just decide to agree that we made a mistake and move on."

"A *mistake,* Jaclyn? You think last night was a mistake?"

She nodded resolutely. "I know it was."

He rubbed his bare chest and looked around as though he was so surprised he didn't know how to respond. "I'm afraid I can't agree with that. I thought it was the most wonderful thing I've ever experienced," he said softly.

Something clamped down on her insides and wouldn't let go, but she refused to acknowledge the hurt. It was better to bear up under the pain and do what had to be done to get over it, than to let any hopeful feelings linger. "I'm sorry. I really am."

"So what am I supposed to do now?" he asked. "Pretend I've never made love to you? That I don't want to do it again, right here, right now?"

"I didn't mislead you, Cole. I told you last night—"

"I'm not accusing you of anything. I just expected…I don't know. Something more."

"I'm sorry to disappoint you," she said. "Maybe it would be better if I just go."

"Wait." He reached out and caught her arm as she tried to slip past him. "Is this about your job? Are you afraid I'll fire you if things go wrong between us on a personal level?"

"Partly," she admitted. "I can't risk losing my job, Cole. It's all I have right now."

"But I'd never leave you high and dry. You know that, don't you?"

Wouldn't he? Could she trust that? Jaclyn remembered the promise she'd made to herself the night she found Terry's truck outside Maxine's—*I will never let myself become so dependent on another human being again*—and knew better than to believe him. She had to keep her promise to herself. That was the only safe way to go.

"I appreciate what you've done for me, Cole," she said. "I hope you know that. You're a generous man. But I won't need you to cover for me much longer. I've started my real-estate classes and will have my license in a month or two. Then no one will be able to leave me high and dry, because I'll be just fine on my own." She gently extricated her arm from his grasp. "I'll see you on Monday."

COLE RAN A HAND through his hair and sank down on the bed. What the hell had just happened? Last night he'd made love to Jackie Wentworth, several times, and relished every passion-filled moment. He'd awakened happy, content, eager to spend more time with her.

And she'd just told him she didn't want anything to do with him.

Had he done something wrong? Had she heard what he said to Terry and grown angry over it? She hadn't mentioned her ex-husband. She hadn't even indicated she knew he'd stopped by. But Cole couldn't figure out what else could have changed in the ten minutes he was gone from the room.

Trust. She obviously had a problem with trust, and after what had happened with Terry, Cole could understand why. He was tempted to try to convince her he was different, that he'd never hurt her the way Terry had, but his own track record wasn't anything to be proud of. What could he really offer her? She had three children, and he didn't want to marry.

"She's right. I'm no good for her," he told himself aloud. Laura had needed more than he could give, and he'd let her go gracefully. He could do the same for Jaclyn, he decided. But when he stood to dress and saw the bed, all the memories of the night before came tumbling back, along with the overwhelming sense of connection he'd felt with Jaclyn—and he knew this time was going to be much harder.

IT WAS ONLY SATURDAY night, less than twelve hours since he'd held Jaclyn in his arms, but it felt to Cole like an eternity. He'd already stopped himself from calling her a dozen times or more, and the battle wasn't over yet. It was only six o'clock. He had the rest of the evening to go, the night that would follow, and tomorrow and the day after….

What was he going to do? He'd never been so consumed with a woman before. He'd tried to occupy his mind with work, tried to take care of some of the things that needed to be done on Rick's desk, but his heart hadn't been in it. He'd been more concerned with the fact that Jaclyn was probably sitting in her house, as alone as he was. The kids were still in Feld. There was nothing to stop them from seeing each other again. So *why* was he helping her turn him away? He couldn't remember anymore. He kept telling himself that it was better for her, but he could no longer say why.

Picking up the telephone, he dialed her number. Then he

rocked back in his leather chair and stared unseeingly at the painting on the wall opposite him, waiting for her to answer.

Her voice came across the line following the third ring. Just the sound of it caused Cole's breath to catch. "Jaclyn?"

She paused. "Hi, Cole."

"What're you doing?"

"I've been studying my *Real Estate Principles* book."

"How far along are you?"

"I've finished my first two open-book tests and mailed them off. I just have three more to go. Then I'm finished with the course and can schedule my state test."

"I have some sample questions you can study beforehand. They'll help you more than the course will."

"Great. I'll have to remember to bring them home with me."

I could bring them over right now, if you want, he thought, and nearly said so, but he wanted to get some idea of how she was feeling toward him first. Last night had definitely spooked her. He was hoping now that she'd had some time to think things over, she'd be more open to continuing their relationship.

Cole took a deep breath. "So what are you doing tonight?"

"I thought I'd go to bed early, get some sleep."

"It's only six o'clock."

"I was planning to study a little more first."

"Have you eaten?"

"Not yet."

"What if I said I'd like to take you to dinner?"

"I don't think that's a good idea."

"Why not?"

She paused. "I wouldn't want it to result in another night like last night, Cole."

"I hate that you regret what happened last night," he said.

"Why? What does it matter to you?" she asked. "You can go out tonight and repeat the experience with someone else."

He sat up straight, feeling as if she'd just slapped him. "Are you saying it didn't mean anything to you when we made love?"

"Why does it always have to mean something to the woman when it never means anything to the man?" she said quietly.

Then the phone clicked and the line went dead.

LAYING HER HEAD on her arms, Jaclyn gave in to the tears that had threatened all day, and let herself sob. Damn Terry for teaching her such hard life lessons. And damn Cole for making her want to forget everything she'd learned.

She'd probably have to find a new job now. How could she continue to see Cole every day? How could she expect to move on with her life when she was so stuck on the wrong man?

Maybe she should take a look at the want ads, she thought. Make a clean break of it. Now that she was getting her real-estate license, she could probably get by waiting tables for a few months. Then she could continue with her original plan to sell houses. Either way, she'd eventually get where she wanted to be if she worked hard and was smart about it. Margaret might even be able to help her find a job; she'd worked at quite a few places.

Jaclyn was just getting up to retrieve the paper, when the doorbell rang. Was it Cole? After their last conversation, she doubted it, but she didn't want to see anyone else, either. She considered pretending she wasn't home, but her car was out in the drive for all to see. She wasn't going to fool anyone who knew her.

Wiping her eyes on the sleeve of her sweatshirt, she

pushed herself away from the table and went to see who was standing on her front porch. A peek through the peephole told her it was Mr. Alder from next door.

"Just what I need," she muttered, then threw the bolt and opened the door, standing as far back in the shadows as possible, hoping he wouldn't notice her red-rimmed eyes.

Unfortunately he did notice. And he mentioned it right away. "What's wrong?" he asked. "Are the kids okay?"

"They're fine. They're with their father this weekend."

"Oh." He hesitated, looking distinctly uncomfortable, then held out the Tupperware containers in his hands. She sometimes had Alex or Mackenzie run some supper over to Mr. Alder to give him a break from frozen dinners. He'd never acted particularly grateful, but her dishes always came back empty and clean.

"Thanks," she said, and started to swing the door closed.

He stopped her with one bony hand. "The bread pudding was good," he said. "Just like my wife, Bonnie, used to make."

Jaclyn raised her brows. A compliment? From Mr. Alder? "I'm glad you liked it," she said.

"I noticed that Alex's bike has a flat. Thought maybe you'd put up the garage door so I can fix it."

"You're going to fix Alex's bike?"

"Just thought he's probably been missing it. Haven't seen him on it for a while."

It had been three weeks, to be exact. Alex kept asking her to have the tire fixed but he always mentioned it after the bike shop was closed, and Jaclyn couldn't seem to remember it any other time.

"He has been missing it. I appreciate the help."

"It's no trouble," he said. "You sure nothing's wrong?"

"Nothing that can be fixed as easily as Alex's bike," she said, and went to open the garage before poring through the want ads.

CHAPTER SIXTEEN

TERRY BROUGHT THE KIDS home late Sunday night. Jaclyn had expected them at dinnertime, but they didn't arrive until after eight.

"How was it?" she asked, as they came trooping in. She brightened her smile as much as possible so no one would suspect the heartache she was experiencing underneath. "Did you have a good time?"

"It was fun," Mackenzie said. "Grandma and Grandpa took us out for ice cream before we left."

"That sounds good. What about you, Alex? Did you have fun?"

Her son didn't answer. He shot her an angry look, nudged past her and went straight to his room.

Jaclyn winced, wondering what she was going to have to deal with this time, then shoved her hurt feelings aside. She was already particularly vulnerable tonight and didn't want to dissolve into tears.

Alyssa had fallen asleep in the car. Terry carried her to her room, and Jaclyn helped him put her to bed.

"Thanks for taking them," she said, following Terry back to the front door. "They like getting to see you and your folks."

"And you like the freedom you have in their absence, right?" he said, pivoting so fast that she nearly ran into him.

Freedom? Jaclyn had spent a long, lonely weekend, at least since Saturday morning, one of the most difficult of her life. But she had managed to do a lot of studying—studying she wouldn't have been able to accomplish if she'd had the kids. "I'm getting my real-estate license. It was good to have some time to study, if that's what you mean."

"We both know you were doing a little more than that."

Jaclyn took a deep breath and counted to ten. She wasn't going to come undone. Eventually Terry's jealousy and his sneering comments would disappear from her life. Besides, his reaction was probably natural enough, considering the fact that her being with another man was a whole new concept for him.

"Thanks again," she said quietly, ignoring his baited words.

Her dogged politeness seemed to diffuse his anger. He stared at her for several seconds. Then his expression softened. "Was being with Cole what you thought it would be?" he asked.

Jaclyn's first instinct was to not reveal anything. But she'd known Terry almost her whole life. He was her high school sweetheart, her husband of twelve years, the father of her children. If he didn't have the right to ask her an intimate question, who did?

She nodded.

"God that hurts," he said, closing his eyes.

"I'm sorry."

"Does that mean you love him?" he asked, acting as though he didn't want to pose the question but couldn't help himself.

Jaclyn considered telling him no to spare his feelings, but there didn't seem to be much point in lying. Whether she loved Cole or not, she wasn't ever going back to Terry. He needed to accept that and move on. She hoped this would help.

"I do," she said.

"Since when?"

Jaclyn wasn't sure she could say, exactly. Since Feld, certainly. Since the day he'd hired her, possibly. Maybe since the day she'd seen him in Joanna's. "It already seems like forever."

Covering his face with one hand, Terry took a deep breath. "I blew it, didn't I, Jackie? When we were together, you tried to tell me what I needed to do to save our marriage. You tried everything to get me to listen, but I wouldn't. And now…"

And now it was too late.

Monday was awkward. Cole kept himself buried in his office, for the most part, and wouldn't even look at Jaclyn when he came to the front office to speak to Margaret. Jaclyn was busy sending faxes to various mortgage companies. She said hello to him when he entered, but he acted as though he didn't hear her, finished his business with Margaret and left. When she made him dinner, he sat down and ate in silence, then went back to his private office before she could even finish the dishes.

"I'm leaving," she said, ducking her head into his office on her way out.

"Good night," he responded without inflection and without looking up.

Jaclyn paused before starting down the hallway, wanting to apologize and explain why she'd said what she had on the phone Saturday night. She wanted to tell him the truth, that the night they'd shared meant too much to her, not too little. But she knew she'd be opening a can of worms. She'd put some distance between them. That was the important thing. It was better to move forward now and let what happened on her birthday fade into the past. She hoped, with time, that Cole would forgive her and forget.

Returning to the office, Jaclyn gathered her jacket and purse, then threw a glance at the avalanche of paper on Rick's desk and sighed. Too many things were falling through the cracks at Perrini Homes, which worried her, for Cole. But he wasn't willing to let her help him, and she couldn't do it on her own. She didn't know where to start.

Locking up, she tried to put those added concerns out of her mind. She had a lot going on already. The kids would be hungry, and she was too tired to think about cooking again. Or maybe she was too depressed. She'd tried to talk with Alex after Terry had left last night, but her son wouldn't open up to her. She knew he held his father's unhappiness against her, but he was too young to understand all the factors that had led to the divorce. She could only love Alex and hope he'd come around, which was easier to do when she wasn't so strung out. In any case, she wanted to climb into bed and pull the covers over her head so she could kick herself, without interruption, for getting involved with Cole in the first place.

WHY HAD COLE CALLED HIM?

Rick stayed in his seat long after the others had filed out of the classroom, staring into space and thinking about the phone call he'd received from his older brother the week before. He'd already analyzed the conversation a dozen times or more, but he still couldn't figure out what it was Cole had wanted. Was there problem at the office? Did his brother need something he was too proud to ask for?

No, Cole had always done just fine on his own. Maybe if Rick were Andrew or Brian, Cole would have called simply because he missed him. But Rick had always been a liability. Cole could only be glad to be rid of him, especially now that he'd had time to make the transition at the office.

At the front of the room near the chalkboard, Professor Hernandez was gathering his teaching materials. ''Don't forget to read the first third of *Les Misérables* for next Monday,'' he said as he left.

Rick waved to acknowledge his words, then unsnapped

the cell phone from his belt. He'd tried to call Chad last weekend to see if he wanted to go do something, but Chad hadn't been home and Rick hadn't talked to him since. Maybe Chad could tell him what was going on with Cole.

"Hey, what's up?" his brother said when he recognized Rick's voice.

"Not a whole lot. What's going on with you?"

"I've been busy, man. It's Thursday already, and we only have until Monday to finish the due diligence on those lots in Sparks. I've been taking care of some customer callbacks on the houses we sold at the last development, and we're starting Phase II at Oak Ranch. It's crazy."

"Sounds like it. So Cole got the funding for the Sparks project?"

"Yeah. Schneider came through. Again."

Rick had never expected to miss the office or what went on there. Before he'd left, he'd been eager enough to break away and branch out on his own so he could correct the mistakes he'd made in his early years. But he felt strange now, as though he wasn't where he was supposed to be. As though he was missing out on something important.

"Cole has never had so many brands in the fire. How's he managing?" he asked. He didn't add *without me,* but that was what he wanted to know. Had his leaving made an impact?

Chad hesitated. "He's getting certain things done. Other things are falling through the cracks."

"Like what?"

"Like just about everything you used to do."

"Why hasn't he hired someone to replace me?"

"I don't think he wants to replace you."

"What about Jaclyn? She could take over some of that stuff—all of it, eventually."

"She's busy."

"Doing what?"

"Cooking and cleaning for Cole."

Cooking and cleaning? What was up with that? It took Rick fifty hours a week to keep up with Cole and his projects. Who was running the office in his absence? "But he can't go on like that. Eventually he'll bury himself in paperwork."

"We've got a real-estate agent selling houses like mad. I think we're there already."

Rick sighed. After all he'd put into his job, it was difficult to watch it go to hell. "This doesn't make sense," he said. "Cole's not one to let things go."

"I don't know, man."

Remembering the call he'd received in the middle of the night, Rick wondered how it tied in to everything he was hearing. Did Cole want him to come back? And if so, was Rick willing to go?

"Push him to train Jaclyn," he said. "It'll save him time in the long run."

"I think he likes what she's doing."

"What's that supposed to mean?"

"Take a wild guess."

"They've got something going on?"

"He took her out to Feld last weekend."

"Cole hates Feld."

"He must not hate it anymore. He just bought a sand rail."

Obviously quite a few things had changed since the first of September. "So what's going to happen next?"

"I wish I knew. Gotta run. Concrete truck's here."

Rick let his brother hang up, then sat tapping his forehead with his phone. Cole had put too much into Perrini Homes to let things slide now. What was happening?

He doubted Chad could tell him any more than he already had. But he knew someone who might have the answers.

THE REST OF THE WEEK wasn't any easier than Monday. Jaclyn thought Cole would eventually lapse into his old self and forget about what had happened between them, but it didn't look as though he was going to do it anytime soon. He barely spoke to her. When he did, his sentences were clipped and formal. And every time his gaze landed on her, he looked quickly away.

He probably disliked her immensely. Jaclyn hated the thought of that, but she told herself it didn't matter. She'd placed some calls to other companies, looking for new employment, and had sent out a few résumés. She would come up with something. She just needed to weather the emotional storm she'd caused by making that one colossal, stupid mistake on her birthday, and keep moving forward.

At least she knew how to survive difficult times. The past fourteen months had taught her to duck her head and keep putting one foot in front of the other. And that was exactly what she planned to do.

Only, sometimes she didn't want to go forward. Sometimes she wanted to go back—back to last Friday night. Regardless of the repercussions, the time she'd spent in Cole's bed had seemed like a once-in-a-lifetime experience. And maybe it was. She'd fallen head-over-heels in love this time. Far more powerful, both physically and emotionally, than what she'd ever shared with Terry. Her compulsion to be with Cole was so strong it hurt.

She picked up the sweatshirt he had tossed on his bedroom floor and held it to her face, pausing in her cleaning to breathe in the scent that lingered on the thick fleece. Spicy and masculine, it conjured Cole in her imagination like nothing else could. The feel of his warm neck when she'd kissed the pulse at his throat...the solid weight of him pressing her into the mattress...the silky feel of his hair between her fingers—

"What are you still doing here? It's after five."

Jaclyn spun to find Cole in the doorway. She was running late, but Margaret had had to leave early and he'd been gone all afternoon, so Jaclyn had been in no hurry to leave. She liked cleaning Cole's house, feeling him all around her in the things he touched and used and owned. But she'd lingered too long.

"I just finished your dinner," she said, swallowing nervously. "I put it in the fridge since I didn't know when you'd be back. Would you like me to reheat it?"

"No, I'll eat later."

"It's meat loaf," she added. His favorite. She'd also made garlic mashed potatoes, asparagus spears and a German chocolate cake for dessert. And she'd finished ironing his shirts and slacks, washing his blue jeans, dusting his room and mopping the kitchen floor. For some reason, she found taking care of him in those personal ways very gratifying.

He didn't answer. He just stared at her standing in the middle of his floor, hugging his sweatshirt, and raised his eyebrows in question.

Jaclyn glanced away, folded the sweatshirt, and put it neatly on his bed, which she'd just made. "Larry Schneider called this afternoon," she said. "He's been waiting for that new set of financial statements for three weeks. He wanted to know what was taking so long."

Cole rubbed his jaw and sighed. "He knows Rick's gone."

"He wanted to know if that meant things were falling apart around here."

"They're not falling apart. I'll get to it in the morning."

"I'd be happy to do it for you, if you'll just show me how."

"I'll take care of it."

"You're not going to hire someone to replace Rick?"

Cole suddenly looked tired, sad. "Rick's not someone I can replace," he said.

"I know." Jaclyn was tempted to put a hand on his arm,

to comfort him in some way, but she didn't dare touch him. "I'm sorry, Cole. Maybe someday he'll come back."

He nodded but held himself rigid as Jaclyn skirted past him.

"See you tomorrow," she murmured.

"Jaclyn?"

She paused at the threshold.

"Sometimes it means something to the man," he said softly.

That simple statement took Jaclyn's breath away. It was exactly what her heart longed to hear, exactly what she'd hoped—that their night together had held meaning for him, too. But how much meaning? And what was he willing to do about it?

She waited, hoping he'd say more. If only he'd mention love…promise that he'd be faithful, that he'd be a good father to her children. But she was wishing for the same elusive moonbeam Rochelle had coveted. Cole didn't want a family, especially a ready-made family. He'd made no secret of that.

Still, the vulnerability that showed in his face at that moment was almost enough to break Jaclyn's resolve. She ached to hold him and whisper that she loved him and knew, if she didn't leave right away, she'd do exactly that.

Marshalling strength she didn't know she possessed, she murmured a quick thanks and left.

COLE STOOD facing Rick's desk and sighed. He'd handled what he could over the past seven weeks, for the most part working nights and weekends. But there simply wasn't enough time in the day to do it all. He was falling behind, and it was starting to become a real problem. The bank was waiting for the financial statements. The payroll company had said they wouldn't cut any checks next week unless they received the income tax deduction forms signed by the construction crew, and Cole had a stack of outstanding bills that needed to be paid—the lumber and concrete companies had both called already. And there was more, lots more. Only, Cole wasn't sure he could handle everything Rick did. His brother had been there from the beginning and had carved out his own niche. Until Rick left, Cole hadn't realized how much he depended on his brother or how lost he'd be without him. There were some things Rick had done that Cole didn't even know how to do—the accounting was one of them.

He'd have to hire that out, too, he decided. He had to get things moving again. They were selling and building houses like mad. He couldn't let the infrastructure of his business collapse.

He glanced at Jaclyn's desk, which was neatly organized, then at Margaret's, which sat next to Jaclyn's and wasn't so neatly organized, and wondered how to restructure the company. Rick wasn't coming back. It was time Cole faced the truth and made the appropriate changes. Too many employees were depending on him for their living. So, should he train Jaclyn to do Rick's job? Could he tolerate having her so close, indefinitely?

He wasn't sure. The way she looked, the way she talked and smiled and dressed drove him nuts. He wanted free access to her. He wanted to take her out to dinner and dancing, buy her things, tell her how gorgeous she was and what she did to him every time he saw her, and make love to her at night. He wanted...

What *did* he want? Sometimes he wanted to make her his own, completely, wholeheartedly, and forever. But that sounded a lot like marriage, which led to the risk of repeating what had happened with Rochelle.

It's just another weak moment, he thought. But he didn't plan on being weak for long. He was going to get over her.

His resolve firmly in place, Cole took Rick's chair and started digging through the stack of papers closest to him, hoping to clear some things away, but the telephone interrupted him before he could get much of a start.

"Hello." He held the receiver to his ear with one shoulder so he could still use both hands.

"Hello? Is this Perrini Homes?"

"Yes, it is. Cole Perrini speaking."

"Ah, Mr. Perrini. I'm glad I caught you. I actually thought your office would be closed by now and was planning to leave a message for—" a pause "—Margaret Huntley."

"I'll be happy to have her call you. Are you in the market for a home?"

"No, actually I'm calling about Jaclyn Wentworth. This is Ronald Greenhaven with Guthrie Real Estate. I just wanted to verify a few items she has listed on her employment application."

Cole dropped the papers in his hand and gripped the phone more tightly. "Her what?"

"Her employment application. She stopped by a few days ago to apply for a job. She doesn't have much experience, but I met her when she came in, and she seems sharp and professional. Would you say she's a reliable worker?"

Cole didn't know what to say. Why was Jaclyn applying for other jobs already? He'd assumed she'd tell him, that he'd have the chance to shift her responsibilities and retain her. So this could only be a result of...

Leaning his elbows on the desk, he pinched the bridge of his nose. "She doesn't have her real-estate license yet. She can't sell houses," he said, his words more direct than he'd meant them to sound.

Greenhaven paused. "Yes, but she indicated that she'd be willing to come on as a receptionist until then."

"Starting when?"

"Right away."

"I'm afraid that's impossible."

"It is?"

"Yes. She already works for me."

Cole slammed down the phone, angrier than he'd been in a long time. Dammit, he'd gotten too close to Jaclyn a week ago, and she was running. To a point, he could understand that. He hadn't exactly made a commitment to her. But he wasn't the one who'd shown up in her bedroom in the middle of the night. Even though he might have coaxed her, he wasn't the one who'd crawled naked into bed. And he'd respected her wishes and left her completely alone since then. Why was she doing this?

Picking up the telephone, he dialed her number, but when he heard her voice, he hung up. What he had to say was better said in person, after the kids went to bed.

CHAPTER SEVENTEEN

WHEN THE PHONE rang again, Jaclyn thought it might be another crank call. She almost let the answering machine take it, but grabbed it at the last second.

"This is *who?*" she asked, surprised when someone spoke and the voice on the other end didn't belong to Terry or one of the kids' friends.

"Rick Perrini."

Cole's brother? Jaclyn hadn't heard from him since he'd quit Perrini Homes almost two months ago. But she was worried enough about Cole and all the things that weren't getting done at the office to be glad to hear his voice.

"Rick, how are you?"

"Fine. And you?"

Jaclyn thought of Cole and wanted to say *miserable,* but returned the customary answer. "Fine."

"Great. Listen, I'm calling because I have a few things I'd like to discuss with you. Is there any chance I could stop by tonight?"

Jaclyn looked at the *Real Estate Principles* textbook open in front of her. She'd finally finished dinner and had the kids at the table around her—Alyssa coloring, and Mackenzie and Alex doing their homework. She needed to get some studying done and spend some time reading to the kids, but she wasn't about to miss the chance to find out what Rick wanted. "What time?"

"Whenever's convenient."

"Is nine too late?"

"No, that'll work."

Jaclyn gave him directions to her house, then hung up, wondering what on earth Rick Perrini wanted with her.

JACLYN HAD ONLY ONE LIGHT burning, when Rick pulled up to her house. He parked parallel to the curb, letting his truck idle, and wondered if it wouldn't be smarter for him to simply turn around and go home. He didn't need to involve himself in Cole's life again. The more he knew, the more responsible he'd feel. And his brother was going to be fine. Cole had always been able to fend for himself, to land on his feet. It was Rick who'd let the problems at home get the best of him when they were teenagers. So what did he think he could do for Cole now?

Probably nothing.

Only, he couldn't forget that late-night phone call. *Did you catch the game?* What the hell did that have to do with anything?

Shoving the gearshift into Park, Rick cut the engine and got out. The night was cool and smelled of autumn. He liked this time of year. It reminded him of the days when he was young and his mother was healthy. She used to make beef stew on chilly nights like this, when the leaves were turning and starting to fall....

Rick closed his eyes and breathed deeply. He could almost smell the stew bubbling on the stove, hear his father's boots on the front stoop as he came home for dinner.

But that seemed like eons ago, another lifetime.

The porch light snapped on, telling Rick that Jaclyn had heard him pull up. He shrugged into his sweatshirt and ambled to the porch, and she opened the door before he could knock.

"Hi, there," she said, smiling and moving back so he could enter.

"Hi." He stepped inside. The light he'd seen from the street was in the kitchen, over a table strewn with one large

textbook, paper and pencils, a few scribbled crayon drawings and two children's backpacks. Evidently the kids were
in bed; the house was quiet. "Is that a real-estate book?
You studying for your license?" he asked.

She pushed up the sleeves on her sweater. "Yeah."

"How's it going?"

"Not too bad. Toughest part is getting enough time to
read. Would you like a cup of coffee or something?"

Rick agreed to the coffee and followed her into the
kitchen. She took a mug out of the cupboard while he
claimed a seat at the table.

"Where do you work now?" Jaclyn asked.

"I'm still looking," he said, because he didn't want to
tell her that he wasn't working, that he was living off his
investments and going to school full time. Why he didn't
want anyone to know, he couldn't really say. He supposed
it was fear of failure. In high school he'd skipped more
days than he'd attended, hadn't read a single assignment,
hadn't learned a thing. So college was definitely an uphill
battle. He was older than everyone else, which made him
a misfit from the start, and he didn't have a good base to
work from in any subject except math, which he'd taught
himself. On top of that, he learned from tinkering, doing.
Textbooks were boring and tedious for him. So he could
easily fail in the end.

"What kind of work are you looking for?" she asked.

"I'm not sure yet."

"I know someone who'd be happy to hire you back,"
she said with a smile. "Cream?"

"No, thanks."

She handed him his coffee. "The sugar's there on the
table."

"What makes you think Cole would hire me back?" he
asked, setting the coffee aside to let it cool.

"He won't let anyone have your desk, for starters. He
frowns if anyone even sits there to use the phone."

Rick smiled, thinking of Cole's scowl. He knew from long experience that it was a fierce one. When they were kids, Rick used to do anything he could to provoke his older brother. Why? Simply because he'd been so angry, always angry. And Cole was the only one who'd fight back.

"Are you thinking about returning to Perrini Homes?" she asked, sitting across from him.

"No, I have other plans. Chad just said…well, I wanted to see how you thought things were going at the office."

"We're on schedule as far as the building goes. And Margaret—she's the real-estate agent Cole hired shortly after you left—is doing a great job of selling houses. But I don't know how to do your job, so the paperwork's not getting done."

"How can you tell?"

"It's not hard. One look at your desk is enough. Besides, the bank and others are starting to scream."

"What does Cole say he's going to do?"

"He doesn't say. You're a sore subject, I think. Anyway, he's putting out fires as they occur, but he doesn't seem to have a long-range plan."

"That doesn't sound like my resourceful brother."

"You've never left him before."

"He can hire someone to do what I did. He's just being stubborn."

"I think it's more than that," she said. "He misses you. He cares about you."

Rick knew his laugh did little to hide his disbelief. "He's not that sentimental. Anyway, he cares about Chad and Brian and Andrew. He can live without me. I wasn't trying to leave him high and dry when I quit. I just have other things to do."

She didn't ask him what, but he knew she had to be thinking it. He'd just told her he didn't even have a job. "I gotta go," he said, standing. "But why don't I give you my number? If a problem crops up that you don't know how to handle, give me a holler. I'll do what I can.''

"Why don't you just call Cole and tell him you'll help him out if he needs it?'' she asked.

"It's complicated,'' he said.

With a frown, she jotted his cell phone number on an erasable board attached to her fridge. As she was putting his empty cup in the sink, the doorbell rang. The way she glanced up at the clock told Rick she wasn't expecting anyone else. And when she opened the door, they were both surprised.

"COLE!'' JACLYN SAID, her eyes widening.

Cole jammed his hands in the pockets of his jeans and tried not to glower, but it wasn't easy. He was feeling many different emotions, none of them pleasant. For starters, he wanted to know what the hell Rick was doing at Jackie's house. She was Cole's employee, Cole's friend from high school, Cole's girlfriend, for crying out loud.

Well, maybe she wasn't exactly his *girlfriend,* but he certainly had some claim on her after last Friday, didn't he? If not, he should. And though he'd wanted to see his brother again, badly, this wasn't exactly the place he'd hoped to find Rick. "I hope I'm not interrupting anything,'' he said coldly.

Rick stiffened, and his movements became jerky. "I was just leaving. Thanks, Jaclyn.''

"No problem,'' she replied, but she wouldn't quite meet Cole's eyes, and he wanted to know why. Was it more of the awkwardness that had gone on between them the past week or…something else?

Cole watched Jackie's face as Rick skirted past him, hoping for a clue as to the depth and meaning of her and his brother's relationship, but her expression gave nothing away.

"Thanks for stopping by,'' she told Rick.

Rick didn't respond. He didn't even look back. He was halfway across the lawn already and seemed eager to be gone.

"There's nothing going on between me and Rick," Jaclyn announced as soon as the taillights of Rick's truck had disappeared down the road. "This is the first time I've seen him since he left Perrini Homes."

"What did he want?" Cole asked.

"To find out about you. He's worried about how you're managing without him. He's willing to help out if you need it."

"Why hasn't he called to tell me that?"

"I don't know. He said it was complicated."

Cole released a long sigh. His jealousy had just made it more complicated. He should have been smarter than to be so obvious. But he hadn't exactly been levelheaded of late. He was doing a lot of things out of character—like mooning over a woman who didn't want him.

"He's right," he said.

She tucked a long strand of hair behind her ear. "What brings you here?"

"I want to talk."

She hesitated. "I'll be at the office in the morning."

"Oh, really? I wasn't sure," he said. "I thought you might take the morning to submit a few more résumés. Or maybe you've already hired on somewhere else. Were you planning to give me any notice? Or were you going to surprise me and simply walk out one day, like Rick?"

Her gaze lowered to the carpet, then lifted to his face again, but the troubled look in her eyes did little to soften his heart. He was angry—angry that he wanted something he couldn't have, angry that he couldn't solve everything by simply taking her in his arms, angry that he'd let his crush on her return after making such a clean getaway from Feld. Wouldn't he ever learn that anything connected to that dusty town was poison to him?

"Come in," she said.

He edged past her, keeping as much distance between them as possible.

"Sit down."

He sat at one end of the couch, while she sat at the other. Wearing a pair of faded blue jeans and a zip-up sweater, and sitting cross-legged facing him, she certainly didn't look like a mother of three. She looked like she had in high school, except for the frown.

"I was going to give you some notice," she said. "I just hadn't decided how or when. It's not like my plans are set."

"Is it because you're tired of cooking and cleaning for me? You know I've never expected that." He'd certainly enjoyed it, but he hadn't expected it.

"No, I like that sort of thing—at least, I like doing it for you. Things between us are just getting too—" she gave him a faint smile "—complicated."

"I seem to inspire that," he said wryly.

Her smile disappeared. "I have three kids, Cole."

"I know."

"And I..." Her voice faded, and she swallowed hard before continuing. "I could love you."

That took Cole by surprise. He'd definitely been getting conflicting signals—her warm willingness in bed that night, seeing her clutch his sweatshirt to her face a few days ago, catching the look in her eyes when she thought he wasn't watching. But the message that had come through most clearly was her desire to push him away.

"You have a funny way of showing it," he said.

"What would you rather I do?"

He thought about that for a minute but couldn't come up with a definitive answer, at least, not one he thought she'd find appealing. He wanted to establish a casual relationship with her similar to the one he'd known with Laura. But there were already too many emotions involved for "casual,'' and it frightened him that his and Jaclyn's experience could follow the same course as his and Rochelle's. If it got so out of balance, someone was bound to get seriously hurt, and he had no way to guarantee that it would be him. What if it were Jaclyn? Jaclyn, who'd already known enough hurt? Jaclyn, who had three children depending on her emotional stability?

"I don't know, but if you care about someone, you don't generally shut them out of your life," he said.

"If you care for someone, you don't generally sleep around on them, either, but Terry did that to me. Does that mean he didn't love me?"

"No. He probably cared for you a great deal."

"If that's true, he wouldn't want to hurt me."

"Maybe he thought you'd never find out. Maybe he thought what you didn't know wouldn't hurt you."

"He didn't stop even after I found out."

"There's no easy answer, Jackie. At least, not one I can give you. Some men are just like that."

She bit her bottom lip and looked down at her hands, clasped in her lap. "Some men," she repeated, then added, "I ran into Rochelle a few years back."

A feeling of dread, of impending doom, came over Cole almost instantly. Where was she going with this?

"Did you hear me?" she asked, when he didn't respond.

"Yeah."

"She said you cheated on her."

Cole stared down at his thumbnails. Rochelle had said a lot of things, launched a thousand accusations, most of which were completely untrue. He'd let her say what she wanted and had ignored her, partly because he'd felt so guilty about the incident with the trucking secretary that he didn't think he had grounds to proclaim his innocence, and partly because he hadn't cared enough to argue the matter. What difference did it make what the people of Feld thought of him? He'd known how hard he'd struggled to be a good husband to Rochelle, a women who'd trapped him, a woman he'd never loved, never wanted. And that was all that had mattered to him. Until now.

"Cole?" There was a plea in Jaclyn's voice that asked him to meet her eyes. "Is it true?"

He wanted to deny it. Lord knew what the truth would do. But the memory of that day with the trucking secretary was still too clear in his mind.

He briefly considered trying to explain the situation: that his marriage had already been over at the time, that the woman had come on unbelievably strong, that it had happened during the lowest point in his life. But he knew Jaclyn didn't want to hear excuses. She'd heard enough from Terry.

"Yes," he said at last.

And then he could say nothing because there was nothing left to say.

So she had the truth at last.

Jaclyn sat alone in her living room long after Cole left, wishing she hadn't asked him about his unfaithfulness to Rochelle. When she hadn't known, she could take his side and pretend, in some secret part of her heart, that the rumors she'd heard were just that—rumors. But now she was faced with the blatant truth, from his own lips, and she knew she could never again risk what she'd risked on her birthday. She had to stay away from Cole Perrini for good. He was too much of a distraction from the goals and plans she'd made for her life, too much of a temptation. Which meant she had to go through with getting another job, even though, in her heart, she wanted to stay right where she was.

"Mommy? What are you doing up? It's late, isn't it?"

Jaclyn glanced over her shoulder to see Alex rubbing his eyes against the light, standing at the mouth of the hallway.

Hair poking up on one side, he yawned while he waited for her to answer.

"I'm going to bed now," she assured him. "What woke you, honey?"

"I don't know. I just can't sleep."

Jaclyn considered her son, remembered when he was little and came so readily to her lap. She missed that boy. She missed his hugs and his unconditional acceptance. And she wondered if he'd ever forgive her for the divorce.

"Would you like some hot chocolate before you go back to bed?" she asked.

He was just turning to go to his room, but he stopped and blinked at her, looking surprised. "I have school in the morning."

"Isn't that my line, kiddo? Come on. A few minutes more won't kill you."

"Okay," he said. "Are you going to have some?"

"Sure. Let's have some together."

They went into the kitchen, and Jaclyn put a pan of milk on the stovetop to warm, then sat across from Alex at the table. "I'm glad you're awake," she said, taking strength from his presence.

He looked at her as though he expected her to add something, but she didn't. Her statement was simple and true just the way it was. She didn't want to think farther than that. As a matter of fact, she didn't want to think at all because when she thought, she thought about Cole, and then she hurt.

"Have I done something wrong?" he asked warily. "Do you want to talk to me about something…serious?"

Jaclyn smiled, wondering if, in her efforts to be Super Mom, always efficient and in charge, she'd bothered to slow down, listen, and simply be Alex's friend. "You haven't done anything wrong. How's school going?"

"Okay, I guess." With a little more prodding, he went

on to tell her about a boy who kept taking his coat at recess and how they'd nearly gotten into a fight the week before.

Jaclyn listened and smiled and refrained from offering too much advice. That she hadn't heard about the situation until now indicated Alex wanted to handle it on his own. And she thought she should let him, provided it didn't get out of hand. "In the future, if you and this boy can't get along, and you feel like you need my help, just let me know," she said.

He nodded. "I think it's going to be okay."

Jaclyn stood to pour their milk into cups, then added the chocolate mix from the pouches she kept in a drawer. Her spoon clinked against the sides of each cup as she stirred, sounding abnormally loud in the quiet house.

"Dad was pretty mad that you went to Cole's last weekend," Alex volunteered, after a few minutes of silence.

"I know."

"He said Cole's ruining our family."

"I thought I'd already done that."

Alex accepted his hot chocolate, his expression thoughtful. "Grandpa and Grandma agreed with him."

"Does that surprise you?"

"No, I guess not."

"They said Cole is trailer trash."

"I don't think that's fair. They don't really know him," she said, sitting down again.

"Do you like him?"

Definitely. Despite everything, she liked him, and she admired him. She doubted, faced with the same situation, Terry would have sat on her couch and told her the truth. "I do."

"What do you like about him?"

She liked too many things too much, so she kept her answer vague. "He's nice, don't you think?"

Alex stared into his cup. "Sometimes I don't want to

like him,'' he admitted. ''I know Dad doesn't want me to. But...''

''But what?''

''I sort of do. He's pretty cool. And it doesn't seem right not to like him just because Dad doesn't.''

Jaclyn smiled. ''You're growing up, honey. You're going to be a good man, and I'm very proud of you.''

Alex finished his hot chocolate and put the cup in the sink. ''I'd better get to bed. It's pretty late.''

''Good idea.''

When he started past her, she reached out to ruffle his hair, but he stopped and gave her a hug, instead. ''I love you, Mom,'' he said, and Jaclyn smiled for the first time since Cole had left.

She had her kids. She was out of Feld. She had a plan for the future. A year ago, she didn't have that much. She needed to be grateful—and forget about begging for the moon.

CHAPTER EIGHTEEN

TWO WEEKS LATER the telephone woke Jaclyn, while it was still dark. She jumped at the sound and lunged to her feet, thinking it was her alarm, then groaned when she saw the time. It was only five o'clock. After tossing and turning half the night, worrying about starting her new job at Guthrie Real Estate this morning, someone was waking her a full hour before she had to get up. Who?

She grabbed the receiver before it could wake the kids, too. "Hello?"

"Jaclyn?"

Burt. Jaclyn tensed. She hadn't talked directly to her ex-father-in-law for months. Why the heck was he calling her now?

"Is Terry okay?"

"He's fine. I'm calling about that man you're seeing, Cole Perrini."

Jaclyn wasn't "seeing" Cole anymore. She'd given him her notice two weeks ago, had finished up at Perrini Homes and was starting a new job today. But the kids hadn't been to Feld since the weekend of her birthday, and Jaclyn hadn't talked to Terry since the change, so the Wentworths wouldn't know.

"What about him?" she asked, wary.

"I want you to stay away from him."

That took a moment to sink in, probably because it sounded so much like a command. When it did, hot, scorching anger replaced Jaclyn's wariness. "*What* did you say?"

"You heard me."

"Have you bumped your head or something, Burt? Because you're not thinking straight. Terry and I are divorced. You have no say over who I date. Thankfully you have no say over anything I do, not anymore."

"I think it's you who's not thinking straight. Terry's still the father of your children. And I'm still their grandpa. That gives me some say in their future, and I don't want a man like Cole Perrini in their lives. He's not a good influence."

"Not a good influence?" Jaclyn repeated. "A man like Cole? You don't know anything about Cole."

"I know enough. I don't need to know any more."

"You pompous..." Jaclyn closed her eyes and tried to rein in her temper, managing to stop before she called him a bastard, a name he'd been called plenty of times behind his back, by many people, but probably never to his face. Peace. She wanted peace between them, for the children's sake. She had to remember that. "And if I tell you to go to hell?" she said, keeping her voice level.

"I'll take you back to court."

Jaclyn couldn't believe it. Court? Hadn't they spent enough time and money on the legal system already? "We've been that route, Burt. Again and again. Everything's resolved."

"It won't be if you don't keep Cole away from my grandchildren, dammit. We'll go back to court until I take every last dime of child support away from you."

"How dare you threaten me with something that's for the kids!" Jaclyn cried. "How can you do that?"

"You don't care about the kids—at least, not as much as you should, or you never would have left here to begin with. They had everything, and now they're living in a dive in Reno, while you work all the time. Tell me that's good for them."

"We wouldn't have to live in a dive if you hadn't done your best to release Terry from his responsibility where they're concerned. He's their father. Why shouldn't he have to help provide for them?''

''You're the one who sued for divorce, Jaclyn. You're going to have to live with the consequences of your actions. And tell Cole if he ever touches Terry, I'll call the cops.''

''Still fighting Terry's battles for him, Burt? I wonder why that doesn't surprise me.''

''Just get rid of Cole, or we'll see you in court,'' he said, and hung up.

Jaclyn sank onto her bed and let the receiver fall into her lap. Burt Wentworth was up to his old tricks again. He was trying to run her life, tell her what to do, punish her if she didn't obey. Would he ever leave her alone?

Shaking with fury and feeling slightly nauseated, she ignored the phone when it started to beep from being off the hook. Part of her wanted nothing more than to call Burt back and tell him to do his damnedest. If he wanted to file for a reduction in child support, she'd go back to court and fight him some more. But the other part of her knew she couldn't win. Burt could hide Terry's income too easily. He could say he'd been laid off, and the judge would probably lower her child support. During the initial separation, he'd claimed that Terry received a drop in wages and substantiated it with copies of his pay stubs. That was why her child support was so low to begin with. Though she knew Burt had to be paying Terry cash under the table, she didn't have any way to prove it. Bottom line, she was better off letting the Wentworths have their way than running up astronomical legal bills she'd never be able to pay. Burt usually won in the end, regardless.

''Damn him. Damn Burt Wentworth,'' she railed, wanting to slug something. Instead, she dropped her head in her hands and kneaded her forehead. She hated that Burt thought he could exert control over her even now. She wasn't seeing Cole anymore. But that didn't matter. What if her ex-in-laws didn't approve of the next guy? Or the guy after that? They wanted her to remarry their son.

"Don't worry about Burt," she whispered to herself, trying to calm down. Considering the way she still felt about Cole, a new boyfriend was probably pretty far into the future. By then, she'd have her real-estate license and be making enough to support her little family, and at that point, the Wentworths would have nothing over her.

Finally hanging up the phone, Jaclyn welcomed the silence. "Enjoy the power while it lasts, Burt," she said, "because you won't have it very much longer."

"HI, JACLYN, how's it going?" Mr. Greenhaven breezed into the office and good-naturedly slapped his palm down on the high counter that circled Jaclyn and one other receptionist.

"Good," Jaclyn responded with a smile. Located in the center of the floor, the receptionists' station was surrounded by cubicles filled with nearly twenty real-estate agents. Sometimes Jaclyn felt as if she were sitting in the eye of a storm. All around her, voices hummed, phones rang, beepers beeped and the monster-size copier and two fax machines along the far wall made their own share of noise. But she liked her new job. It was only her second week, but things were going well. She was getting to know the agents, handling the calls that came in and thriving on what she was learning about loans and mortgage companies and other aspects of selling houses.

Most of all she liked the fact that she finally had a job with a future. No more waitressing. No more wondering what she was going to do for a career. Her life had a sense of direction and lots of hope—even more than when she'd worked for Cole. He'd hired her out of the goodness of his heart; technically, he hadn't even had a position for her. But Mr. Greenhaven had hired her for completely different reasons. He thought she had potential in real estate, and she was determined to prove him right.

"Any messages for me this morning?" Greenhaven asked.

"You had two calls. I put them through to your voice-mail."

"You're doing great. Thanks." He greeted Nancy, her petite, dark-haired counterpart at the phones, then started toward his office. He'd only gone a few steps when he turned back. "When do you take the test, Jaclyn?"

"On Monday."

"Good. You've got the weekend to study. How do you feel? You think you're ready?"

"I think so. Do you know how long it takes to get the results?"

"About three weeks. Good luck."

He strode to his office, leaving Jaclyn to pick up the call that was just coming in and to think about his answer. Three weeks. Providing she passed the test, she could have her real-estate license before Christmas and be a full-fledged agent. Of course, she'd only be selling homes part time at first. She needed to keep her position as receptionist until she earned enough commissions to let her salary go. But with any luck...

"Deirdre, you have a call on line one," she said, patching the incoming call through to their top agent.

Nancy transferred a call of her own, then swiveled to face her. "You're taking the real-estate test on Monday?"

"Yeah."

"You nervous?"

"Maybe a little," Jaclyn lied. In truth she was terrified. Her whole future was riding on this test. If she failed her first try, she could always retake it, but she'd lose significant time, and she risked losing Mr. Greenhaven's confidence, as well.

"What did you do before you came here?" Nancy asked.

"I worked for a developer."

"That should give you a good background for real estate. Which developer?"

"Cole Perrini."

Nancy's eyes lit up. "I've heard of him. Deirdre and a few of the girls love to take their buyers to see his stuff. His homes are beautiful—and he's a real looker, from what I hear."

Jaclyn had seen a few Guthrie agents at Oak Ranch, as well as agents from other companies, but when she switched jobs she pictured herself selling older homes. She hadn't really anticipated the possibility of doing business with Cole in the future, probably because she didn't want to think about it. She was trying to put him in the past and leave him there, not that she was succeeding. She thought about him all the time, missed working for him, missed *him,* to the point of buying ingredients for meals she wanted to make him but never would. "He's a nice man," she said vaguely.

"How nice?" Nancy asked, grinning in a way that told Jaclyn she'd grill her until she heard something interesting.

"Very nice," Jaclyn responded. "He's also a confirmed bachelor."

"That's better than saying he's married," Nancy said, grinning. "I mean, what woman can resist the challenge of a confirmed bachelor?"

"I can," Jaclyn grumbled. But it wasn't the challenge of catching Cole that frightened her. It was the risk of what might happen if she caught him. If he'd stepped out on Rochelle, chances were good he'd do the same to her.

COLE WAS DAMN LONELY. For one thing, he missed Rick. He hadn't contacted his brother after seeing him at Jackie's over a month ago and had no plans to do so. Rick had to make the first move—Cole knew that instinctively, had felt it when he'd seen him. But it didn't make life any easier to realize that the only thing he could do to help the situation was wait, wait and hope Rick would come around. Meanwhile he had to move on with his life.

A week before Jaclyn's last day, he'd hired Brandon Johnson, fresh out of college, to take over as controller. Johnson was getting the accounting and other paperwork flowing again. And Margaret was continuing to do her job. Phase I had completely sold out. Phase II was close, and they were taking orders on Phase III. In addition, the Sparks project had closed escrow—they were breaking ground on the model homes this week—and Cole had received the funding to buy the lots Chad wanted him to pick up in Sacramento. All things considered, Cole thought he should be happy. His business had never been quite so large or so successful.

But no one was baking him bread anymore. Ever since Jaclyn had quit and hired on at Guthrie, the office and his part of the house, *especially* his part of the house, had seemed empty and impersonal, as though she'd stripped away all the cheer and warmth he'd ever felt there and taken it with her. He and Jaclyn had managed to tiptoe around each other before the job change, had kept any interaction between them very formal, but now she was gone and Cole felt her absence like a hole in the side of an airplane at thirty thousand feet.

I'll get over her, he told himself firmly, but he'd been telling himself that for weeks—ever since October seventh, the night he made love to her—and six weeks later, living without her wasn't getting any easier. He'd tried throwing himself more deeply into his work, but he was drowning in phone calls and title searches and home inspections already, and it was all starting to feel pretty pointless. Jackie was the thing he cared most about, which was why he'd driven past her house twice already tonight and, against his better judgment, was heading back for another pass.

"I hate this. I feel like I'm in high school again," he

grumbled, circling the block. He used to drive by the trim wooden house where she'd been raised in Feld, hoping for a glimpse of her. The most he usually saw was Terry's truck parked at the curb, but occasionally he got lucky and she passed him on the street in her parents' car, or he saw her out front talking to someone. It happened enough to keep him coming back. But never did he think he'd be driving by her place again at the age of thirty-two.

God, wouldn't Chad and Rick get a laugh out of him spending his Friday evening like this, he thought, slowing. Jackie's house was coming up on his left, but no one was outside, not even Alex. The only thing moving on the street was the old man next door, and he wasn't moving very fast. He was standing at the curb, sifting through the mail he'd just retrieved from his mailbox, and he gave Cole a distinctly suspicious glare when Cole passed.

Cole waved and smiled. He didn't want to alarm anyone. He just wanted to see Jackie.

Her car was parked in her driveway. This time of night, she was probably making dinner—spaghetti or teriyaki chicken…or meat loaf. Heaven help him if it was meat loaf. Cole thought he could smell it from the road, could almost taste it—but then, he was probably imagining things. He hadn't been himself lately. He hadn't been thinking straight. There were times, late at night, when he actually considered asking Jackie to marry him—pretty funny, since he'd sworn he'd never marry. And he knew she'd turn him down, anyway.

What if she didn't turn him down? he wondered, parking in front of the neighbor's a few houses away, where he wouldn't be so obvious but still had a clear view of her place. What if he asked her to be Mrs. Cole Perrini and she said yes?

Scrunching down in his seat, he leaned his head back and let himself imagine the wedding. Him waiting at the altar, all stiff and formal and nervous in a tux. His brothers spit-polished and standing next to him.

Part of his brain tried to interrupt at this point, to remind him that Rick wouldn't be there, but he refused to listen. This was a dream—*his* dream—which meant he could paint it any way he liked. And he liked what he was seeing. Rick was there, and so was Jackie, coming up the aisle, dressed in white.

Butterflies fluttered in Cole's stomach at the look he pictured on her face. Imagined or not, it did something to him, something that moved him. It was a smile of trust and love and promise.

Closing his eyes to more fully enjoy the vision, he heard himself agree to love and honor Jaclyn his whole life.

Then he waited for claustrophobia to overwhelm him. But it didn't. He had no desire to pull and yank on his tie or run screaming for the hills the way he had the moment he'd said "I do" to Rochelle. He felt happy and eager to hear Jaclyn return the same promises to him.

Next came the good part—the kiss, which was soft and sweet at first, then bordered on passionate. And he knew what to expect from the wedding night—

A fist rapped on his window. "Cole? Cole, why are you sleeping out here?"

Cole opened his eyes and blinked at the face that went with the fist, and wished he could have talked himself into going home fifteen minutes earlier.

It was Alex.

"MOM! HEY, MOM!" Alex called, charging into the house.

Jaclyn had just finished the dishes and was hurrying to get her jacket and purse. Scooping her keys off the counter, she rounded the corner.

"What is it?" she asked. "You're supposed to be helping me get the girls in their seat belts. We're going to be late for your game."

"Guess who's here? Guess who's coming with us?" he cried.

Jaclyn didn't need to guess. By now she was standing in the living room nose to nose with Cole Perrini.

He grinned, and her heart leaped into her throat. "Cole?"

"Yeah, it's Cole," Alex continued excitedly. "He said he'd come watch my game. Isn't that great?"

"Yeah, it's great," Jaclyn managed to say, but she couldn't inject any enthusiasm into her words. Terry, Burt and Dolores were meeting her at Alex's indoor soccer game in fifteen minutes. Burt would interpret her showing up with Cole as a direct challenge. He'd have her back in court before she could say "child support."

"These games can get kind of long," she said, stalling while she tried to figure out what to do.

"I don't mind," he said.

"Terry and his folks will be there."

He shrugged. "Okay."

Okay? He still wanted to go? "You're fine with that?"

"Sure. Want me to drive?"

Oh God, what now? Showing up with Cole would create complications she wasn't prepared to deal with—not when she was already dealing with the stress of her new job and the real-estate test looming first thing Monday morning.

On the other hand, Jaclyn hated to let Burt Wentworth dictate whom she could see and what she could do. Maybe it would do him some good to see her with Cole and to think something was still going on between them. Maybe it would do him some good to spend the whole game sitting right next to Cole.

Giving in to a devilish impulse, Jaclyn smiled. Burt's reaction was going to be worth every penny she stood to lose. "That would be great," she said.

CHAPTER NINETEEN

"THERE THEY ARE," Mackenzie cried, pointing at Grandpa and Grandma Wentworth and Terry sitting together in the bleachers overlooking the indoor soccer field.

The Wentworths hadn't yet spotted them coming in the door. Burt was actually smiling for a change, and saying something to Dolores, who was nodding in agreement. Even Terry seemed to be in good spirits.

Jaclyn suspected that would soon change.

Hauling in a deep breath, she slipped her hand in Cole's, looking for the alliance and support she'd known when they visited Feld. *Here we go,* she thought.

At her touch, Cole glanced at her in surprise. Until tonight, they hadn't spoken since she'd left Perrini Homes. They hadn't so much as brushed up against each other since the night they'd made love. But he didn't seem to mind the liberty she'd taken. His fingers curled around hers, warm and strong and comforting.

Alex had already headed to the locker room to join his teammates, but Alyssa and Mackenzie raced ahead, dodging the other soccer moms and various spectators as they climbed the stands to greet Terry and his folks.

"Is something wrong?" Cole murmured, leading Jaclyn up behind them.

Jaclyn kept her eyes on Burt, or what she could see of him around Cole's broad shoulders, waiting for him to notice their approach. Excited and strangely empowered, she was frightened, too. Was she crazy to provoke her ex-father-in-law? Probably. But she had to do it for her own self-respect. She wasn't the same woman she'd been a year ago. She was stronger, more confident. The time had come to let Burt know he hadn't quelled the fight in her, after all, at least not yet.

"They're not going to be happy to see you here," she said.

"I'm not expecting a lot of hugging and kissing."

"It's actually more than that. Your presence here is sort of making a statement."

"What's the statement?"

The children had reached the Wentworths, and Burt, Dolores and Terry were watching them now. Terry looked grim, troubled. Dolores looked shocked. And Burt was nearly apoplectic.

"Never mind," Cole muttered. "I think I get it."

"Look, Daddy, Cole's here," Mackenzie said, as they drew even with them, her enthusiasm for Cole's presence inadvertently rubbing salt in the wound.

Jaclyn bit the inside of her cheek to keep from smiling. She could almost see steam coming out of Burt's ears. "Hi," she said, imbuing her voice with as much confidence and friendliness as she could muster. "You guys got here early, huh? How was the drive?"

No one answered. Terry tore his gaze away from Cole and focused on the empty field below, which was circled by a half-wall like that of a skating rink. Dolores flushed and put a hand on her husband's arm. Burt stood.

"What the hell is he doing here?" he demanded.

"Who?" Jaclyn asked, feigning innocence.

Cole stiffened. "I think he means me."

"Damn right, I mean you," Burt growled. "I told you, Jaclyn. I told you I wouldn't have him around my grandchildren, and I won't!"

The momentary thrill of victory quickly dissipated, leaving Jaclyn worried and anxious. She'd thought Burt would glower and pout—and get back at her later—but she'd never expected him to cause a scene. Not in front of the other soccer parents, and most certainly not in front of the children.

"Alyssa and Mackenzie are here," she said, keeping her voice low. "And Alex is expecting us to watch his game. Let's not ruin it for him. We'll talk about other issues later, okay?"

Frowning, Mackenzie and Alyssa scrutinized the adults. "What's wrong, Grandpa?" Mackenzie asked.

"Your mother's what's wrong, young lady," Burt answered, a vein throbbing in his forehead. "She doesn't have sense enough to do what's best for you, even when someone spells it out for her."

"What, exactly, is she doing wrong?" Cole demanded. "Maybe it's time someone spelled it out for me. Because I'm having a hard time understanding why you guys can't simply enjoy your time with the children and leave her the hell alone."

Jaclyn wanted to warn Cole to stay out of the line of fire. She'd seen Burt's temper a number of times, knew he could get real ugly real fast, and didn't think it fair for Cole to be on the receiving end of it. She'd brought him. This whole thing was her fault. Besides, people were starting to stare. Jaclyn could feel their eyes, their interest. And she was concerned about the confusion on her daughters' faces and the possible embarrassment such a scene was going to cause Alex when he found out about it.

"Cole, let's go sit somewhere else. The game's about to start," she said, but no one paid any attention to her. The smell of popcorn and hot dogs filled the air. Footsteps tramped up and down the wooden bleachers while others found seats. And the opposing team was already pouring onto the field. But Cole and the Wentworths seemed oblivious to it all.

"If she had any sense, she'd come back to Feld, settle

down and raise these kids like she should,'' Burt was saying. ''If she had any sense, she'd leave men like you alone.''

Cole cocked an eyebrow at him, challenge apparent in his expression. ''Men like me? You mean trailer trash, Burt? You think a poor man can't be as good as a rich one?''

''Don't play games with me,'' Burt snapped. ''This isn't about rich and poor. I know who and what you are. I know your reputation—the liquor and the women and what you did to that poor girl you married. You nearly drove her to take her own life, for God's sake. I can't say what you've done since you left Feld, but I doubt you've changed much. An apple doesn't fall far from the tree, now does it. You think I want my grandchildren growing up around you?''

Terry stood up then and hovered at his father's shoulder, much the way his friends had hovered at his back during the confrontation at the Starlight Motel. Jaclyn wondered if it was because he expected Cole to start a fight, and she began to worry about that very thing.

Not here, she chanted silently. *Please, not here.*

''Cole,'' she said again, but he was already talking.

''You're implying they'd be around what, Burt? A poor example? A heavy drinker? An adulterer?'' His gaze cut to Terry, who suddenly seemed ill at ease. ''That's funny. I thought they escaped a man who was all those things when they left Feld. And if I were you, I don't think I'd run around spouting off about the apple and the tree. I'm not sure it reflects well on you.''

''I've made my mistakes, but so have you,'' Terry started, entering the argument for the first time, but his father cut him off.

''How dare you!'' he yelled at Cole. ''This is none of your business. You have no say in any of it!''

''I have more say than you think,'' Cole replied. ''I'm going to marry Jaclyn, which would make her my wife *and* my business, and there's not a damn thing you can do about it!''

This announcement was met with stunned silence. For Jaclyn, the drone of voices fell away. The tramping of feet fell away. She could only hear the furious pumping of her own heart. Had Cole just said what she thought he said?

Surely he hadn't meant it. He *couldn't* have meant it.

''This is getting out of hand,'' she finally managed to say, hoping to diffuse the situation to the point where they could all think rationally again. ''Cole and I don't have any plans, but we have the right to make them if we want. Now, I suggest we all calm down and think about what's going on—''

''There's nothing to think about,'' Burt said, pointing a thick finger at her. ''You marry this guy, and I'll see that your kids are taken away from you if it's the last thing I do.''

''Mommy!'' Mackenzie cried, clinging to Jaclyn's leg the way Alyssa had done almost from the start.

''It's okay, love,'' she said, patting her back. ''Grandpa's just angry. He doesn't mean it.''

''Try me,'' Burt spat, glaring at Cole.

Cole chuckled humorlessly and shook his head. ''You folks need to take a long look in the mirror and decide what it is you're trying to achieve because you're certainly not helping your grandchildren.''

White-faced, her brow crinkled with concern, Dolores looked frustrated and helpless at the same time. ''Burt, he's right,'' she said, but her husband shook off the hand she laid on his arm.

''He's not right about anything!'' he cried.

''We'll see,'' Cole said. ''But don't say I didn't warn you. You take Jaclyn to court, and you'll be sorry. We'll fight to achieve full custody of the kids, and we'll triple Terry's child support. I've got the time and the money and the inclination to do it. I know the right lawyers. So you need to ask yourself something, Burt. Is this really a war you think you can win?''

Burt's jaw sagged. Before he could gather his thoughts and respond, Cole shot a condemning glance at Terry, who looked as if he wanted to say something more but was still deferring to Burt. ''Why don't you ever stand up to your father?'' Cole demanded. ''Are you that sure you'll fail without him?''

Then he lifted Alyssa into his arms, took Jaclyn's hand and led her and Mackenzie to the opposite end of the bleachers.

HOLY HELL, what had he done? Cole wondered. He'd just announced to Jaclyn, her ex-husband, her ex-in-laws, and her two daughters that he was going to marry her. *Marry* her! He hadn't even asked her, for crying out loud. He wasn't even sure he *wanted* to marry. Furthermore, he and Rick still weren't speaking, proof positive that he lacked any kind of good parenting skills. But his competitive spirit and defensive instincts had simply taken over. He'd established territory where he possessed none. And now he could only look back in horror and amazement.

Cole felt Jackie's presence at his side but refused to look at her. Fortunately she didn't seem any more eager to draw his attention than he was to give it. Following the argument with the Wentworths, she hadn't said a word. She'd sat down next to him and focused strictly on the game—a game in which her ten-year-old son was playing. Mackenzie was sitting on the other side of her, and Alyssa was on Cole's lap, and all Cole could think about was the prospect of raising them to adulthood while trying to avoid all the mistakes he'd made the first time around.

He couldn't do it. He simply couldn't do it.

Cheers reverberated around him—wild, excited cries diametrically opposed to Cole's own emotions. He wanted to groan and drop his head into his hands. He wanted to go back in time and relive the past thirty minutes.

Cole clapped automatically for the goal Alex's team must have scored, but he was thinking about Rick, and the way their relationship stood, and the reasons for it. He'd failed Rick somewhere along the line. He hadn't given him enough love or positive attention or any one of a thousand other things a child needs, which meant he should quit while he was ahead—or at least not too far behind. He'd just have to apologize to Jaclyn and her kids for his impulsive mistake and move on.

Except moving on meant *moving on*. He wouldn't get to see Jaclyn anymore. He couldn't ask her for the same kind of relationship he'd had with Laura. Jaclyn wasn't the same type of woman. She'd never put up with it, for one thing. And her situation was too different, besides.

"Would you like some popcorn?" she asked. "I'm going to the snack bar."

Cole shook his head mutely, only now noticing that the playing field was empty. It had to be half-time. He'd been sitting in the stands for half the game and hadn't seen any of it. Distantly he wondered if Alex had played well.

"Want to come with Mommy and Mackenzie, Alyssa?"

"No, I'm staying here with Cole," Alyssa answered, and slipped her arms tightly around his neck.

For a moment Cole was tempted to peel her away, hand her to her mother and get out of Dodge, fast. The child felt sweet and soft in his arms, and smelled like baby shampoo, but he didn't need her blue eyes fixed on him, making him feel that much guiltier for planning to walk away after the game. He'd always had a weakness for Jackie. He'd always wanted her. But he couldn't let that tempt him into screwing up the rest of his life. He'd just unsnarled the damage caused by the first twenty years.

Taking Mackenzie with her, Jaclyn scaled the bleachers, then disappeared around the corner. Cole glanced across the stands to see what the Wentworths were doing and caught Terry watching him. Only he didn't look angry, as Cole expected. He looked...thoughtful, almost sad.

Sighing, Cole shifted Alyssa on his lap. "Don't you want to go see your daddy?" he asked.

She peeked around at Terry, then shook her head. "I'm going to stay here. With you."

"Great," he muttered.

Fortunately she didn't question this response. She just curled up in his lap as content as a cat bathing in the sun, until her mother returned.

"I brought you a cola," Jaclyn said.

"Thanks." Cole accepted the drink and shared it with Alyssa and Mackenzie, both of whom clamored for it immediately.

"Grandma and Grandpa and Daddy came all the way from Feld to see you," Jaclyn told the girls. "Why don't you take them some of your popcorn?"

Alyssa was still reluctant to get down, but when Mackenzie ran off with the popcorn, she finally followed her sister, which left Cole and Jaclyn alone for the first time since Alex had brought him to her door.

"I'm sorry about what happened when we arrived," Jaclyn said.

Cole took a sip of his soda. "No problem."

"I should have told you that Burt threatened to cut off the child support if I saw you anymore. Then you could have been prepared."

"It wouldn't have changed anything," he said, but he wondered if that was true. Would he have opened his big mouth and shouted out that he was going to marry Jaclyn if he'd known he was walking into an ambush?

"About what I said up there." He cleared his throat, which suddenly felt rather tight, then plunged ahead, deciding that it was best to address the subject as soon as possible and clear the air. "About...you know, marriage."

"Yes?" She faced him, her expression blank enough to make Cole believe there was still hope for an easy out. She didn't seem hopeful or upset or overly eager. She seemed perfectly okay.

Taking heart, he went on. "I shouldn't have said what I did. There's a lot we'd have to consider before making a big decision like that one."

"I understand," she replied. "We all say things we don't mean once in a while." She shrugged. "I enjoyed seeing the shock on Burt's face. It was worth it. Anyway, we'll just wait a few weeks and reinforce that our plans have changed. It won't be a big deal."

She smiled reassuringly, but it was her indifference and willingness to let him backpedal that bothered Cole. After what had happened between them, wasn't Jackie even remotely tempted to make their relationship permanent? Isn't that what most women wanted? Rochelle had used sex to trap him, she'd lied to him and manipulated him, all for a ring on her finger. Jackie, on the other hand, had much more reason to want the financial and emotional support of a spouse, yet she asked for nothing. Was it because of the mistake he'd made with the trucking secretary? He'd known it would affect Jackie's opinion of him, but he also believed a woman who cared about him would be willing to forgive him. Had *she* been the one who'd made the mistake, he'd definitely let the past go and give her a chance to prove herself. But then, he hadn't gone through what she'd gone through.

"What are you saying?" he asked. "That you wouldn't want to marry me even if I asked you?"

She looked down at the field and started clapping. Alex's team was just coming back on. "I don't have to worry about you asking me," she said after a moment. "You don't want to get married, remember?"

"Yeah, right," he said, sorely missing the determination behind that conviction. He'd been going back and forth on the marriage issue for weeks now, but the more Jackie slipped away from him, the more eager he was to bind her to him.

And the less committed he became to bachelorhood.

"THAT WAS QUITE A GAME," Jaclyn said, standing outside her house with Cole beneath the pale arc of a streetlight. "I'm so glad Alex's team won."

Alex had gone inside to change out of his soccer uniform, and the girls had soon followed, convinced, when Cole and Jaclyn did nothing more than talk in the chilly night air, that there had to be something more interesting on television.

"Terry and Burt weren't too happy when they left the game," Cole said.

Folding her arms across her body to help her lightweight jacket keep her warm, Jaclyn tilted her head back to admire the night sky. It was only eight o'clock, but the days were getting shorter. Thanksgiving was less than a week away. She could hardly believe how fast the months were passing. When she'd started working for Cole in mid-August, getting her real-estate license had seemed so far into the future. Now she was two days away from taking the test.

"Poor Alex. He was hoping to go with them. But they said goodbye and hurried off," she said. "And I doubt they'll be coming back again very soon."

"Do you think Burt will call once they reach home?"

"There's no telling what Burt will do."

Cole shoved his hands in his pockets and leaned against the side of his Navigator. "Do you want me to stay for a while, just in case?"

The words were spoken casually enough, as though he was merely being polite, but Jaclyn got the distinct impression his offer stemmed from something deeper than courtesy. He wanted to stay, and as much as Jaclyn wished otherwise, her desire to let him had nothing to do with protection from Burt Wentworth. When she was with Cole, the whole world seemed right, as though she'd started a journey long ago and finally reached the ideal destination.

But that's my heart talking, not my head, and my heart's been wrong before.

"There's nothing Burt can do to hurt me, at least not tonight." She offered him a weak smile. "It will take him a few days to marshal his force of attorneys."

"You don't think he'll back off?"

"Maybe." She grinned. "Now that he believes we're getting married."

She thought she saw Cole blush, which wasn't something that happened often, but the shadows covering his face made it difficult to tell for sure. She did know he hadn't been his smooth-talking, confident self ever since claiming he was going to marry her. Fortunately she understood that he'd said it in the heat of the argument. Even if she'd taken him at his word, she would have realized he regretted what he'd said when he clammed up and wouldn't talk through most of the game.

"What about Terry? He'll just let his dad do whatever he wants?" Cole asked.

"I don't know. Terry was very bitter last year and very much a part of the court battles, but he seems to be losing his zeal for the fight. Maybe he's finally reconciling himself to the fact that I'm not coming back, no matter what he does."

"Or maybe he's met someone else."

Jaclyn thought about that. "I doubt it," she said after a moment. "The kids never mention anyone. Neither does Terry."

"Would it upset you?"

"If he was seeing someone else? No. I keep hoping he'll do exactly that and move on with his life, but he claims there will never be anyone to replace me. When he says things like that, I can't help wondering what happened to all the other women he wanted when we were married."

"I guess they were more desirable to him when they were off-limits."

Jaclyn wanted to know if Cole could identify with those feelings. Is that what had enticed him to break his own marriage vows? Is that what appealed to most philanderers? If so, she couldn't relate. To her, an affair seemed fleeting and selfish and cheap.

"I guess," she said. She really didn't want to dwell on Terry's extracurricular activities because she had to face the fact that Cole had the same reputation. And there were times—lots of times—when she didn't want to acknowledge that. Times like now, when he looked so appealing in his faded blue jeans and Ralph Lauren sweater, the dark stubble of a day's beard on his jaw.

"What about Alex?" he asked. "You think he'll be okay? He didn't seem to know what to do when he had his father and grandparents on one side of the bleachers, and you and me on the other."

"I know. I'm sure he was afraid his father would take it personally or get angry if he spent too much time with us, but he likes you, so he was naturally drawn our way."

"He's a good boy."

"He's coming along. He still has some issues with the divorce, but he knows I love him and want what's best for him. I'm hoping that will eventually conquer the negative. It has to, doesn't it? I mean, otherwise, parents wouldn't stand a chance of raising healthy, well-adjusted individuals—not with all the things that go wrong in life. Very few people have a perfect childhood."

Cole's gaze fell to the ground. Taking one hand out of his pocket, he kneaded the back of his neck as he asked, "You think love is enough?"

"I think it can compensate for a lot of things. It's a lack of love that really hurts a child—or anyone, really."

He nodded but didn't say anything, his expression serious, as though he was pondering something important.

"What are you thinking about?" Jaclyn asked.

"I was just wondering if it's ever too late."

"For what?"

"For someone to receive the love they need."

Surely some people received too little love too late, she thought. But weren't there others out there, millions, who could still be whole and healthy if only they had someone to care about them? "That would probably depend on a lot of things," she finally replied.

"Yeah." He sighed and jammed his hand back in his pocket, then looked at her. "I want to see you," he said.

The sudden change in topic took Jaclyn by surprise. His statement was simple and sincere, and she wanted to respond to it. Except that dating Cole went against everything she'd been telling herself for the past three months. She was finally out and on her own. Why break down now?

"I think we've already established that it's probably best—"

"To what?" he interrupted. "Give up on what we feel?"

Evidently Jaclyn was far more transparent than she thought. "What do we feel?" she asked.

"That's what I want to find out. And don't tell me you don't feel anything. I know better."

"How?"

"From your birthday."

Jaclyn raised a challenging eyebrow. She hadn't made any protestations that night.

"Come on," he said. "When we made love, I wasn't alone emotionally any more than I was alone physically."

It was Jaclyn's turn to blush. She might not have made any protestations of love on her birthday, but she hadn't held anything else back. To get the conversation on safe ground again, she said, "I'm just trying to make good choices. It's so important now that I'm on my own with the kids.''

"I understand. That's why I let you pull away the first time. But now, I'm not sure it's such a good choice.''

"So what do you want? To see a movie once in a while, you and me? Or are you interested in including the kids?''

He shrugged and gazed toward a car turning at the corner. Headlights swung toward them, then away as the vehicle pulled into a driveway up the street.

"Why can't we do both?'' he asked. "I don't have any expectations. Let's just start at ground zero and try not to decide the ending before we finish the beginning. I'll promise to take things slow, if you'll promise to trust me.''

Trust him? A known philanderer?

"I'm not sure I can do that.''

"I'm not like Terry,'' he said.

Jaclyn had wanted him to say those words ever since she'd run into him at Joanna's. She'd wanted to hear him claim his innocence, or at least declare his reformation, but he'd never offered any justification for his past, and he didn't now. He just looked at her with hope shining in his eyes, willing her to believe him.

Somehow his silence went a lot farther toward breaking down her defenses than any amount of talking could have done.

"I know you're a lot stronger than Terry in many ways,'' she said. "You wouldn't have been able to accomplish what you've accomplished if you weren't, but—''

He grasped her by the shoulders and stared down at her. "I won't cheat on you, Jackie,'' he said, then he kissed her.

Jaclyn closed her eyes, savoring the feel of Cole's lips on hers. His breath fanned her cheek and his hand cupped the back of her head, but it wasn't a passionate kiss. It was soft and sweet and endearing, and it begged her to believe in him.

The smell of his aftershave filled her nostrils as his

tongue met hers, tasting like mint, and Jaclyn felt her resistance crumble. She could *try* to trust him, couldn't she? It wasn't so much to ask.

Breaking off the kiss long before Jaclyn wanted him to, he lifted his head and smiled down at her. "Can I see you tomorrow?"

Heart beating in her throat, Jaclyn gazed into eyes that were dark and intense beneath an unruly lock of black hair, and knew she couldn't refuse him. *It's only a date,* she told herself. *No big deal. I can back out at the first sign of trouble.*

Oh God, who was she kidding?

"Why don't you come for dinner at six?" she heard herself say.

"I'll be here," he promised with a grin. Then he got in his truck and drove away, leaving Jaclyn standing in the street, still hungry for his touch, still aching for his embrace.

CHAPTER TWENTY

HE'D BEEN A FOOL to insist Rick make the first move to heal the breach between them.

Letting his engine idle, Cole sat outside Rick's place and stared at his own reflection in the dark windows of the house. He'd left Jackie's nearly two hours ago, but it had taken him that long, and nearly four cups of coffee at the local Denny's, to work up the nerve to come out to his brother's. Now he just needed to summon the courage to approach the door.

It's a lack of love that really hurts a child....

Cole took a deep breath and let that statement swirl around in his mind some more. Is that where he'd failed Rick? Did Rick know how important he was to Cole? Or had Cole given his brother everything except what a child needed most?

It was certainly possible. Cole wasn't much for psychology. After surviving his childhood with his sanity intact, he hadn't wanted to delve inside his head or anyone else's, for fear of what he might unearth there. But looking back, he could certainly see how a young boy in Rick's situation—acting out like he was—could get his signals crossed. For years every exchange Cole had with his brother had been negative. Maybe Rick didn't know Cole cared. Maybe he'd never known.

"Shit," Cole grumbled, killing the engine. If Rick didn't know, he needed to tell him, but it wasn't going to be easy.

He and his brother just didn't communicate on that level. They never had.

But if that's what stood between them...

Getting out, Cole approached the door and rang the bell. Rick's car was in the driveway, but all the lights were out. He was probably asleep, which meant Cole would wake him—again. He considered waiting for morning, an option that was certainly growing in appeal, but decided he'd better say what he'd come to say and be done with it. Or he might never get it said.

Nothing happened for several minutes, so Cole rang the bell again.

Finally the porch light came on and Rick opened the door, wearing nothing but a pair of sweatpants. "Cole?" he said, scratching his head.

"Yeah."

"Tell me you're not here to ask about the game last Sunday."

"No." This time Cole wasn't going to say anything about sports or business or the past. This time he was going to set the record straight between them, once and for all.

Except, he couldn't talk. Now that the moment had arrived, his heart was making such a racket, he could scarcely hear above it, and his eyes—damn them—were starting to water.

"I wanted to tell you something," he said.

Rick's expression remained guarded. "What? If it's about work—"

"It's not about work. It's..."

Suddenly Cole couldn't fight the tears filling his eyes, and his chest tightened to the point that he could scarcely breathe. But he wouldn't let himself turn away. Because worse than being a thirty-two-year-old man standing on his brother's doorstep and crying like a baby was the fear that his brother didn't know, had never known, how he truly felt.

Hands clenching and unclenching, he said, "I love you, dammit."

It came out as a hoarse whisper. A pathetic attempt. Cole cleared his throat and forced his next words, loud and clear, past the lump that threatened to choke him. "I...have always...loved you."

Then, too embarrassed to wait for Rick's reaction, he turned on his heel and left.

STUNNED, RICK STOOD in the doorway and watched the taillights of Cole's Navigator disappear from sight. He'd never seen his brother cry—not when their mother died, not when their father died a year later, and not when he divorced Rochelle. Through the most difficult part of his life, Cole had always been strong and aloof and practical. The entire family had leaned on him, and he'd pulled them through.

Yet he'd just knocked on Rick's door with tears in his eyes and said, "I love you."

Rick rubbed the whiskers on his jaw and shook his head. His first instinct was to go after Cole, but he knew, for the moment, his brother would rather be alone. Rick didn't know what he'd say if he caught up with him, anyway. The problems between them weren't going to disappear overnight, but Rick knew he loved his brother back. There was no doubt about that. He'd always loved him, had admired Cole like no one else. Maybe that was enough to make things right. Maybe if they agreed to clear away all the resentment from the past and build on that foundation...

It was certainly worth a shot. Rick wanted to feel like part of the family again. And missed Perrini Homes. He'd actually been thinking, now that he had his classes rolling along, that he'd like to go back to work part time. School was a challenge, but he'd talked Abby, the girl from his English class, into studying with him, and she was helping him a great deal. He was gaining confidence, starting to believe he could handle it—just as long as he could handle her. Abby was a feisty number who made no secret of the fact that she planned to wear his ring someday. But he'd managed to keep things from getting too serious. The two of them were spending a lot of time together, but they were still wearing the label "friends."

Finally closing the door, he went to the phone in his kitchen and dialed the office at Perrini Homes. He knew Cole wouldn't be there yet, but he wanted to leave a message on his answering machine.

"You've reached Oak Ranch, another fine development by Perrini Homes," a woman's voice said. Was it Jaclyn? No. Had to be the new real-estate agent. What was her name? Margaret? The fact that Rick didn't know her brought back that poignant feeling that he was missing out on something important.

"We're located near the beautiful Washoe County Golf Course...."

Impatiently tapping his finger against the table, Rick waited through the address and office hours for the *beep*. When it sounded, he said, "Cole, this is Rick. I hear the Forty-niners are playing the Vikings this weekend. Any chance you'd like to come over and watch the game?"

DINNER HAD BEEN GREAT. Perfect, in fact. The whole evening had been ideal. Jaclyn couldn't remember a time when she'd enjoyed herself more. But after spending another four hours in Cole's company, she found herself more hesitant than ever before to trust him. Ironically enough, it was because he was doing everything *right*.

True to his word, he was taking things slow. He hadn't touched her all night, hadn't kissed her when he left at the surprisingly early hour of ten o'clock. He'd simply talked and laughed and let everyone enjoy his presence. He'd brought the makings for ice cream sundaes. He'd helped with dinner. He'd pulled out a new Nintendo game he'd bought for the kids, then played it with them for more than an hour.

By the time he left, Alex was asking when he'd be coming over again. Mackenzie was begging him to stay longer. And Alyssa, poor little Alyssa, who missed the physical contact she'd once had with her father, was demanding hug after hug goodbye. Cole was capturing her children's hearts as effortlessly as he'd won her own, and it was making Jaclyn nervous. They didn't understand what was at risk here. It was up to her to protect them.

But if she shut Cole out of their lives, she might be denying herself and her children something wonderful.

Good or bad? How did she decide?

With a groan, Jaclyn rolled onto her back and stared at the ceiling above her bed. Had Cole changed since his days with Rochelle? And if so, had he changed enough?

I ran into Rochelle a few years back... She said you cheated on her... Is it true?

And then Cole's response: *Yes.*

Jaclyn rubbed her eyes. *If he's done it once, he could certainly do it again.*

He won't, regardless of what came before. He said he'll never cheat on me.

Kicking off the covers, she sat up and stared at the phone. She needed to talk to Cole, and she needed to do it tonight. Her real-estate test was only one day away. She had to make a decision about him so she could concentrate on something else.

The glowing digits on her alarm clock said it wasn't quite eleven. Hoping he'd still be up, and thinking it likely considering he'd left only forty-five minutes earlier, she called him.

Cole answered on the second ring. "Hello?"

"Cole?"

"Jaclyn. I thought you were going to bed early so you'd be all set to study tomorrow."

"I'm in bed. I just can't sleep," she admitted.

"Is something wrong?"

Jaclyn had fully planned to ask Cole about his marriage to Rochelle and what had happened with the other women during that time. She needed to know, to make an informed decision. Was it an isolated incidence? A long-term affair with one woman? Brief affairs with many women? It made a difference. But at the sound of Cole's voice, the desire to see him hit Jaclyn so strong that she couldn't frame a single one of those difficult questions. She could only marvel at the fact that he'd been gone less than an hour and already she felt willing to walk across a bed of nails to be with him again, if need be.

"I—I just wanted to thank you for treating the kids so nicely tonight," she said, stalling in the hope she'd be able to summon the nerve before they hung up.

"You have great kids. It's easy to treat them nicely."

"That was an expensive Nintendo game you bought. I feel I should pay you for it."

"Why? I wanted to buy it. I thought Alex might like it."

"He does."

There was a short silence. "Dinner was good," he said.

"Thanks."

"Do you need me to quiz you on your real-estate facts tomorrow? I'm watching the game with Rick, but I could come by afterward."

Jaclyn sat up taller. "You and Rick are talking again?"

"Yeah."

"How did that happen?"

"Last night you said something that wised me up. I went over to his place after I left your house and tried to clear the air."

"Wow, what did I say that had such an impact?"

"You said love can compensate for a lot. That sort of simplified things for me."

Love could compensate for a lot. Love and forgiveness.

Was there a message in that for her, too? "I'm glad. So you and Rick have decided to put your differences behind you?"

"Old habits and grudges die hard, but we talked on the phone for nearly an hour this morning. We're going to work on it."

"Is he coming back to Perrini Homes?"

"He's thinking about it. Maybe part-time. He hasn't decided for sure."

"That would be great. Would you still keep the new guy, Brandon?

"Yeah. We're growing fast. I think I can keep them both busy. So how 'bout it, Jackie?"

"How 'bout what?" she echoed.

"You want me to come over tomorrow?"

Jaclyn wanted him to come over *now*. She wanted to lose herself in his arms and let love do the rest. Somehow the future and the dangers that loving Cole entailed seemed so much farther away in the dark, with the children fast asleep in their beds. But she and Cole had agreed to take things slowly, and she knew that was by far the wiser course. Besides, she didn't want the children to wake in the middle of the night and find him in her bed.

"Cole?" she asked, without answering his question.

"Yeah?"

"Did you love the other woman?"

"What other woman?"

"The one you stepped out with?"

Silence, then, "I thought you were going to try and trust me."

"I am trying. But I have to know your side of things. I'm hoping the truth isn't as bad as what I've been imagining."

Jaclyn heard him sigh softly. "Haven't you ever done something you regret the moment it's done, Jackie? Something you've promised yourself you'll never repeat?"

"Yes," she said, grabbing onto the sincerity in his voice and letting it ring through her. "Everybody makes those kind of mistakes now and then. Is that what it was, Cole? Is that all it was?"

"Yes. A one-time thing. A mistake. And, no, I didn't love her. I got into the situation in the first place because I didn't love Rochelle, either."

Jaclyn felt a twinge of pity for Cole. He'd married Rochelle because of the baby. He'd done what he considered to be right even though he *didn't* love her. Surely that spoke volumes about the kind of man he was, didn't it? Didn't that say as much for him as a brief affair said against him?

"Have you ever been in love?" she asked.

This time he paused so long that Jaclyn was beginning to fear he'd hung up. "Only once," he said at last.

"With Laura?"

"No. With a girl I met in my high school English class."

Warmth filled Jaclyn, starting from somewhere deep inside and radiating outward all the way to her fingers and toes. She let the grin that warmth brought with it break across her face. "The one you saw on your first day? The one who looked up and smiled at you?"

"That's the one."

"Do you think you could ever love her again?"

"I don't think I ever stopped."

"YOU'RE A HELL OF A ONE for a party today, Cole. Are you thinking about work or something?" Rick asked, muting the sound while he flipped through the channels on his television during a commercial break in the football game.

"Cole's always thinking about work, ain't that right, Cole?" Chad said from where he lay stretched out on the couch. So far it had been a leisurely Sunday, cool but clear outside. Cole, Chad and Rick were all lounging around Rick's living room, full of pizza and nachos and beer. The stereo played an old rock station softly in the background, and the whole place smelled like pepperoni and onions, the two most abundant toppings on their pizza.

But Cole hadn't been thinking about work. Not today. Or yesterday, for that matter. Or the day before. Ever since Jaclyn reappeared in his life, he'd had trouble thinking about anything but her, and considered it no small miracle that his business was doing as well as it was, given his sudden lack of interest.

"Actually I was thinking about kids," he said, because it was true. He hadn't been able to get the subject off his mind. Ever since the night before, when he'd had dinner with Alex, Mackenzie and Alyssa and enjoyed them almost as much as he had Jaclyn, he'd been imagining what it would be like to have a baby of his own—with Jackie. Raising four small children seemed as terrifying and overwhelming as it always had. But there was something about the thought of a baby that stirred an inexplicable excitement in him.

"Kids?" Rick nearly choked on the peanuts he'd tossed into his mouth and jumped out of his easy chair to save himself. Most of the rooms in his house were bare, but here he had what mattered most—a big-screen television, a great sound system, two easy chairs, a soft leather couch and a coffee table for snacks and drinks and old copies of *Sports Illustrated.* "Whose kids? Certainly not your own?"

Cole shrugged, suddenly feeling irritable, defensive. "Why not?"

"Because you don't plan on getting married. Isn't that a little bit of a problem?"

Cole was starting to believe marriage in general wasn't such a distasteful thing—not if it meant he could be with Jaclyn for the rest of his life—but he didn't want to say so out loud. He knew what his brothers' reaction would be and wasn't ready to take the ribbing. "I wasn't thinking about right away. I was just thinking about…someday," he said.

Chad arched his eyebrows at Rick. "It's Jaclyn. She's the one who's putting these crazy thoughts into his head."

"See what happens when I leave for a few months?" Rick said, finally sitting back and making himself comfortable in his easy chair. "Cole starts doing the unthinkable—he considers relinquishing his freedom."

"Don't you want kids?" Cole asked, wishing he'd never brought up the subject in the first place. It was one thing to think about marriage; it was another to hear his brothers talk about him like he was standing in line with his head bowed, ready to be put on a leash.

"Someday. But I gotta meet the right woman first," Rick said. He was staring at the screen, watching the Fortyniners punt the ball. "And I don't think that's going to happen anytime soon."

"You've got to be doing something with your days and nights," Chad responded. "What's the matter? Are you afraid to let whoever you're seeing meet one of us? You think she'll throw you over?"

Rick scowled. "The day I lose a girl to one of you ugly bastards is the day I enter the priesthood."

Cole and Chad both laughed. "Come on. Tell us who she is," Cole said.

"The only girl I see with any regularity is barely twenty," Rick told them.

The Forty-niners nearly fumbled. Cole reclaimed his beer from the coffee table and pretended to watch them recover the ball while trying to read his brother's face.

"Eight years isn't that big a difference," Chad said above the voice of the announcer.

"It's nearly thirty percent of my life," Rick replied. "Wow! Look at that run!"

They all leaned forward to watch the running back get tackled near the fifty-yard line.

"She still lives at home, for Pete's sake," Rick continued. "I bet she's still a virgin."

"At twenty?" Chad grabbed a fistful of peanuts. "What, does she weigh five hundred pounds?"

"No. She's…" Rick whistled low, under his breath. "She's gorgeous. And she's a real fireball." He turned and smiled wistfully, then shrugged. "She's just too young."

"At this rate, Andrew and Brian will marry before you two do," Cole said, then took a drink of his beer.

Rick and Chad both looked at him in surprise.

"Before *us?*" Rick threw a peanut at Chad. "I think he's making an announcement. What do you think?"

Chad nodded. "That sounded pretty serious to me."

Cole hadn't meant to assume he'd marry soon and they wouldn't. It had just come out that way. Feeling himself flush, he opened his mouth to deny having any immediate plans, but was saved by the ringing of his cell phone. Waving their attention back to the game, he said a grateful hello and was surprised to hear a child's voice.

"Is this Cole?"

"Yes."

"This is Alex."

Alex? Why was Jaclyn's son calling him? "Hi, buddy. What's up?"

"Nothing. I found your number on the bulletin board in the kitchen."

Before they'd hung up last night, Jaclyn had told Cole she'd better not see him today. She wanted to devote herself wholly to her studies. But hearing Alex's voice made him hope she'd changed her mind. "What are you guys doing?"

"Nothing. My mom's studying. She's been studying all day. She has a big test tomorrow."

"Yeah. It's pretty important. She'll get her license if she passes."

"That's what she said."

"Is something wrong?"

"No, I'm just bored. There's nothing to do around here."

"What are the girls doing?"

"Playing Barbies."

Cole couldn't help but chuckle at the disdain in Alex's voice. "Would you like to come over and watch the football game with me and my brothers?"

"Yeah!"

"Do you think your mom will let you?"

"I'll ask her."

The phone *thunked,* then Alex called to Jackie in the distance. After a moment, Jaclyn picked up an extension.

"Cole?"

"Hi."

"I'm sorry Alex bothered you. I didn't know he had your number." She sounded slightly embarrassed.

"There's nothing to apologize for," Cole assured her. "He said he'd like to come watch the game with me. Is that okay with you?"

"You wouldn't mind?"

"I invited him. Why don't I take the girls, too? That way you can study without interruption."

"You don't have to do that," she said, obviously surprised at the offer.

"I want to. Maybe once you get licensed, you'll bring a few of your buyers by Oak Ranch." *Or maybe you'll be living there yourself—with me.* "I'll be over in a few minutes to pick them up."

"Cole?"

"Yeah?"

"Are you sure?"

"I'm sure," he said, but he wasn't quite so sure after he hung up and had to face his brothers, who were giving him their best you're-so-full-of-bullshit look.

"I'm just helping her out," he said innocently.

"You're going to baby-sit her kids?" Rick asked.

"I thought they could play here, while we watch the game. That's not a big deal, is it? If you'd rather not, I can always take them to my house."

"It's not the house I'm worried about—it's the future." Rick looked at Chad. "How many kids does she have? Three?"

"Yeah," Chad responded.

"God, our days of peace are over." Rick shook his head. "We'd better get fitted for tuxes."

CHAPTER TWENTY-ONE

MONDAY WAS BITING COLD and completely gray, but Jaclyn was smiling when she arrived home after taking her real-estate test. The test had been long, nearly thirty pages containing 350 multiple-choice questions, but she'd done well. She could tell. She'd known most of the answers right away, thanks to Cole's sample tests and her hours of study.

Wanting to dance and twirl in the yard when she thought about having it behind her, she fit her key into the lock on the front door and was just about to let herself in, when Mr. Alder called to her from over the fence.

"Jaclyn? Alex is riding his bike on my lawn again," he said.

Jaclyn stifled a groan at letting the man catch her outside, and forced a smile. "I'm sorry, Mr. Alder. I'll have another talk with him."

"He really shouldn't ride on your grass, either. It makes ruts."

"I realize it's probably not a good thing, but we don't have much of a lawn right now, anyway." Alex was only young for a short time. And there were no other children in the neighborhood for him to play with. What were a few ruts compared to the enjoyment he got out of biking? The lawn had had more than its share of ruts and weeds *before* they moved in. "It's pretty dry and brown," she said.

"It wouldn't be if you threw a little seed out there every once in a while."

"I'll try to remember that." She slid closer to the door and blessed privacy.

"I've got seed in my shed. If you like, I can toss some on today."

This surprised Jaclyn, even though ever since he'd fixed Alex's bike, Mr. Alder had been almost kind at times. "I'd be grateful. If you're sure it's not too much trouble."

"No trouble."

She paused when he didn't turn away, wondering if there was something else. Did he want to return her plate from the lasagna she'd sent a few days ago? The basket from the cookies? Or was he hoping for some little goody for dinner tonight?

"You've been busy trimming your roses, I see," she said, trying to make polite conversation, instead of hurrying inside and closing the door as she wanted to do.

"There's a certain way to prune a rosebush. You have to know what you're doing."

"I bet that's true. They'll look nice come spring, I'm sure."

"I can show you how to prune your roses, if you like."

"That would be nice. Maybe on a Saturday when it warms up a little?" She glanced above her at the gray sky and wondered if it was going to rain later.

"Saturday's as good a day as any," he said.

"Okay, well, I'd better go in. I have to be to work in an hour. Have a nice day, Mr. Alder." This time she got the door open and had nearly stepped across the threshold, when he called her name again.

"Jaclyn?"

"Yes?" she asked, turning back.

"I don't know if it's anything important," he said, watching her closely, "but some man came snoopin' around your place 'bout an hour ago."

"Some man?"

"An older gentleman, 'bout sixty. Drove a Lincoln Towncar."

Burt! Jaclyn hadn't heard from him since Alex's game on Friday. She'd assumed he had cooled off and let the matter of Cole drop. But what if he hadn't? Why had he driven all the way from Feld on a Monday morning without letting her or the children know he was coming? "Are you sure it was a Lincoln Towncar?" she asked.

"Sure as I'm standing here."

"What color?"

"Silver."

It *was* Burt. It had to be. He was the only sixtyish man she knew who drove a silver Towncar. "What did he do?"

"Knocked on the door. When no one answered, he looked in the windows, then went around to the back."

"Did you see what he did there?"

"No. I walked over just as he was coming to the front again. I told him you were gone and asked if he wanted to leave a message with me, but he said that wouldn't be necessary."

"And then he left?"

"No, he asked me a few things first."

Jaclyn resisted putting a hand to her stomach to massage the knot of tension she felt growing there. "What did he want to know?"

"If you ever entertain men at your place."

Briefly, Jaclyn squeezed her eyes shut and willed away the anger that flooded her at the audacity of her ex-father-in-law. He'd gone to her neighbors and asked them about her? God, that rankled.

"And?"

"And I told him you were a dedicated mother. That you rarely entertain anyone and never throw wild parties or stay out late."

"You did?" Jaclyn couldn't keep the amazement out of her voice. Mr. Alder hadn't been happy about having her as a neighbor. What had motivated him to come to her defense? "Did he ask about anything else?"

"Just a black Lincoln Navigator."

"What did you tell him?"

"That I'd already told him what kind of person you are. For anything beyond that, he'd have to ask you."

"Really?" At that moment, Jaclyn could have kissed Mr. Alder's lined forehead. He might not have taken to having a divorcee with three children living next door at first, but he seemed to be warming to the idea. At any rate, he took to strangers even less.

"And I told him if he comes nosing around here again, I'd call the police."

Jaclyn couldn't believe it. Burt must have been fuming when he left. "What did he do then?"

"He got in his car and drove away."

Grateful for Mr. Alder's stand, Jaclyn smiled despite her renewed worry and anger. "I appreciate your support, Mr. Alder. That man is my ex-father-in-law, and I think he's trying to take the kids away from me again. He tried once before, but he could never get anything against me. I guess he's trying to see if he can dig up something now that I've spent a year on my own."

"Well, he can try and take your kids all he wants, but he's not going to manage it. You're a good mother," Mr. Alder stated matter-of-factly, just the way he stated everything. "I've got your lasagna plate, by the way. I'll bring it by later tonight."

"Fine. Thanks," Jaclyn added, but her mind was a million miles away from food or dishes or anything so mundane. Burt was snooping around, asking questions, a sure sign he was on the rampage again. Just when she was pulling her life together, she was going to have to turn her attention to fighting her ex-in-laws one more time. What a mess!

Instead of going in the front door, Jaclyn walked around

the side and into the backyard, retracing the steps Burt had to have taken to reach her back door. What, exactly, had he been looking for? Some sign that Cole was living with her? That Cole sometimes stayed overnight? No doubt Burt would have loved nothing more than to find her home unlocked so he could search her bedroom in hopes of finding some condoms or men's underwear.

She thought of her overtaxed bank account and all she'd already been through, and wondered how she was going to summon the strength and the money to finance yet another defense. Somehow she'd do what she had to do. She'd pay her attorney in small installments, sign away the next ten years of her working life, borrow what money she could—whatever it took. Terry and Burt wouldn't take her kids away unless it was over her dead body.

The yard looked normal enough—just grass and a few shrubs enclosed by a wooden fence. There was a small screened-in porch off the back of the house, but she didn't own any patio furniture, so it usually contained nothing but her stationary bicycle, a toy box for the girls, and Alex's scooter and in-line skates. Today, however, there was something more. Poking out from under the worn welcome mat at the back door was a manila envelope.

Jaclyn's hands shook as she retrieved it. She didn't want any more trouble. She just wanted to be left in peace.

Tearing open the flap, she pulled out the document inside, then wished she'd waited until she was in the kitchen and had someplace to sit down. Burt was making good on his threats. He was suing her again for custody of the kids. But there was something else in the envelope, something she hadn't expected—a list of women all claiming they'd had an affair with Cole Perrini.

WHAT WAS IT ABOUT HOLIDAYS? First her birthday and now Thanksgiving.

Jaclyn pushed the channel changer on the remote and

halfheartedly watched the news, MTV and an old sitcom. The kids were with Terry in Feld—he'd finally deigned to come for them. And while she was happy that they were seeing their father again, she'd let them go reluctantly. This past week, while she'd been dodging Cole's calls and pretending to be too busy to see him, her kids had been her mainstay, her only friends, her only support. Now that they were gone, she felt bereft and alone and far weaker than she deemed safe.

Call him.

No! Just in case the temptation proved too great, Jaclyn crossed the room and returned the cordless phone to its cradle, just to get it out of her lap. Then she went to the kitchen and stared into the refrigerator. She wasn't exactly hungry. She'd had a peanut butter and jelly sandwich a little earlier—there wasn't any point in making a big Thanksgiving dinner with Mr. Alder visiting his eldest son for the day and the kids gone until Sunday—but she was bored and seeking solace in *something.*

Disappointed to find that the foil-covered plate, which had stored the lemon squares she'd made the day before, was empty, Jaclyn settled for a bag of chocolate chips. Carrying them back to the living room, she sank onto the couch and tried to drown her sorrows in chocolate while once again searching for a program on television that interested her.

Nothing, she decided twenty minutes later. There was nothing on she wanted to watch. Nothing she wanted to do. Except to see Cole. She wanted him so badly that she thought she might go crazy if the impulse to call him didn't stop shooting from her brain to her arm every few seconds.

To bolster her resistance, Jaclyn threw away the empty chocolate-chip bag, went to her bedroom and retrieved the envelope Burt had left at her door. Then she looked down the list of Cole's lovers again. There were thirteen. She'd counted them the day she'd received it. Thirteen women who'd written and signed a short paragraph detailing the nature of their intimacy with Cole when he was married to Rochelle. Twelve more than he'd admitted to her. Twelve in nine months! Certainly that had to beat even Terry's record!

If it was true... But that was the problem, wasn't it? Jaclyn didn't know what to believe, didn't need the second-guessing and pain of getting involved with someone who had a bad track record. The statements looked legitimate, so believable, especially when she remembered what Cole used to be like—wild and reckless and definitely a favorite with the ladies.

Damn Burt Wentworth, Jaclyn thought, shaking her head. Just when she'd been feeling some hope again, just when she'd been trying to trust love again, he had to plant seeds of doubt.

The doorbell rang, and Jaclyn started in surprise and dropped the list on her bed. *It was Cole.* She knew it instantly, before she even left her bedroom. He hadn't called since last night, when Alex had told him she was too busy to come to the phone, but it was too much to hope that he'd go through the weekend without some attempt to reach her. He probably wanted to know what was wrong, why she was shutting him out. And she didn't want to go into it. She'd been through enough of that kind of hell already, with Terry.

"Here we go again," she muttered, summoning the courage to answer the door.

Sure enough, Jaclyn could see Cole through her peephole. He was standing on her porch in a pair of faded blue jeans and an oversize sweatshirt, holding something in his hand.

For a moment she considered pretending she wasn't home, but her car was in the drive. Swinging the door open, she offered him a tentative smile.

"Hi, Cole."

He didn't return the smile. He studied her, his jaw set. "Can I come in?"

Jaclyn stepped out of the way, and he moved past her.

"What's going on?" he asked, turning to face her as she closed the door.

She couldn't quite meet his eyes when she turned herself. "What do you mean?"

"You took your test on Monday and never called to tell me how it went. I tried to call you on Tuesday at work. The woman there took a message, but you never returned it. Then I talked to Alex last night, and again you never called me back."

Jaclyn didn't respond.

"Did the kids say something about the time they spent with me last Sunday that upset you?" he prompted.

"No." Actually the opposite had occurred. The children had loved their time with Cole and had talked of little else since then. "I'm sorry," she said. "I appreciate you baby-sitting. I should have thanked you earlier, but—"

"I didn't do it for the thanks," he said. "I wanted to help you."

Jaclyn crossed her arms, suddenly feeling chilled despite the sweater she was wearing. "And you did. The test went well."

"That's it? That's all you have to say?"

"What do you want me to say?"

He stabbed a hand through his hair. "Nothing, I guess. I don't want you to say anything you don't feel, but if you're asking what I'd *like* to hear, I'd like to hear that you've missed me as much as I've missed you. God, Jackie, I'm crazy about you. I sit home at night and think about you, remember your birthday, want to be with you. Do you know what I'd give to make love to you again? Anything! Yet you won't even return my calls."

What could she say? *I'm confused? I don't know if you've been lying to me? I'm afraid to take the chance?*

"Burt sent me something. I got it on Monday," she said, when Cole didn't speak and seemed determined to hear an answer from her first.

"What is it?"

"He's suing for custody, of course."

"Why didn't you tell me? If that's all it is, I can fix it. We'll get a good lawyer. I know someone who can help us."

He said he could fix it, just like that—easily, confidently. He'd used the word *us*. Jaclyn wanted to grab hold of the support he offered like a drowning man longs for breath, but she wouldn't let herself. Trusting left her too vulnerable.

Remember that night outside Maxine's? It's better not to trust, not to lean on someone else.

"If I can afford him," she said. "Otherwise, I'll have to find someone who will take payments."

"Money isn't the issue. I'll help you, babe." He stepped toward her, as though he'd take her in his arms, but she moved away.

"Cole, I…" Briefly she closed her eyes, then tried again. "Burt sent something else with the court papers."

Cole's face darkened, the gravity of her tone no doubt giving him some inkling that what Burt had sent wasn't good. "What?"

Without answering, Jaclyn returned to her bedroom and retrieved the list of women and their sickening, accusing words. She didn't want to show it to Cole. She wanted to burn it and pretend she'd never seen it. But she'd spent her first three years with Terry in denial, and to do that again was stupid. Whether it caused her pleasure or pain, she had to face the truth head-on.

When she returned, she handed the paper to Cole, then watched his reaction as he read. At first his eyebrows knitted together in what looked like confusion; then they lifted high, almost to his hairline in—what? Surprise? Guilt? Outrage?

Finally he looked at her. "I don't know these women," he said.

The hope that had smoldered deep inside Jaclyn threatened to burst into flame, but she tempered her reaction with the memory of how many times Terry had proved her a fool for believing him. "We went to high school with some of them," she said.

"Maybe I'd remember them if I saw them again," he said, "but I didn't have sex with any of these women."

Silence fell between them, during which Jaclyn tried to read Cole's eyes. She wished she could see inside his heart and mind so she'd know what to believe. She loved him. She wanted to trust him and forget the past. But what if she was wrong—again?

He watched her for a moment. When he spoke, his voice was low. "I haven't been a saint, Jackie. I've slept with my share of women, and I'm certainly not proud of the number. But I didn't sleep with anyone else when I was married, except the one I told you about."

Jaclyn didn't say anything. She couldn't. She was so torn, so confused. Were Burt and thirteen women lying? Or was it Cole? Burt had a reason to make her believe one thing. But Cole had his own reasons for wanting her to believe another.

Cole waited several seconds, his eyes pleading for some sign that she believed him. But when she didn't say anything, made no move, he set the paper she'd shown him on the coffee table and put the small blue velvet box he'd been carrying on top of it. "If you don't believe me now, you never will, Jackie. And we can't base a relationship on that," he said.

Hesitating for only a second, as though he wished there was something more he could say, something he could do to convince her, he kissed her softly on the temple and left.

Jaclyn stared at the little box on the coffee table, the clock ticking on the wall the only sound. Cole had brought her something. Jewelry?

Sitting on the couch, Jaclyn picked up the box, still holding her breath against the pain she'd felt the moment Cole had walked out the door, and opened the lid. It was a gold locket. Inside she found a picture of her children.

Tears filled Jaclyn's eyes as she glanced from the locket to the list of women. Burt had caused this. Burt had purposely undermined her trust because he knew he could. He knew where she was most vulnerable. He'd lived with her, heard the arguments, witnessed her pain.

After clasping the chain of the locket around her neck, Jaclyn grabbed the list and tore it into shreds. She wouldn't let Burt win. She wouldn't allow him to hurt her anymore or cost her the one man she loved more than any other. She might be an utter and complete fool, but she had to go with her heart, or she knew, this time, it would break and never heal.

CHAPTER TWENTY-TWO

COLE COULDN'T GO HOME. Not after what had just happened with Jackie. He knew he'd be too alone, too miserable. Besides, Andrew and Chad were in town for the holidays. He wanted to see them as often as possible before they headed back to school. So he got on the freeway and drove to Rick's, where he and his four brothers had spent the day eating the turkey dinner they'd purchased hot and ready-made from the grocery store.

Trying not to think about Jackie, telling himself he'd deal with that painful issue later, Cole wound his way through the neighborhood where Rick lived. But when he arrived at his brother's place, all vehicles were gone but Rick's Pathfinder and a Monte Carlo he didn't recognize.

Where were Chad, Andrew and Brian? And who was this?

Cole parked across the street and went to the door. He felt comfortable enough at Rick's place, having spent so many hours there today, that he almost walked in. Except that this time Cole was afraid of what he might see. Was the person who owned the other car Rick's love interest? Was it the twenty-year-old girl his brother had mentioned?

Cole heard Rick laugh from inside the house and decided to leave. Obviously his brother had company. He was just turning to head back to his car, when the door flew open and he found himself staring into the widest brown eyes he'd ever seen, blinking at him from behind a pair of glasses.

"I told you someone was here," the woman said to Rick, who came up behind her.

"Cole, what's up?" Rick said. "I thought you went to see Jackie."

Cole didn't want to explain. He was still too angry. He wanted to sue Burt for slander or bust Terry's lip, or both. But he knew doing so wouldn't help anything. The problem was Jackie's inability to trust him. What others said or did wouldn't have any effect on their relationship, if only she could believe in *him*.

"She wasn't home," he lied, to put a quick end to the subject.

"Oh." Rick shifted, looking ill at ease.

The girl standing next to him nudged him in the ribs. "Aren't you going to introduce me?"

When Rick hesitated, she stuck out her hand and introduced herself. "Hi, I'm Abby Walters. I'm Rick's study partner."

"His what?" Cole repeated, shaking her hand.

"His study part—"

"She's just a friend of mine," Rick interrupted.

"I'm his older brother," Cole said, wondering what the hell was going on. From the looks of her, Abby could easily be the twenty-year-old Rick had mentioned. But unless Cole was mistaken, she'd just said something about being Rick's study partner. What would Rick be studying? He hadn't even graduated from high school.

"Sorry to interrupt," Cole said, getting the impression that his brother wanted him gone. "It was nice to meet you, Abby. I'll leave you two to—" he glanced at Rick "—your studies or whatever."

"Rick's always talking about you," Abby called after him. "I feel like I know you already. Maybe the three of us can go to dinner sometime."

"That would be great," Cole said over his shoulder. He got in his car and shut the door, but he didn't leave right away. Instead, he stared at Rick's house as the front door closed, trying to figure out the riddle of his brother's behavior.

But while he was more confused now than before, he also felt a great deal of hope.

WHEN COLE LET HIMSELF into his house, he knew he hadn't drunk nearly enough. He was still conscious and functioning, which meant he still wanted Jackie, still couldn't quit thinking about her. He considered calling Chad on his cell phone to see if he and Andrew and Brian had left the bar where they'd spent the past hour, thinking he should have had one more drink with them, after all. But the taxi that had brought him home was gone, and calling another one seemed altogether too much effort. It was better that he'd come home. Maybe if he could just fall asleep, he'd forget Jaclyn, at least until morning.

So much for the plans he'd had for Thanksgiving, he thought morosely. He'd wanted to give Jaclyn the locket he'd bought her and tell her he loved her. He'd said as much on the phone, but not directly, and for the first time in his life he was excited to tell a woman that—to feel strongly enough that nothing she asked of him would be too much. Marriage. Anything. Instead, he'd been confronted with Burt's letter and rejected, and he'd gone barhopping with his brothers.

At least he'd enjoyed seeing Brian and Andrew. They were doing well in school, were dating and happy. There had been times when he'd thought he'd never get them raised, but they were adults now, and good men besides. He was proud of them.

Stripping off his shirt and pants as he made his way down the hall, he didn't bother with any lights. They'd only hurt his eyes, and he wasn't particularly worried about putting anything away. His bed was waiting for him. But when he crawled beneath the covers, his sheets weren't cool and crisp. They were warm and—

Cole almost jumped out of his skin when his bare thighs brushed up against something warm and wonderful and very much like a woman.

"Cole? You're home?" Jackie mumbled, when he cried out in surprise.

"Jackie?" he responded, the buzz he'd been feeling instantly dissipated by the shot of adrenaline that finding her sent through his system. "Where's your car?"

"It's right out front. Didn't you see it?"

Cole hadn't noticed, but then he hadn't really looked. Sometimes the construction crew parked cars out front and left them overnight. He hadn't expected Jackie and hadn't been paying attention to make or model.

"What are you doing here?" he asked. Jaclyn was still wearing her clothes. She'd obviously fallen asleep while waiting for him.

"I wanted to talk to you."

Talk. She wanted to *talk*. But Cole wasn't sure what she was going to say, and he didn't want to take the risk that he might not like it. Not when he already had her in his bed, within the circle of his arms. She'd come to him. That's what mattered. They could talk in the morning, after he'd given her a few more things to think about.

"Can't we talk later?" he asked, kissing her neck and pulling her to him at the same time.

She closed her eyes and seemed to give herself over to him, but just as his hand slipped beneath her shirt, she stopped him with a question. "Don't you think we should settle some things first?"

He withdrew his hand and tilted her chin to the left so that the moonlight illuminated her face. "I just need to know one thing, Jackie," he said. "It's as simple as that. Are you willing to trust me?"

She hesitated. "I'm willing to try."

"Then, we'll go from there."

"Where? Where will we go, Cole?" she asked.

"You don't know?"

"I need you to tell me."

"What do you want to hear, Jackie? That I love you?" He felt her body tense.

"If it's true."

"It's true," he admitted. "There's never been anyone else for me. Only you." Then he lowered his lips to hers, tasted the sweet moistness of her mouth and felt desire slam through him when she moaned and arched against him.

That was when she quit trying to talk and simply let go. Cole could feel her start to respond, and vowed in some tiny corner of his mind that he was going to make love to her like this every night for the rest of his life.

JACLYN WAS EMBARRASSED when she woke up. She'd come to Cole's house to talk to him, to apologize for doubting him and to promise to work on her issues of trust. But she'd been cold and tired and had fallen asleep in his bed waiting for him. And then she hadn't gotten very far when he came home. Cole had wanted to communicate in a different way and had made love to her again and again, as though he feared she'd leave him before he could get enough. Their time together had been passionate and heady, but now Jaclyn was left to face the day and wonder if she was going to regret what she'd done....

What had she been thinking? She started to berate herself, but when she lifted her eyelids and found Cole watching her intently, the panic and the worry evaporated almost instantly.

"I love you," he said, as soon as their eyes met. "I never dreamed I could love a woman so much."

Jaclyn smiled. How could she not trust this man? She loved him, too, couldn't imagine life without him. Surely everything would be all right.

"Will you marry me?" he asked without moving, his eyes still caressing her face. "I know I said I'd take things slow, but they don't really want to go that way, and I don't see any point in waiting. I want to build you and the kids a house, right here in Oak Ranch, or in the Sparks development, if you like it better. And I want to come home to you every night."

The mention of marriage brought back a flicker of the old fear. Marriage equaled vulnerability, and vulnerability frightened Jaclyn like nothing else. What if she and Cole married and it didn't work out? She'd be right back where she had been after her divorce from Terry, only this time she was sure she'd be even more emotionally devastated. She wasn't sure she could go through that again.

"I may not be the best man in the world," Cole was saying, "but I'll put everything I have toward being a good husband and a good father, Jackie. I'll make you happy."

"Do you think you can love the kids?" she asked.

"I know I can. I already do."

"And what about my work?"

"What about it?" he said. "That's really your decision, but if you're going to work, I'd want you to work with me. I'll build the houses. You sell them."

A team. A partnership. That was something she'd never been able to establish with Terry.

"What do you say?" he asked. "Will you be Mrs. Perrini?"

Could she do it? Could she trust him enough? It was like standing on the edge of a cliff with Cole standing across from her on another, prompting her to jump to him. In between them was a deep gorge with a rock-strewn bottom. If she fell…

"Say something," he prompted. "You're scaring the hell out of me."

Jaclyn squeezed her eyes shut and fisted her hands. *Don't*

look down, she told herself, then shoved the doubts and fear aside and made the leap. "I will," she said.

He pulled her into his arms, his chin above her head, the beat of his heart thrumming a steady cadence in her ear. It seemed to say, *You've made the right choice, the right choice, the only choice.*

"We'll make it, Jackie," he murmured. "We'll do it together."

"I know," she said. "I love you, Cole."

"YOU'RE *WHAT?*" Chad and Rick stared up at Cole from where they were sitting around his kitchen table, their mouths agape.

"I'm getting married," he told them, putting the frying pan he'd used to cook eggs into the sink to soak. "Just after Christmas."

Rick whistled and drummed his fingers on the table. "Jeez, Cole, I was only joking that day I said we should get fitted for tuxes. I never dreamed you'd tie the knot so soon. Are you sure you know what you're doing?"

"I'm sure," he told him, putting the orange juice away and wiping off the counters.

Cole had invited his brothers over for steak and eggs, but it was Thursday, a workday, and he knew Chad had a construction crew waiting to pour concrete for the driveways of the model homes over at the Sparks development.

Chad shoved the rest of his breakfast into the center of the table and stood. "Isn't this a little sudden?" he asked. "I mean, what happened to an engagement period and all that?"

Bottom line, there didn't seem to be any point in waiting. He and Jackie knew what they wanted. They were only trying to hold off long enough to give the kids time to adjust. They'd broken the news to them together on Sunday night after Terry had dropped them off, and in the four days since, Cole had been spending a lot of time at their place to ease them into having him around on a permanent basis.

At first Alex had seemed resentful of having another man in his mother's life, especially when Cole touched Jackie or kissed her. But Cole had taken Alex to the stock car races this week, and they were planning a trip to Sand Mountain with the dune buggy over the Christmas holidays, which helped show him some of the positives to the arrangement. Fortunately the little girls had been happy about having Cole as a stepdad from the beginning. They didn't perceive him as a threat. Alyssa, especially, saw him as another adult willing to give her love and attention, which was exactly what he planned to do.

Cole was starting over. Amazingly enough, the responsibility of raising Jackie's kids no longer frightened him as it once had. He'd be part of a team this time—a team of three because he had to include Terry, the children's father, in their lives. With sufficient goodwill they'd manage…. It was a second chance for Cole, a chance to do better than he had at eighteen. And though he was marrying the girl from his high school English class, Feld and what had happened there had never felt farther away.

"We'll do it before Andrew and Brian have to go back to school," Cole told them. "It'll be a small, intimate church wedding."

Rick and Chad looked at each other and shrugged. "We're with you, if that's what you want," Chad said.

"That's what I want." Cole smiled, feeling happier than he'd ever been in his life. He remembered the many times he'd sworn he wouldn't marry. He'd eat those words when he stood at the altar by Jackie's side, but he'd be grinning like a fool when he did it.

"Is Jaclyn going to come back to work at the office?" Rick asked.

"She's not sure. We both think it might be good for her to get experience elsewhere for a while, working with dif-

ferent types of buyers and loans and other real-estate trans-
fers. But I hope she'll want to come back eventually. I'd
like to have her here with me.''

Rick's chair scraped the floor as he scooted back to cross
his legs. "So where are you going to live? Here?''

"No. Jackie likes the house at the end of Golden Leaf
Court. We need to get it finished so we can move in come
January.''

"The one with the big backyard?'' Chad asked.

"Yeah. I'm going to put in a pool for the kids this summer.''

"Well, don't worry about the house. I'll get it finished
before you're even married. It'll be my wedding present.''
He downed the rest of his orange juice and headed to the
door. "But for now I gotta run. Congratulations, big
brother.''

Cole said good-bye and watched Chad go, then stared
across the table at Rick. Silence fell, and for a moment
Cole feared Rick would leave, too. He didn't want him to.
There was still some awkwardness between them, and he
hoped to say something that would make it go away, for
good. Something that would open the channels of communication between them at last.

But it was Rick who spoke first. "I've decided I'd like
to come back to work on a part-time basis, if that's okay,''
he said, leaning forward again and pushing the last of his
food around with his fork. "I'm draining my savings account pretty fast, and I've got more time than I thought I'd
have.''

"Studies are going pretty well then, huh?'' Cole asked,
taking a chance.

Rick didn't look at him. "Yeah.''

"When do you get your G.E.D.?''

"I got it a while ago.''

Cole tried not to show his surprise. Rick was acting as
though he wanted his going to school to be taken in stride,

and Cole was doing his best to play along. "So this is college?"

"Yeah."

"I'm proud of you," Cole said, and he meant it. But he was a little amazed that such praise came so easily to his lips. Maybe he was making more progress where Rick was concerned than he'd thought.

Rick looked embarrassed, but Cole could tell he was pleased with himself, too.

"I'll get another desk out front for Brandon," Cole went on, so it wouldn't seem as though he was making too big of an issue of it. "Are you eventually coming back to stay? After you graduate?"

Rick shook his head. "I doubt it. I know you want me to, Cole, but I'm not like the others. I have to do my own thing."

Cole sipped his coffee. "And what's that?" he asked.

There was a slight hesitation, but finally Rick met his gaze. "Computer Programming."

Computer Programming. So his little brother, a high school dropout, had big plans indeed. "I understand," Cole said, smiling in spite of his effects to act as though nothing had changed. "The job will be here if you want it, but whatever you do with your life, I know you'll be successful. You're one of those rare individuals with the ability to do anything."

Surprise reflected in the depths of Rick's blue eyes. Though Cole had said similar things over the years, this was probably the first time he wasn't using it to beat Rick over the head for something he'd done wrong. *You have so much potential. You could do anything, be anything and, instead, you quit almost before you start....* Now Cole was on the level and simply meant what he said, every word of it, and somehow Rick knew the difference, because surprise wasn't the only thing in his eyes. There was hope, as well, and a willingness, at last, to believe.

CHAPTER TWENTY-THREE

"I'M BACK HERE, Jaclyn hollered when she heard Cole call her name from the front of the house.

His tread sounded in the hall, then he opened her bedroom door.

"Burt Wentworth just called here, trying to get hold of you," she told him as he bent to kiss her. It was just days before Christmas, and she was sitting in the middle of the floor, wrapping the presents they'd bought for the kids on one of their many shopping excursions over the previous week. "What's going on?"

"Why are you wrapping presents today?" he asked above the Christmas carols playing on her radio. "School's out for the holidays. Alex or Mackenzie could walk in on you."

"They know to knock first. Besides, Alex is next door having Mr. Alder help him raise his bicycle seat, and Mackenzie and Alyssa are at their baby-sitter's house making gingerbread men." She left the wrapping, stood and stretched her back. "Aren't you going to answer me? Burt's trying to reach you."

He smiled. "I know. He's been trying to reach me at the office, too. But I've been over at the Sparks project, meeting with decorators who are bidding on the models. Why didn't you give him my cell phone number?"

"Because I wasn't sure I wanted him to have it," she said, bending to peel a piece of tape off the carpet. "What do you think he wants? And why am I lucky enough to see you at this time of day? It's just after noon.''

Cole shrugged. ''I couldn't go any longer without seeing you.''

''You came over for breakfast this morning,'' Jaclyn said, laughing. ''It's only been four hours.''

''I know, but eight seems like an eternity. I decided to break it in the middle.''

She grinned and hugged him. ''I love you.''

''You're going to love me even more after I talk to Burt.''

''I am?''

He nodded, looking smug.

''Why? What's going on?''

''Burt's had things easy for too long,'' he told her. ''I decided to give him a little scare, go on the offensive for a while and see if I can't get him to drop this child custody issue before it ever goes to court.''

''How?'' she asked, feeling a surge of excitement. Just talking about taking charge felt good after being on the defensive for so long.

He cocked an eyebrow at her. ''I would have been able to threaten him with a libel suit, but someone I know tore the evidence up and threw it away.''

Her financé was wearing a suit today, a beautiful black one Jaclyn knew was hand-tailored, with a pair of Italian loafers. He looked suave and debonair, too sophisticated for the reflection she saw of herself in the mirror behind him: her hair was in a ponytail, she was barefoot and wearing sweats. But Cole didn't seem to care. When he looked at her, he smiled as though she was the most beautiful woman in the world.

Jaclyn bit her lip. ''That wasn't too smart, I guess,'' she said sheepishly.

''So I had to come up with something else,'' he went on.

"Like?"

"First let's see if it's going to work." He unsnapped his cell phone from his belt and dialed the number to the ranch.

"Is Burt there?" he asked. "No, I'll wait. He's been trying to reach me. Tell him this is Cole Perrini."

He winked at her, and Jaclyn moved closer so she could put her ear next to the phone and hear what Burt had to say. As it turned out, she didn't need to get quite that close.

"You rotten son of a bitch, how dare you!" Burt's voice blasted through the phone, causing Jaclyn and Cole to yank their heads back in an effort to protect their eardrums.

"I think I got his attention," Cole said wryly.

Jaclyn was mystified. What was going on? She bent her head next to Cole's to find out.

"Is there a problem, Burt?" Cole asked. "You seem upset about something."

"You know what the problem is," he growled. "You tied up my land. You tied up the land I was going to use to build my car dealership."

"I did? That's odd. Billy Hagler there in Feld said you'd let your option lapse. He said the property was available."

"Available? He knew I still wanted it. He knew I was going to buy it, dammit."

"Then, I guess you should've had something in writing. I'm afraid intentions don't mean much in real estate."

"They will when I take you to court!" he cried.

"For what?" Cole asked. "I paid five thousand dollars to option that land, and I have a contract. I negotiated for some very appealing terms, by the way. If I don't decide to buy it in the next year, I have the right to option it again. The way I look at it, I can tie it up indefinitely, unless I see good reason not to."

Jaclyn was smiling now, too. Cole had hit Burt where it hurt most. Terry's father had wanted a car dealership for years. It was all he'd talked about when she was living with him and Dolores.

"You don't want that land," Burt said. "You'd go bank-rupt trying to build houses out here in the middle of no-where. It's not zoned for it, anyway."

"That's why I'd probably put a car dealership there."

"You wouldn't." This time Burt's voice was flat, the bluster gone.

"Actually I might. It's a prime piece of real estate, per-fectly situated. And you've already gone to the trouble of meeting with the city planners and having the zoning changed. Everyone's expecting a car dealership, everyone's looking forward to it. And dealerships can turn quite a profit, from what I hear. Why *wouldn't* I want to do it, Burt?"

Silence. Panicked silence, if Jaclyn had her guess. Burt was probably busy imagining Cole moving to town, steal-ing his status as the richest, most successful man in Feld. The Perrini name would go up in lights at the corner of Third and Main, instead of the Wentworth one.

Heaven forbid, she thought mockingly, and slipped her arms around Cole's waist to give him a squeeze, never happier to see someone get what they deserved.

"What do you want for it?" Burt finally choked out, sounding like a man with a gun to his head.

Cole didn't answer right away. He kissed her forehead and then, as though intentionally prolonging his hesitation, said, "I'm not sure I *want* to sell the option, Burt. I mean, I just got it a few days ago. I haven't had time to look into the full potential of the piece. And with Christmas only a week away, I won't have a chance to do much until January. But if someone wanted it badly enough—" He covered the phone and asked Jaclyn how much she still owed in attor-ney bills from the divorce.

"About forty-six hundred dollars," she whispered.

"Ten thousand would probably do it," he told Burt. "If someone were to act quickly."

It was Burt's turn to pause. Jaclyn could easily picture

him pacing in his home office, grinding his teeth in agitation.

"Fine," he said at last. "I'll do it. I'll give you the damn ten thousand. You just keep your nose out of Feld and away from my son."

"I didn't know I was any threat to your son, but now that you bring him up, we should probably discuss one other small matter," Cole replied. "If you want the land, you're going to have to drop the child custody suit, too. I don't think Jackie would feel very good about marrying me in a few weeks with that hanging over her head. It's kind of negative, if you know what I mean."

"I don't give a damn how negative it is. It's Jaclyn and her self-pity that's been the problem from the start. She had it good here, and she threw it all away."

"And you've done your best to punish her for it. Tell me, did it make you feel like a big man, Burt, to push around a woman with three little children to support?"

"You dirty—"

"I'm going to hang up," Cole said as calmly as ever. "We have a lot of Christmas presents to wrap."

"Wait!"

Jaclyn could hear Burt's labored breathing, could envision him clenching his fists and trying to rein in his temper. She knew it wasn't an easy thing for him. He wasn't used to having to curb his tongue for anyone. "Ten thousand dollars is more than enough to put that land back in my control. This has nothing to do with the children. I think we should keep them out of it."

"Sorry, that's the deal. You're going to lose the case, anyway. You can't prove abuse, neglect or abandonment, and that's the only way a judge would give you what you want. You may as well get your land back and save us both the attorney fees and hassle of fighting about the children— because we will fight, Burt, and this time my attorneys will

be every bit as good as yours. If I'm lucky—and I'm usually pretty lucky—they'll be better.''

Several seconds of silence passed, then Burt muttered a
curse and said, ''If I pay the money and drop the case,
you'll assign the option to me?''

''I will.''

''When? When will you meet me so we can put everything in writing?''

''Call Brandon Johnson at my office and set up a time.
And don't forget your checkbook.''

''I hope you rot in hell for this, Perrini.''

Cole's laughter was genuine. ''You can thank me later,
after the wedding,'' he said, and hung up.

With a scream of delight, Jaclyn threw herself into
Cole's arms. ''You did it,'' she cried. ''We've won!''

''Merry Christmas, sweetheart,'' he said.

TERRY WAS ON THE PHONE. Jaclyn grimaced at the sound
of his voice, thinking his intrusion the only defect in an
otherwise perfect Christmas morning. Cole had arrived
early, before the kids were even up, and built a fire. The
smell of it mingled with that of the fir tree and the freshly
backed cinnamon rolls to create a scent that brought back
all the Christmases of Jaclyn's youth.

She and Cole and the kids were sitting in a circle as if
they were already a family, unwrapping presents. Alex's
favorite gift so far seemed to be his new Gameboy, which
Cole had insisted on buying for him. Alyssa and Mackenzie
were thrilled with their play kitchen, which had been
Jaclyn's idea. Cole had wanted to build them an entire play-
house, but Jaclyn had asked him to wait until next year, or
at least until summer. With the upcoming move, they had
enough going on already.

''It's your father,'' she told the children, holding the
phone out for whoever grabbed it first.

Mackenzie was closest. She took the receiver and started

to list everything Santa had brought and to tell Terry about what Mommy and Cole had given her, then Alyssa did the same.

Meanwhile, Jaclyn listened to Cole, who was sitting next to her in a pair of jeans, a flannel shirt and a Santa hat Mackenzie had brought home from school and insisted he wear. He was helping Alex figure out the new game for his Gameboy. She felt a profound sense of gratitude to him. She wouldn't have been able to provide this kind of Christmas for the children on her own. It was Cole who had made the difference—not just because of his generosity, though the presents were wonderful, but because of the feelings of contentment and unity that his presence seemed to nurture in them all. Terry was coming to pick up the kids this evening, but Jaclyn didn't mind. She knew they'd be happy to see their father.

And she wouldn't be alone. She'd be with Cole.

She put her hand on his leg, and he took it immediately, glancing back to smile at her before finishing what he was saying to Alex.

"It's Daddy, Alex," Alyssa said, passing him the phone.

Jaclyn had just begun gathering up the jewelry, sweaters, perfume and shoes the kids and Cole had given her, when Alex said goodbye and handed the phone to her.

"Dad wants to talk to you," he said, going right back to Cole and his Gameboy.

"Would you rather I handle it?" Cole asked, at her slight hesitation.

"No, it's fine." She put the receiver to her ear. "Hi Terry."

"Hi, Jackie. Are you having a nice Christmas?"

"Yeah. You?"

"It would be better if I had my family here."

"Terry, you're picking the kids up today, so you'll see them soon, right?"

"What time can I come?"

"Is six o'clock okay?"

"Six o'clock? The day will be over by then."

"You had the kids for Thanksgiving. Anyway, I'm fixing dinner for Cole and his brothers, and I don't want the kids to miss it."

There was silence, then he said, "Oh, we wouldn't want that."

Jaclyn ignored the sarcasm. "Two of his brothers are only home from college for a few days," she explained. "They have a ski trip planned, then they have to go back to school. This may be their only chance to get to know the kids before the wedding."

"So you're going through with it?"

"The wedding?"

"Yeah. I bet it doesn't last a year."

"I wouldn't put a lot of money on that if I were you."

He chuckled. "Why? The odds are with me. Eventually he'll treat you just like he treated Rochelle. He's a man, Jackie. A man doesn't change that much."

"Yes, that's what I found out," she said, turning his words back on him. He was still bitter and trying to undermine her happiness, but Jaclyn refused to let him. She'd already given Cole her heart. She was going to give him her complete faith and confidence, as well. Sometimes it still felt as if she was gambling everything on one big roll of the dice—Cole's word against the rumors, against Burt's claims—but her love for Cole made the risk worth taking.

"We'll see," he said. "Merry Christmas."

"Merry Christmas," she replied and hung up.

"Everything okay?" Cole asked, watching her curiously.

She smiled, telling herself to shake off the pall Terry's words had cast on her spirits. "Fine."

"Then, it's time."

"Time for what?"

"To give you your big surprise," Alex interjected.

Jaclyn surveyed the gifts already stacked around her. "There's more?"

"This one's special," Mackenzie said. "It's from all of us."

"Where is it?" Jaclyn asked.

"You'll see," Cole said. "Everyone get dressed."

THEY WERE HEADING to Oak Ranch. Evidently Cole's big surprise had something to do with the new house. Maybe he'd put in a hot tub or upgraded the carpet or drapes or something, but Jaclyn couldn't really believe he'd do that. She'd already picked out everything she wanted, and she was happy with her choices. So what was it?

"Did you have the landscaping done already?" she asked, trying to solve the mystery.

"Not yet," he told her.

"Did you start digging out the pool?"

"Nope. Too much mud for that. We need to wait for the ground to dry out. We'll do it closer to spring."

In the back seat, the girls giggled at her failed attempts to discover the secret.

"Tell me what it is, Alex," Jaclyn said, trying to put some authority in her voice.

Cole gave her son a quick "don't you dare" look in the rearview mirror, but when Alex answered, Jaclyn could tell he wasn't even tempted. "You have to wait and see, Mom. We'll be there soon."

"Will I like it?" Jaclyn asked.

"You'll probably cry," Alex told her.

Cry? Why would she cry?

They parked at the curb of their new home and picked their way through the melting snow and mud to reach the heavy oak doors that had been hung just a few days earlier. Now nearly finished, the house was beautiful. Jaclyn had walked through it two days ago, right after the carpeting and hardwood floors had gone in, feeling like a fairy princess. Never had she dreamed she'd own something quite so lovely or so large.

But what about the house had changed in the past two days?

"Close your eyes," Alex said, as soon as they reached the entry.

The smell of fresh paint and cut lumber assaulted Jaclyn's nostrils as soon as she stepped inside. Cole took one hand and Alex took the other, and they guided her slowly through the high-vaulted entryway and around to the sunken living room. Without any curtains or furnishings to absorb and soften the sound, their footsteps echoed loudly.

"Now you can open them," Cole said, when they stopped.

Slowly Jaclyn lifted her eyelids. There, sitting on an expensive-looking Turkish rug, right in front of the bay window facing the street, was a shiny black grand piano.

"Oh! You bought me a piano!" she breathed, too awed to speak in more than a whisper.

Cole smiled, obviously enjoying the amazement on her face. "Do you like it?"

"I love it. I've never seen anything more beautiful."

"Then, you haven't looked in the mirror lately," he said, and gathered her in his arms.

"Yuck," Alex complained when Cole kissed her. "Do we have to see this?"

"Shh," Mackenzie replied, a dreamy smile on her face. "Mommy's kissing Santa Claus."

Laughing, Jaclyn pulled the kids close for a hug, knowing she could never be happier or feel more complete than she did at that moment.

And then she proved Alex right. She cried.

EPILOGUE

HER BACK HURT. Jaclyn relinquished her seat on the hard cement and stood up to stretch, but at seven months' pregnant, she wasn't exactly at her most mobile.

The cold didn't help. It was almost Christmas again. A couple of inches of snow covered the ground outside, and a chill wind blew. It crept through the cracks of the garage, seeping through her sweater. Jaclyn knew Cole wasn't going to be happy when he got home and learned she'd been out moving boxes and shifting stuff around in her condition. He'd told her not to bother with what they had in storage, that he'd take care of it, but the kids were with Terry, Cole was at work, and Jaclyn didn't want to wait. The garage was the last part of the house she had yet to organize, and she wanted to finish. Then she could decorate for the holidays and enjoy her leave of absence from Guthrie until after the baby arrived and she was ready to go back.

Problem was, most of the boxes belonged to Cole, and she didn't know what to do with the stuff inside them. Did he really want to keep the old sweaters she found? They didn't look nearly large enough for him, but maybe they'd belonged to his father or something.

Digging a little deeper, Jaclyn uncovered some old pictures. She smiled as she studied a black-and-white photograph of Cole and all four brothers. He was in the middle, with one arm around Rick and another around...who? It had to be Chad, judging by the size, but he looked so different. There were holes in the knees of their blue jeans, the toddler had his sneakers untied, and the oldest three were in various stages of getting their permanent teeth, but it had to be the cutest picture Jaclyn had ever seen. She set it aside to have it framed and added to the hallway, where pictures of their family already hung in vast array, and moved on to the next box.

This one contained odds and ends, a pocket screwdriver, a video, a small sewing kit, loose photographs of houses and land, keys, even some loose change. It looked as if Cole had emptied his junk drawer and carried it with him when he moved, instead of sorting through it.

Finding a piece of crumpled paper, Jaclyn ironed it out to see if it was something she could throw away, and was surprised to find a handwritten letter.

Dear Cole,

If you ever get this, I know it will come as quite a surprise. After everything we've been through, you may not even want to hear it. But I have to tell you I'm sorry, for me, if not for you. You were right. I did lie about the baby....

By the time Jaclyn finished Rochelle's letter, she had tears in her eyes. Finally she understood Cole's past. He'd married a woman he didn't love and tried to stay with her even after he learned she'd trapped him. Then he'd protected Rochelle by not telling anyone what she'd done and had carried the brunt of the blame himself. What kind of a man did that?

A very fine man, she thought, swiping at her eyes with the back of her hand. Her husband.

Remembering Terry's bet that their marriage wouldn't last a year, Jaclyn wanted to call him and read him Rochelle's letter, so he'd know just how wrong he'd been about Cole. How wrong they'd all been.

But Cole had kept Rochelle's secret all these years, had proved himself honorable in spite of everything. And she admired his integrity enough to stand by his decision.

What Terry thought didn't matter. She refolded the letter and tossed it back in the box. Burt's opinion didn't matter, either, nor did that of all the folks in Feld.

Because she knew Cole's heart.

Thank God it belonged to her.

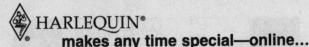

In November 2001, bestselling Harlequin author

JUDITH ARNOLD

provides help for dads... at *The Daddy School*

Three single fathers are out to show three wonderful
women that, when it comes to babies *and* romance...

*Father
Knows
Best*

Three complete novels.
Look for it at your favorite retail outlet.

HARLEQUIN®
Makes any time special®

Visit us at www.eHarlequin.com
BR3FKB

*H*ugh Blake,
soon to become stepfather to
the Maitland clan, has produced three
high-performing offspring of his own. But
at the rate they're going, they're never going to
make him a grandpa!

There's *Suzanne*, a work-obsessed CEO whose Christmas spirit
could use a little topping up....

And *Thomas*, a lawyer whose ability to hold on to the woman
he loves is evaporating by the minute....

And *Diane*, a teacher so dedicated to her teenage students she
hasn't noticed she's put her own life on hold.

But there's a Christmas wake-up call in store
for the Blake siblings. Love *and* Christmas miracles
are in store for all three!

Maitland Maternity Christmas

A collection from three of Harlequin's favorite authors

Muriel Jensen
Judy Christenberry
&Tina Leonard

Look for it in November 2001.

WITH HARLEQUIN AND SILHOUETTE

There's a romance to fit your every mood.

Passion

Harlequin Temptation

Harlequin Presents

Silhouette Desire

Pure Romance

Harlequin Romance

Silhouette Romance

Home & Family

Harlequin American Romance

Silhouette Special Edition

A Longer Story With More

Harlequin Superromance

Suspense & Adventure

Harlequin Intrigue

Silhouette Intimate Moments

Humor

Harlequin Duets

Historical

Harlequin Historicals

Special Releases

Other great romances to explore